HIDDEN CANYON

A CHARLES BLOOM MURDER MYSTERY

MARK SUBLETTE

 JUST ME PUBLISHING

Published by Just Me Publishing, LLC.

Library of Congress Control Number: 2013952666
Hidden Canyon / Mark Sublette
ISBN 978-0-9855448-4-3
1. Fiction I. Title

Quantity Purchases
Companies, professional groups, clubs, and other organizations may
qualify for special terms when ordering quantities of this title. For
more information, contact us through www.marksublette.com.

Cover painting: Billy Schenck, *Fire in the Sky*
Jacket and book design: Jaime Gould
Author photo: Dan Budnik

Printed in the USA by KnockOut
Minneapolis, MN · www.knockoutpub.com

AUTHOR'S NOTE

The books in the Bloom murder mystery series are all works of fiction. All characters are fictional as are all the art galleries, artists, and art dealers. The Native American characters in my book are fictional and any resemblance by name, clan, or description to real life is pure coincidence.

The best fiction has its roots in reality and I would like to thank two experts in their respective fields who helped bring this book to life.

Larry Cansler, whose decades of experience working in Hollywood composing and writing songs, including one of my favorites, "Wildfire" (with Michael Martin Murphey), gave me a deeper understanding of a working composer's life from 1960 to 1980. Dr. Jon French, PhD, shared his insights of the working mind of a psychopath over a dinner at the Plaza Café in Santa Fe. The conversation was compelling as were the blue corn enchiladas.

The Toadlena Trading Post, a central component of all the Bloom books, is a real-life working trading post that exists as described on Navajoland. The historic post specializes in Toadlena/Two Grey Hills weavings and is well worth the effort to visit. I would like to thank its proprietors, author Mark Winter and wife Linda, for their wonderful hospitality and helpful editing comments.

No book is complete without a great cover and I'm most appreciative to Billy Schenck for so graciously allowing me to use his painting "Fire in the Sky" to capture the essence of *Hidden Canyon* and to Jaime Gould for her graphic design and editing skills.

All the photographs are taken by me and serve as points of reference that correlate to those chapters. Hopefully they help to give the reader the sense of place and moment in time I experienced when I took them.

CHAPTER 1

#2 PENCIL PLEASE

Prison forensic psychologists recognize the fastest way to spot a true psychopath: ask the other cons. They all know. These broken individuals are loners, people to fear, with no gang or personal affiliation of any kind. They *think* their emotions, unable to experience feelings.

All languages across the world have a word to describe a psychopath, except for the Navajo. Psychopaths are exceedingly rare. Their ability to blend in and seem normal while being anything but, makes detection difficult and destruction of unsuspecting lives a given. Specialists in this psychiatric field believe these individuals are outliers in man's genetic code: unique humans born mentally deranged.

Fallon Scriber was such an individual. His physical and social environment only helped accentuate an inherent tendency toward destructive behavior.

His mother had exceptional intelligence and if not for her alcohol addiction, could have been a good mother to Fallon, though it probably wouldn't have mattered. Her only child was damaged goods from the start. Fallon's father was a non-issue. He came and went, an odd man with a bad temper whose only interaction was always some puzzle to be unraveled. He was never a stable

1

component in either of their lives and by 1970 had disappeared for good.

Growing up in a rough neighborhood in Oakland, California, didn't help. It undoubtedly fostered Fallon's perverted outlook on life at a young age. Fallon was a short white kid in a sea of athletic color. He might have skated by on his personality, which was chameleon-like, if not for an unrelenting medical condition. His untreatable disease caused him to stick out, resulting in extreme taunting and pain.

Fallon's porcelain-colored flesh was cursed with one of the most severe cases of dermatographia ever recorded. Usually this condition is just a benign problem, more an oddity than an affliction. With dermatographia, the slightest touch of the skin causes red welts to emerge. These eruptions generally remain for only a couple of minutes and are associated with some transient mild pain in the affected area, but not for Fallon Scriber. His skin was so reactive the slightest scratch would cause deep welts lasting 30 minutes or even longer. The deeper the scratch, the more painful and long lasting the welt. He was a human Etch A Sketch, and everyone on Oakland's poor side of town in the rebellious sixties and seventies wanted to play.

Children can be downright vicious, especially ones with little parental supervision. A victim is singled out and taunting goes on until something breaks the cycle. Fallon was such a victim, which is ironic as he was already a full-blown psychopath who could have easily been the tormenter, making notes on whom to punish severely later in life.

The game he was subjected to was called Red Man Writes and the object was to see which contestant could write the most words on Fallon's skin that were readable. Each participant was allowed one minute to accumulate points. The game started when Willy Bellows would scream: "Red Man Writes!" Points were awarded for the amount legibly written and multiplied by the minutes for which they remained visible. It was like blowing soap bubbles and watching them pop. Great transient fun for all, except Fallon, who was never a willing participant.

In the game, curse words scored double as these were guaranteed to get Fallon in serious trouble with the teachers as well as give him severe discomfort. Fallon always wore long-sleeved shirts no matter how hot the weather. The cloth dampened his skin's reactivity and served as a weak attempt to ward off bullies who loved to see the painful lines appear instantaneously on his albino-like skin. Contestants of Red Man Writes would overpower the small kid, pull up his sleeves, and lift Fallon's shirt over his head, using his stomach as a human chalkboard. Let the game begin. Part of the fun was watching Fallon struggle to defend himself. That added a physicality certain boys loved.

The first semester of eighth grade was the worst. Fallon's saving grace was growing seven inches over summer break, pushing his new height to six feet. Bullies were now less likely to pick on a tough, tall white kid, even one they had tormented for years. The game took a new turn. Fallon decided he would no longer be the object of terror. He would stop being tormented no matter what the cost to his own freedom. Fallon's life force which had grown with his height would now embrace the dark side, something he had kept suppressed for far too long.

The aim of his anger was pointed at Willy Bellows, a mean child who was the official game starter of Red Man Writes. He viciously attacked Fallon under the school bleachers during the Halloween school party. Willy decided to give Fallon a red man's costume by making Fallon's skin into a single welt, one that would last all of the school day, which it did. Willy's sharp pencil tore into Fallon's fragile skin and left not only the usual reactive welts, but permanent scars, binding Willy the tormentor with Fallon the psychopath for eternity.

Fallon took time to work out his revenge plan. He would ambush Willy, who hadn't had the same luck of growth-hormone production. He waited until Valentine's Day. He would leave Willy his own heartfelt card, one for all to read. Fallon's calm demeanor was a great disguise. He seemed normal in every way, with no indication of his murderous side. This was unfortunate for his victim, whose only concern that morning was if he would receive any Valentine's cards. He would. One he didn't expect.

Fallon showed up early to shadow Willy as he left his home in the projects. He ambushed his prey at his usual short cut, an isolated alleyway behind the ramshackle abandoned homes in the poverty-stricken neighborhood. At first Willy challenged him, "Get out of my way, fool, or I'm going write my name on your face!"

Fallon's unflinching black eyes told the story to a boy who had seen plenty of violence in his life, even at 14. Two yellow pencils, razor sharp, suddenly appeared, each gripped tightly in Fallon's gloved hands. He was as quick as a rattlesnake, fangs ready for action. Pencils would be Fallon's calling cards to the police if they could figure out the crime. Death by #2 lead, carried out by a young psychopath named Scriber, derived from the German word for "writer." He was fulfilling his fate. The first in a long line of deaths by the boy whose skin was a painful piece of paper.

Realizing he was in serious trouble too late, Willy tried to run but tripped over his feet, the only part of his body that had grown during puberty. He fell hard. Fallon aggressively jumped on top of Willy, stabbing the boy in the neck and upper torso, the sharp lead breaking off as it hit cartilage and bone in Willy's still-developing cervical spine. Fallon's rage continued, using the dull pencil ends, plunging them violently into Willy's neck, deep into the blood vessels. Fallon was a pro at killing even his first time. He had worn gloves, knowing he would be murdering today, and had watched enough television to learn about fingerprints. He left none. However, Fallon purposefully left the two pencils sticking out of Willy's neck to see how well the police detectives would do their jobs.

At school, Fallon changed into a fresh set of clothes he had brought, cleaned his face with a wet towel, and then proceeded to have the best day of school ever. He could hardly wait for someone else to upset his natural order of life again. Fallon found himself exhilarated. He decided his lot in life was cast. No more the fool with the red, painful skin. He was in charge of his destiny and if anyone got in his way he would take care of them in his own fashion. Pencils, writing, and death were his new calling cards if anyone ever cared to look.

In the case of Willy Bellows, the police did not do their jobs well at all. They classified the killing as gang-related, like his deceased brother before him. Case closed. Another black child's murder unsolved, the Bellows name dying out with little Willy.

For the rest of eighth grade, Fallon took Willy's old short cut to school. He loved walking by the place he had become a man.

4

Unfortunately for his victims, Fallon Scriber would never go to prison. No easy diagnosis of psychopath would ever be rendered by his fellow inmates. The unlucky few who would encounter Fallon's dark side would not know they had experienced a rare breed of human, a true psychopath and the most dangerous type: a serial killer. The only question was could he ever be stopped?

CHAPTER 2

SUMMER OF LOVE

A native Arizonan, Samuel Houston Hubbard moved to the Golden State during the Summer of Love, 1967. Unlike most of his peers who came to Haight Ashbury for free love, drugs, and rock and roll, he arrived for school at Stanford University. Although his campus was south of San Francisco, he came up to the city frequently. It was where the action was. He drank, but no drugs other than an occasional drag of dope when a girl would push. His tendencies were more conservative than those of most of his peers, but he agreed with his free love brethren when it came to Vietnam. The war was raging in Southeast Asia and Sammy—as he was still going by at that time—had no intention of getting caught up in a fight that didn't seem right. It wasn't as if he was afraid to stand up for his principles. He was more willing than most to do that. But this war smacked of politics, something he despised.

Sammy had a remarkable brain. He could easily put together complex thoughts in many fields. He was particularly gifted in science but found the technical lab work a grind, just busy work. Field investigation was more to his liking. Research had been his parents' path. Both of them were research scientists, and Sammy was expected to follow in the Hubbard footsteps. A long line of doctors and scientists had come before, and it was assumed his journey would be no different. He was a Hubbard, after all.

His aptitude in science had allowed him to get into the highly competitive Stanford University. He had been very successful at his public high school, winning the national science fairs in both his junior and senior years, something unheard of.

His project, which he worked tirelessly on for two consecutive years, was titled, "The Life Cycle of the Javelina (*Pecari tajacu*) of the Southern Sonoran Desert." Sammy followed a family of approximately 20 javelinas around the desert daily for two years. He was careful not to affect the natural setting and behavior by bringing in food or by his own presence, which might change their normal routine. Sammy had the luxury of his father owning a huge tract of virgin Sonoran Desert just outside Tucson's city limits. Tucson during the mid-sixties was still a small town with less than 100,000 people. Land was cheap and the desert untouched.

Sammy set numerous stations along the javelinas' well-worn tracks and patiently waited for them to come by and feed, to play and just be javelinas. He had three stations along a four-mile route, which was the range of the wild peccaries that most Arizonans incorrectly refer to as pigs. He made detailed records of dominance behavior, sexual interaction, and eating habits. He worked on his project daily for two years, never once missing a day of data on his prized javelinas. The data was so well compiled it set a new standard for biologists in the field, which is uncommon coming from a 17-year-old. This dedication to getting it right had won him the golden ticket to Stanford.

The Summer of Love became the summer of study for Sammy. He was not the typical Stanford student; grades didn't come easily. He threw himself into what he cared about, but he did not care about everything. Sammy's first year and a half in the Bay Area was spent learning and experiencing life, and looking for a field of study that could captivate him for life. Any person who for two years could maintain a fascination with observing pigs cavorting in the hot Arizona desert would not settle for a run-of-the-mill job.

The answer to what he would do for the rest of his life came just before the start of his junior year. He was leaning toward becoming a marine biologist, envisioning himself following whales cavorting around in the ocean for the rest of his life.

He was planning to declare this field his major when fate stepped in the week before, in the form of a newspaper headline dated August 1, 1969. It would change everything. It was a missive from a serial murderer who would soon be referring to himself as Zodiac, and it was published in the *San Francisco Examiner* on page three. The killer sent his proclamation to the press in the form of a 408-symbol cryptogram, declaring his presence as a force to be reckoned with. Seven days later the first of many ensuing letters arrived from the murderer, the Zodiac Killer.

Sammy's interest faded completely from humpback whales, switching to bound-and-gagged victims right here in the Bay Area. He watched as the rest of the country did in morbid fascination the actions of this unknown Zodiac Killer, a person who was systematically murdering for pleasure. The killer bragged of possessing supernatural power and invisibility, demanding others to bow to his will or face his wrath. The Zodiac's cryptogram was believed to be the declaration of a deranged person who wanted to hunt humans as the ultimate prey that would become his slaves in the afterworld, and the seven victims so far (two survived) were all between 16 and 29, Sammy's age group.

When the last confirmed person was killed in San Francisco's Presidio on October 11, 1969, Sammy was having dinner not far from the murder scene. For months he had pictured his path crossing with that of the deranged killer, and had wondered how he would have fared. Did he have what was required to recognize such a killer? Humans are not like whales or javelinas. They are complex organisms with a superior intellect.

The thought was haunting Sammy. He was afraid he didn't have what was needed to recognize evil in the human form. Then, like the proverbial light bulb going on, he had an epiphany. He would become like the Zodiac Killer. He would study (hunt) humans, not to kill but to help rid society of these evil people. The mentally sick of our society, those individuals who are the far outliers in the social bell curve of humanity, would become his study population. Sammy realized his fascination with the Zodiac case was more about his successfully identifying the person who had such severely aberrant behavior than it was about the details of murders. What made Zodiac tick, and how did he become so totally deranged? The year 1969 was the summer of fear for Northern California, but for Sammy it was when he found his voice. He would become a forensic psychologist and pursue the Zodiacs of the world.

CHAPTER 3

SHOTGUN WEDDING?

Charles Bloom's life was gearing up for fatherhood. It was 2012, his first son was due any moment, and he still had not addressed his own hesitancy to marry Rachael Yellowhorse. She was getting pressure from all sides of her clans on the marriage issue, especially since she was about to bring a child into the world. Charles on the other hand was quite happy with their relationship. He was in his 40s and he was involved with a great woman whom he loved, who was soon to be the mother of his child. It wasn't that he had a problem with marriage. It was great for other people, like his parents, just not for him.

The couple decided to wait a little longer to get married, which was Bloom's idea. A formal proposal had yet to be offered by the reluctant art dealer. He had however purchased a small silver band from Sal Lito, the old trader at Toadlena. The ring was Navajo-made and was over a hundred years old. The wear on the ring had made it feel as smooth as wet marble. It was apparent this ring had lived. Bloom liked the thought that a couple of generations of Navajo grandmothers had already worn the ring, giving it a soul. It was being recycled once again into the next generation of Navajo women, this one with a white boyfriend. Now all he needed was the right time to propose, assuming he could get past his hesitancy. A sign was needed, he decided.

The unspoken understanding became that once their child was delivered and everything got back to normal, Bloom and Rachael would set a date and he would commit. Still, maybe there was some way he could avoid it. He knew it was weak of him, but he was who he was and marriage scared the shit out him. Being in love and upcoming fatherhood seemed right, but not wanting to sanctify the relationship by getting married was causing him a great deal of stress in a world he otherwise viewed as near perfect.

The baby was due in less than a week. They had asked Dr. Riddly over in Kayenta, Arizona, on the Navajo Reservation to deliver their child. They lived on the rez across the state line in New Mexico, but Rachael's maternal family was all from Arizona, and Rachael had been born in their ancestral hogan near Canyon de Chelly. When the baby came it would be a long drive over to Kayenta and there was no way to predict when the little Bloom would make his appearance. After all, he was half Navajo and might be on Indian time.

They decided to splurge and get a room for two weeks at the Kayenta Hampton Inn, room 2B, their lucky number. This would allow for medicine man Hastiin Johnson to give a blessing to the new child, who was going to be called Willy Randal Yellowhorse Bloom. Willy was in honor of his late uncle Willard Yellowhorse, and Randal was for Randal Begay, Hastiin Johnson's late grandson, who had been a great weaver. Randal Begay and Rachael had shown together at Bloom's Santa Fe gallery during last year's Indian Market. Randal had died afterwards in a sudden and tragic murder. They considered seriously giving the baby a third name, Carson, in honor of Carson Riddly, and also to try and break the Indian prejudice against those named Carson, Kit Carson being an anathema figure with most Navajos, but they decided to put that concept on hold. Maybe they would revisit it with the next Yellowhorse-Bloom child.

Rachael was craving Taco Bell burritos with green sauce so the time in Kayenta would give her a while to fatten up the baby before delivery. She had gained only 20 pounds, and Dr. Riddly had given her permission to consume as much comfort food as wanted. The baby's arrival would be perfect timing, as early May wasn't busy at

Toadlena or Santa Fe. Plenty of time to take care of marriage, baby delivery, and get ready for the next Indian Market. Bloom still needed a great rug from Rachael to showcase during August.

Bloom's gallery in Santa Fe was working out well. Dr. James, Bloom's only employee, was a better hire than Bloom could have imagined. The gallery was actually producing money without Bloom being there. Bloom was now working almost full time at the Toadlena Trading Post, something he had requested as it helped occupy his time and he earned extra money. He was exceptionally good at selling weavings and for Bloom that was more fun than retail work off the rez.

CHAPTER 4

PAST AND PRESENT

The world of Navajo textiles was fascinating to Bloom. He could see correlations between the weavers' designs and the contemporary paintings he had dealt in for so long. He was surprised at his own intense interest in the history of this Southwest art form. The contemporary art scene in Santa Fe was still his bread and butter, but Bloom now could better understand why so many of his Native artists brought traditional concepts of their life into their contemporary artwork.

It also had finally dawned on him how Dr. James, his anthropologist employee, could sell the living artists' works so well even though he didn't have an art background. Dr. James had gained such an appreciation for the early art of Southwest man that he could relate its symbolism to Bloom's contemporary Native artwork. His passion rubbed off on Bloom's clients and allowed the old professor to make sales. Dr. James loved prehistoric cultures of the Southwest, particularly prehistoric rock art. He was considered a specialist on the images in Canyon de Chelly, one of the largest petroglyph sites in

North America. He had one of the most extensive libraries of photographs of petroglyphs and pictographs in private hands.

Teaching anthropology at Eastern New Mexico University, which also had a very strong archeology department, gave Dr. James his introduction into the world of the Anasazi. An ancient civilization that thrived for a thousand years in the harsh environment that makes up the desert Southwest, the Anasazi disappeared around 1350 CE, leaving only their ruins and descriptive rock art as testimony of their struggles and ingenuity. Dr. James found himself spending a great deal of time in the archeology department and before he knew it he was the resident expert in Southwest rock art. The type of art produced by early man was created in two distinct ways: petroglyphs, which are images picked out in stone, and pictographs, which are painted images. Petroglyphs are much more common and durable and can be found at most Anasazi sites, which are numerous in the Southwest.

Dr. James had been sharing his love with Bloom, who was living in the heart of the ancient Anasazi world. *Anasazi* comes from the Navajo word meaning *enemy ancestors*. Even today, there are many undiscovered ruins throughout the Navajo Reservation. Federal and state laws forbid any of these sites from being disturbed, which is just fine with most Navajos, as they look at these places as taboo and avoid contact whenever possible.

Often it is hard not to come in contact with the ancient culture, with pottery shards strewn about the rez. So common are they, it is nearly impossible to walk and not step on the multicolored clay fragments dotting the landscape. Most Navajos do their best to ignore the ancient artifacts present in daily life.

Rachael Yellowhorse was intimately familiar with many of these ruins from her explorations along the canyon floors tending sheep when younger. Before her pregnancy, she had shared with Bloom one exceptional wall that was special to her family. It was located in a remote canyon, 40 minutes from Toadlena. The hard-to-find location, which was behind a hairpin turn, had thousands of images never seen before except by those tending sheep. Bloom was amazed at the variety of images jammed together on the high sheet of sandstone. The images were still powerful and untouched for over a thousand years. These petroglyphs were etched on a southern wall with a large stone overhang that acted like a visor and had protected the art masterpieces from the ages.

Unfortunately the ultimate fate of the images was already sealed by the hand of Mother Earth. The magnificent wall would be destroyed as the momentous rock precipice that had protected it so well for a thousand years was starting to crack. Soon its sheer weight combined with nature's own lubricant, water, would take it down, covering the secret writings for eternity. A few slabs of the wall had already given in to the elements, their images lost forever.

Exploring the site with Rachael had given Bloom goose bumps. To be able to put his hand on the handprints of another human who had left evidence of his existence a millennium ago was magical. He felt the energy produced from touching another man's signature and he could understand how an anthropologist could dedicate their life to the passages of human expression.

Bloom, who was in awe of the spectacle, knowing he might have been the first white man to see the grandeur of a people long extinct, wondered if the rock protector overhang might give way at any minute, crushing those non-Indians who dared to view its strong medicine. He knew his reasoning was faulty and the sandstone wall could easily be in place for another hundred years, but it brought out a spiritual awareness in him to see such heartfelt abstract art in its earliest form. He noticed Rachael preferred to stay a safe distance from the huge rock outcropping, not wanting to disturb her Indian enemies of long ago. Maybe she knew more than she was saying.

"You go ahead, my *bilagaana* nonbeliever. Enjoy ancient Indian history. I had all I wanted of that Nasazi wall as a kid," shrugged Rachael, using the Diné word for Anasazi. "You can take photos for old Dr. James and your dad. I'm sure they would be interested for their records. Good luck to them if they ever want to find the place, since only a handful of the locals even know about Hidden Canyon. I doubt Google maps knows about this one yet. I wouldn't have ever discovered it myself, if it wasn't for a lost sheep when I was 12."

She explained, "I knew if I lost one of my grandmother's prized wool sheep I better not come home or both my mom and grandmother would have my butt. This little camel-colored devil had slipped away from the flock, blending in against the canyon walls. The grass grows

15

well down here in the summer, and the lamb must have smelled its juices. My old dog Naja had been chasing some ravens and hadn't noticed one of my sheep had slipped away. I remember finding this spot for the first time. This tree was not much different in size then than it is now. I would have missed the canyon completely if the lamb hadn't started baa-ing 'come find me.'"

Rachael motioned, "I saw that long line of ancient bighorn sheep chiseled in the wall and I knew this was some kind of sacred place. I sang to help ward off any bad *chindi* that might still be hanging around. Over the years I would come here to graze the flock, but I always got a funny feeling of danger." Rachael started singing in perfect pitch a high, soft song. The words were in Navajo, their meaning lost to those who shouldn't know. The melody bounced off the red rocks.

Bloom respected Rachael's spiritual aesthetics, but he felt exhilaration along with trepidation. Painted onto the rock's surface was a still-vibrant red mineral color. He assumed the red was a mineral paint, but couldn't help but think maybe a blood binder might have been used as well.

Bloom stared at a horned figure carved in the wall, wondering about its meaning. He knew it was impossible to know, yet it seemed to be central to the overall design. There were many repetitive symbols on the wall, but only one of the horned-devil-looking being. "Who was this man or god?" he thought to himself. Staring at the powerful medicine art gave Bloom chills. He retreated over to the shade where Rachael rested. "OK, I've seen enough. Time to let these images rest," he said.

"Told you, Bloom. Don't screw with spirits. Maybe you're starting to hear their voices?"

As they hiked back to their truck under the searing sun, she commented, "There's a faster way back. It's a little escape hatch you can climb up if you follow the wall to the end. Look up, you'll see it. We're probably both too big, though. It was pretty tight even when I was 12." She linked arms with Bloom. By now she had had enough reminiscing. So they left the cliff precipice behind, Bloom not bothering to observe one of the most important aspects of Hidden Canyon.

CHAPTER 5

MAY 7TH

Waking up at 5 am in a cold sweat, Bloom sensed today would be a special day. He took an early morning run, the sun just peaking over the Red Mountains as he finished the three-mile course. Entering the room completely soaked with sweat, he saw Rachael sitting fully clothed, bags packed and waiting for him on the end of the queen bed in room 2B.

"Bloom, I wish you wouldn't run so much. That is what got me in trouble to begin with," Rachael teased, referring to their first romantic encounter when they both fell into a puddle of water at Newcomb High School. That fateful day Bloom had also just finished a long run, arriving to meet Rachael after school, sweating profusely. Any time Bloom finished a run he was fair game to pounce on as far as Rachael was concerned. Except this day, she was not interested.

"What's up?" Bloom, sweating and still breathing hard, looked at Rachael intently, his stout chest and abdominal muscles working overtime.

"Charles, it's time. I've already called Carson and he's canceling morning clinic and is going to meet us at the hospital in 30 minutes. I'm having contractions about eight minutes apart and my water broke. Luckily for our hotel maid, it was while I was taking a shower. You've got time to take a quick shower, but you need to get going. We Yellowhorses usually go pretty fast, or so my mom told me once."

"OK, shit, this is really happening. OK, I'll shower. Where are my clothes, and my wallet? Should I call anyone? Damn, I'm going to be a father and on May 7 th!"

"Yes you are, Charles Bloom. Should we stop by the court house first and get hitched?" Rachael said, taking a last stab at her discombobulated boyfriend before their son was born.

"You want to go to the court house? I don't think there is one in Kayenta."

"Honey, I'm pulling your leg. Now get your white, sweaty ass in the shower. This is my tenth contraction and they seem to be coming faster." With that, Rachael lied back down and started her Lamaze breathing to ease the pain. She imagined working on her rug, the heddle and batons working their magic. It seemed to ease the discomfort of her uterine muscles' exertion.

✻ ✻ ✻ ✻

Brenda Wildhorse checked in the expecting couple. She had most of the paperwork already filled out, as Rachael was meticulous when it came to details, having completed most of the forms the day she arrived at Kayenta. There were only 10 beds in the hospital and the delivery would take place inside one of the rooms. No birthing suites, but at least it was private for now.

Dr. Carson Riddly had just signed on for an additional year's contract with the I.H.S to work at Kayenta Main Clinic. He had had been counting the days until his contract was fulfilled at Kayenta, but that was before he had fallen in love with his Navajo girlfriend, Brenda. She and he were inseparable and it looked as if he too might become a *bilagaana* to bite the marriage bullet. As far as Bloom was concerned, he hoped Carson beat him to it.

"So how's the happy couple? Excited about becoming a father, Bloom?" asked Carson.

Rachael, who was bearing down going through another much more intense contraction, didn't answer.

"Sure, except I'm even more scared than I was when I saw your face next to that rattlesnake," Bloom said, referring to Carson's own near-death experience at Buck Wilson's house a year ago. Bloom had helped stabilize the situation and saved Carson's life.

"Don't you worry, I remember that day. I haven't forgotten your help. Why do you think I agreed to deliver your child? I hate deliveries. Obstetrics was always my weakest subject in school." Dr. Riddly winked at Rachael to let her in on the joke.

"Shit, that's sucks. Anybody else around more competent? Could of told me that a few months ago when we were still deciding who should do the delivery," Bloom responded.

Before Dr. Riddly could answer, Rachael politely said in a very Navajo way, her voice calm and collected, "OK it's time for you two boys to get to work. I'm about to deliver."

Within a few minutes, a healthy seven pound, zero ounces boy was born on May 7th, precisely at 7:55 am. Carson Riddly filled out the pertinent information on the birth certificate and read it out loud so Bloom could take it all in.

It was ironic that the newest Yellowhorse-Bloom decided to come into the world the exact same day as his father, Charles Bloom, had almost checked out three years ago. Bloom had nearly lost his life in New York City trying to solve the mystery of Willard Yellowhorse's death.

Bloom had been changed by that event in New York. May 7th was a special day which had taken on meaning in his life. He believed it had brought him a second chance at life. Now he knew it had brought even more than that. It had brought the chance to see his son born, and of all places, in an Indian hospital on the Navajo Reservation. No one could have foreseen that. Willard would have been very proud of what in death his life had brought, the coming together of his little sister and his first art dealer to start a new generation of Yellowhorses, delivered by of all people, a man named Carson!

Now Charles had a healthy son—Willy Randal Yellowhorse Bloom. Charles Bloom could now legitimately say his business was Indian-owned and run, his own 1/16th Cherokee blood only a drip compared to the strong Navajo bloodline that made up half his son's genetic code. Bloom couldn't help but wonder if it wasn't all meant to be, some preordained prophecy that Willy's great-grandfather Hastiin Sherman had seen back when he first met Bloom. What else did life have in store for the Bloom family and young Willy?

CHAPTER 6

IN THE NAVY

Fallon Scriber enlisted with the United States Navy as seaman E3. His scores on his entrance exam were in the upper 99th percentile. His medical condition of dermatographia, while quite severe, did not exclude him from service but did eliminate certain job categories that required his skin to be irritated, like scuba diving and anything related to water works. His routine entrance physical into the military included a psychiatric evaluation.

The psychiatrist did note some egotistical ideations, but nothing significant enough to exclude him from active duty. His rough background, which was well documented, might explain some of his peculiar beliefs. The physician's comments section read: "While Mr. Scriber does exhibit some ideas of grandeur, his overall personality is pleasant and he is generally a likable individual whose above-average intellect and positive attitude should help him assimilate well with the rigors of the Navy."

Little did the physician know he had just let in a homicidal psychopath capable of almost anything. Scriber's main goals were to get a G.I. Bill and learn a trade: bomb-making.

The course in explosives and ordinances was boring to most of the recruits who were not at war in the late seventies and wondered if the training could ever have any benefit in the outside world. For Fallon the information he learned would serve his higher purposes in life, which he was still trying to figure out. He knew his life was destined for greatness and his god would have a need for the intimate knowledge of bomb making, a skill that could impact the world in a big way.

Scriber the seaman was made for the Navy. By the time he was 22 he had earned the rank of petty officer third-class. Scriber had few friends but was well liked by his commanders for his intellect and organizational skills. His duty station was a four-year stint at Seal Beach, just south of Los Angeles. The base was a throwback to the 1940s. No building was newer than the late thirties in construction, and its mission was ordinance production and storage facility. It required special clearance to get through the gates. Its idyllic setting allowed for nice runs near the ocean and a feeling of what L.A. must have once been like. The command was small and expected its men to be some of the best the Navy had to offer in all fields, not only in the way they performed their jobs but also when it came to moral fiber.

Fallon Scriber liked his job and he learned everything there was to know about handling explosives. However, the system of saluting higher-ranking individuals bothered the egocentric Scriber. He innately knew his own personality could only take so much saluting. It would only be a matter of time before he would snap and murder another one of his fellow soldiers who made too big a deal of their superior rank. He had been lucky that he hadn't gotten caught when he killed Petty Officer Smith, but the killing gods had looked after him. They always did.

Mat Smith was a lifer, one of those individuals who loved the lifestyle the military provided. Smith had found his niche and it was as a petty officer second-class. He had no intention of become a first-class petty officer, as the responsibilities increase dramatically with the higher rank. He couldn't be made to take the test to improve his rank and he couldn't be involuntarily released as a petty officer with the second-class rank. He was safe and he liked it. Some 25% of the Navy falls into this pay grade.

Smith's greatest joy was pulling rank on those of lower pay grade. He knew that almost all those he picked on would either get out of the Navy or surpass him and move on. He loved to isolate those individuals who didn't seem like they would make it a career, and then work them over, enjoying what little power a petty officer second-class would ever have. Smith decided Fallon Scriber fell into the category of a sailor that would leave the Navy after four years. "Too smart for the military, won't ever make it a career," Smith told himself.

The Navy has a ritual that was supposed to have been outlawed. When a seaman makes the rate of petty officer, his fellow petty officers give him an initiation of blood stripe. The rate of petty officer third-class has one stripe, a V-shaped insignia. The ritual is for all the other petty officers to punch the shit out of the initiate's arm, causing it to become red and swollen over the stripe of the shirt. This was highly discouraged by the upper brass of the military, as it was causing too many lost workdays for those making the grade and discouraging seamen to try and become petty officers.

Seal Beach had been good about keeping the sick bay clear of these individuals. The doctors were to report anyone who went in sick because of an arm beating. The blood stripe ritual had been avoided for the most part at Seal Beach, except with P.O. Second Class Smith. He had been in the Navy for 15 years, just five away from retirement, and he loved the old traditions and didn't give a shit what any officer said about "no blood stripe."

Smith and a civilian buddy grabbed the unsuspecting Fallon, who had been celebrating his promotion by himself at a local bar in the city of Seal Beach. The dive was a favorite of the enlisted types. They manhandled Fallon quietly to a remote location behind the bar.

Smith's drunken friend Bill held Scriber's arm as Smith began interrogating.

"So Petty Officer Scriber, do you know about blood stripes?" the inebriated Smith asked Fallon.

"Listen Petty Officer Smith, I understand you're old school and want to punch the shit out of me, but it's been outlawed by the Navy and doesn't seem like a very good idea to start something you know will end badly. You've had your fun by dragging me out back to scare me. Let's call it enough," Fallon protested.

"Shut the fuck up, you scum bag officer third-class, I'm your superior officer. You need to show a little respect, you dipshit. We're just getting started." Smith was drunk but still understood that he was in charge of the situation.

"I don't like people touching my skin." Scriber pulled his arm from the other drunk's grasp and rolled up his loose sleeve showing his tormentor's fingerprints that were now raised welts where he had been grabbed. "I've got a documented medical problem as you can see and you hitting me is only going to make my condition much worse and then you will be damaging government property, ME," warned Fallon.

"Whatever Scriber, you are in the Navy not the Air Force, you little pussy. Wait till you see what I do with my fist." Smith took his whole 200-pound frame and whaled into Scriber's right deltoid, leaving knuckle marks that rose almost immediately into inflamed welts visible through his windbreaker.

"YOU ASSHOLE, YOU'RE DAMAGING MY SKIN! I AM GOING TO KILL YOU!"

Smith was taken aback by Fallon's anger and how his eyes turned dark instantaneously. The Fallon Scriber he knew had disappeared, and someone very different was now standing in front of him.

The drunken buddy helping Petty Officer Smith force Scriber outside started to slowly retreat, seeing the man he was dealing with was not a normal human being. "I'm out of here, Smith. I agree you're an asshole anyway. Leave the guy alone. He's got a medical problem."

The buddy turned and stumbled away, leaving Scriber and Smith alone in the isolated alleyway to work out their problem.

"Smith, you may be bigger than me but I've been taking deadly force classes for the last two years. You know how painful it is to take combat training classes with my skin condition? It hurts a whole fucking lot, but I'm sure glad I did it. Now let's find out how well the Navy trained me and more importantly if they trained you, Petty Officer Second Class, soon to be Dead Class Smith," Fallon threatened.

Smith realized, just like Willy had seven years ago, that he was in over his head and tried to back away. Even being a sizable foe, his intoxicated condition was no match for the rage of a psychopath who had keyed in on his prey. Scriber used a single karate chop to Smith's carotid area followed by a sweeping move with his lower leg, and Smith was incapacitated, laying sprawled out on the ground, moaning.

"Wow, that was incredibly easy. I should make the Navy a career. Now let's see what I want to do with you." Eyeing a large trashcan, Scriber, like a superhuman, lifted it over his head, then catapulted the metal weapon downward directly onto Smith's cranium, crushing his skull like a watermelon in a Gallagher performance. "I like this badass stuff. Now Petty Officer Smith, I've got to be getting back to the base before curfew. Looks like you're going to be AWOL. Hope you don't get in trouble."

Scriber removed one of his special #2 pencils he always carried in a slim silver box from the inside of his jacket pocket. The pencils were a constant reminder of who he was and the power he could wield. The box rarely left his presence. It was his crucifix. He had discovered the custom case in a L.A. pawn shop. According to the shop owner, an elderly rich woman who smoked Virginia Slims had commissioned it from a Navajo silversmith. She had died of lung cancer and the kids brought it in to pawn. Fallon wouldn't have given the curio box a second glace, except he saw the initials F.S. etched in between two nugget-sized turquoise stones. Removing the pencil from its sacred holder as if it were a holy sacrament, he wiped off his fingerprints and placed the pencil in Smith's front pocket. He then cleaned the trashcan handles where he had grabbed them.

"Let's see if these asshole military cops are any better than Oakland's," Scriber thought, exiting the alley at a trot, his arm aching from the blood punch, his fragile skin still forming additional welts, but his pain dampened by the exhilaration that was pumping through his system, an exciting rush for the man who rarely felt anything.

✹ ✹ ✹ ✹

His next stop was for the second murder of the night. "A twofer," he thought to himself, smiling at the visualization of killing Smith's buddy, Bill, who was the only witness. Scriber found him halfway down the street, wobbling home. Bill never saw the pumped-up Scriber, who made short order of him. Scriber dumped the body in the ocean off a high beach cliff after placing a sharpened pencil in Bill's inside jacket pocket, buttoning it to keep it from falling out on the ride down. The body would not be discovered for a week, and determined an accidental fall, drowning secondary to alcohol intoxication.

Smith's case was solved by the Navy's military police, or so they thought. Scriber was never a suspect. Petty Officer Smith, who was known for his poor motivation and lackadaisical attitude, was not particularly missed or mourned. He simply was dead and a non-issue. His replacement was ironically Petty Officer Third Class Scriber, a better seaman and liked by most, plus he never complained.

Fallon Scriber could have worked his way up the military ladder making a career, but he found the military too rigid for a lifetime commitment. The military had served its purpose. Bomb making and the G.I. bill were his military aspirations and they had been filled. He had even gotten to hone his murdering skills thanks to Uncle Sam's dollars. He left the military with two medals for marksmanship, both in pistol and rifle. He laughed to himself when he received the awards: "Too bad they don't give one for killing fellow seamen in hand-to-hand combat. That one would be much harder to achieve."

After leaving the Navy, Fallon's path was first and foremost to get an education. Complete college, followed by law school, where a psychopath could learn the intricacies of jurisprudence, something that would be important in his career path. Law might even bring him in contact with others of his own kind like Ted Bundy who had used his knowledge of the law to help elude capture. Bundy inspired Fallon, who had read Bundy's quote, "I guess I am in the enviable position of not having to deal with guilt." The two men shared a brotherhood few could ever understand. Fallon could hardly wait to start his career and fulfill his own destiny.

CHAPTER 7

PARTY SCHOOL

Determining which college to attend was mostly a matter of where Fallon could get admitted. He had a G.I. Bill, which made it financially possible to go to more than a California school. It was an article in *Playboy* magazine that helped him make up his mind. Its review of party schools listed A.S.U. in Tempe, Arizona, as the number-three party school in the country. It was also ranked second in student population, with over 60,000 kids. This meant Fallon could easily disappear into a sea of long hair and wild tee shirts. A.S.U. promised the added benefits of being able to get laid and if desired, murder anyone who irritated him. A large student population meant Fallon didn't have much to worry about. All the ingredients a psychopathic killer could hope for. It also helped that A.S.U.'s acceptance rate was over 95% for those that applied. He had matured a great deal intellectually during his four years in the military, but he still had a weak transcript from his Oakland public school days. Fallon Scriber would happily become a Sun Devil. How could you beat a school name like that? He loved the spear logo. It was a sign, one that emulated his own brand: a sharpened #2 pencil.

His goals were simple. Do well enough in college to get into law school. Don't get caught for any criminal activities. Fulfill his sexual urges, which had been growing since his last two murders.

He entered the freshman class in 1981 at 23 years of age, older than his peers. And yet he still had work to do on his personal interactions; skills he hoped to better hone. Being able to blend in and have conversational skills would allow Fallon to be a better attorney. You need to be able to schmooze to get ahead in any profession, but in law it is critical. The more believable his personality sounded, the easier to obtain a client base. A client who is confident in your abilities and cares about you is less likely to ask a lot of questions and becomes a much easier target.

The best place for interactions that are short-lived yet intense is elevators. Elevators hold up to 10 strangers in a closed claustrophobic setting for short durations. Discomfort is a given. Human behavior is intensified in this unnatural setting. Nervous people show their concern, happy people laugh, and criminals watch each other. It was a nice laboratory of human emotion and Fallon made it his job to go up and down at least 20 elevators three times a week, honing skills of interaction and small talk. He would vary his locations so as to find different types of individuals. His favorite was the county court house. There he got to observe criminals and lawyers at close range, his two favorite groups. Besides observing, he worked on becoming a chameleon. Changing hairstyles, clothing, even accents, helped him figure out how best to blend in. Bundy had been a master at this, so Fallon simply borrowed a page out of his hero's psychopath book.

He was amazed how much better his communication skills became as his elevator time multiplied. He could easily manipulate his own emotions to fit the mood of each load of a unique mix of people. He also pushed the boundaries of decency to find out what his limits should be, making politically or racially incorrect comments or jokes to see what the reaction would be. He learned what would take the conversation just over the line of decorum, and shut the whole group down until he was gone.

After three years of "elevatorology," as he called it, Fallon was able to rapidly assess any given situation and deal with what his milieu of human participants threw at him. He figured this must be how many comedians worked on their skills: comedians for joke telling, Fallon for deceiving. His sense of personal power grew as his undergraduate days ran out. By the time he had finished his senior year, he had used his skills to see how many girls' phone numbers he could obtain, 37. He loved to open his silver box and hand them a pencil when they gave him their number, knowing someday that same pencil would be a clue in a death. After all the pencils had been touched he would bundle them up except for one and start over, working on additional fingerprints for the future, his bank account for killing so to speak. Keeping each #2 pencil in order allowed him to have other peoples' fingerprints in case he wanted to screw with the cops. The control was good. Getting so many numbers from interested women attested to his skill with words, not bad for a man whom most would call average in looks.

Fallon had grown to six-foot-one, and the years of physicality in the Navy had helped bring about an athletic build and confidence. An undersized chin with a slight overbite led to a rather odd combination. Growing a beard helped and also made him less likely to stand out in a crowd. His outgoing personality helped him to seem more handsome than he was. This added to his bravado and egotistical nature, which college girls found attractive, thereby allowing him to get laid on a regular basis.

He often toyed with the idea of becoming a serial killer of young college girls as it would have been so easy, but Fallon was waiting for his calling. Killing just to kill was not his modus operandi. He needed a reason. Fallon was still searching for his purpose on earth. Who he was supposed to be, and what legacy he would leave mankind.

The only part of Fallon's life that was not improving was his skin disease. It did seem to be easing in pain just a bit, even though his reactivity was still amazing. He thought maybe this was a sign from god to key in on his skin disorder. It made sense. After all, he might not have ever killed if weren't for Red Men Writes and Willy Bellows.

Fallon made it through college with a 3.5 grade point average, and didn't murder a single person, even with ample opportunities. Next stop, Tucson's law school. Time to take it up a notch.

CHAPTER 8

I SHALL DEFEND MY LIFE

The University of Arizona in 1985 was much smaller than Tempe and Fallon hated its mascots: The Wildcats. He'd rather be a devil. It fit his personality better. Fallon planned to be careful in Tucson, as it was a smaller town and campus. Concentrate on his studies and whatever time he had left over could be used to work on bomb projects and the occasional girl.

Estate law became his field of choice. It was fairly uncomplicated. The best part was it dealt with those individuals who had enough money to plan ahead and generally would be dead in short order. It would allow him to make plenty of money and lay low until the word of god made itself clearer.

Law school was fascinating for the boy from the wrong side of the tracks. He learned that most individuals that need a lawyer seem to be poor or damaged. Rarely did the rich go to prison, or so it seemed from case law. Fallon attacked law differently than most. From day one he was looking for those areas in which he could use his god-given talents of deceit and murder to the fullest of his ability with the least chance of being discovered and still make a good living. He had come to realize his god had a role for him when it came to taking lives, but also understood his gift in this area could help him make an above average living.

Taking human life at will had made Fallon's sense of invincibility grow. He knew he was human, but believed that he was not a normal mortal. After all, why would he have such a painful skin disorder if some higher power weren't trying to guide his hand? The fact that emotions were rarely felt allowed him to act clearly no matter what the situation. This was a gift. Slaughtering his fellow man could be done without remorse. One of few true feelings Fallon could experience was excitement, which occurred after taking another's life or with sex. Murdering was the stronger of those two instigating factors. He wondered if sex and death were combined would they amplify the other sensation? Could this be why Bundy had killed so many, hooked on a feeling, as in the 1974 Blue Swede song? It was a road he was not ready to take just yet, but the song, like others, did play loudly in his mind.

Experiencing emotion even if it was in relation to murder felt good and right. He was certain that his higher power was rewarding him for a job well done by letting him feel something in a world of the unemotional. Happiness and sadness were emotions to be mimicked, not felt. Besides excitement, he did understand anger and pain. Especially pain.

The pain was the focal point of his developing obsession as to why he had been chosen to bear such a burden. He convinced himself it was related to his name Scriber, and the punishment he had experienced as a child at the hands of other children. As his own thoughts of murder and his role in life solidified he developed a mantra: "Those individuals who have wronged me must be punished. If the law is unable to stop my actions even when I give them bountiful clues then I will continue my crusade, my power multiplying. It is up to *them* to stop me, so help me god."

The first three murders were good experience for the more challenging tests ahead. He would be prepared for what the future brought him. Law would let him deal with others in his profession, and more importantly the cops. These were his mortal enemies. The more he understood the mind of his foes—the police—the better he could fight and taunt them. It would be up to them to stop him. The greatest victories were those when you are not only the hunter but also the hunted. He would be both. He took his lawyer's oath seriously, at least some of it: to act at all times within his right to defend his life, liberty, and property. It would be his life and he was at liberty to take property as he saw fit.

Scriber felt his ultimate purpose would be revealed to him in some sort of great message from god, and when he received it, he would need to be ready to battle those he deemed the axis of evil. Years later when President Bush spoke at his State of the Union, Fallon realized it was for him alone: he was the chosen one to deal with those who had caused him so much pain, it was his axis of evil.

CHAPTER 9

GOOD GUYS 0, BAD GUYS 5

Sammy was now Dr. Sam Hubbard. College life was a distant memory as he entered his ninth year of work as a forensic psychologist for the state of California in 1980. His job was straightforward enough: evaluate inmates with psychiatric disorders to find out their state of mind and if they were fit for prison, to be released for parole, or destined for a mental institution. Sam enjoyed his job for the most part. It was interesting and always changing. The human mind was a complex animal, much more than a javelina's, and its range of disease was broad and wide.

The Zodiac Killer that had steered him to his current profession had never left Sam's subconscious. He secretly hoped to discover the killer's identity and bring him to justice. The only thing really known was Zodiac was a male and probably lived somewhere in the San Francisco-Oakland area. The likelihood of actually capturing the elusive killer was minimal. Sam was pretty sure he was a psychopath, and these were the hardest criminals to corner. Their intellect and charming outer appearance made them difficult if not impossible to isolate, unless they got too confident in their abilities to elude the law.

Five large poster boards dominated the small government office of Dr. Hubbard, each covered with the history of one of San Francisco's potentially psychopathic-related serial murders. The almond-colored paper mosaics were designated at the top by a title. Some were public names like "Zodiac," and others were secret code names kept by the police and those closest to the case. Possible serial murderers are better not shared with the general public.

Currently the cops had no serious leads on any of the five separate files. Sam would add any potential information to the charts as it became available. In his spare time he would stare at the chronologically placed forensic images of now deceased loved ones and make a pledge to find these vermin of society.

The Zodiac's case had gone cold for over 10 years and like the police Sam had all but given up hope on solving what seemed to be the most disturbing killer of the group. These collages of death were

Sam's playtime. He knew the probability of making a dent in these cases was slim. His real work was dealing with institutionalized convicts, which took up the majority of his day.

Sam had discovered his early childhood talents of observation served him well into adulthood. He was the best in his field of forensic psychology. He was an expert at listening and processing his observations and then coming up with an unbiased opinion.

Currently his workload was mostly gang-related. You spend enough time working in big American cities as a forensic psychologist, you will become a gang expert by default. The day's agenda: crack a suspected Vietnamese murder suspect who was claiming innocence but appeared from his demeanor to be anything but. The language barrier was significant and he was working with one of the best interpreters in the field. The accused murderer was a small, wiry Asian man of 20 who had eyes that danced like dice on a craps table. He was dirty but so far had clung to his story.

The interrogation process lasted for two hours and nothing of use materialized. Then the suspect slipped and said a word even Sam's Anglo ears recognized, "Lotus." He knew after years as a psychologist if the hair on the back of his neck stood up he had just hit pay dirt, and "lotus" elicited the hair response.

The interpreter didn't catch the importance of the word but Sam did. An oriental lotus pot has the same visual appearance as that of a gun's cylinder and was a slang word used by gangs to describe just such a use. Sam jumped on the word and started to pound away. He knew using lotus had been a Vietnamese Freudian slip. The man was indeed the shooter.

"Ask him, no tell him, I know he was involved. Press him hard! Say I know what 'lotus' means!" The anger was seething out of Sam toward the suspect, who had been wasting a good portion of Sam's morning, all the while feigning innocence. Standing directly behind the interpreter, Sam locked eyes with his young evil opponent and waited for his response. He listened for the interpreter to say "lotus" and watched.

"Bingo!" he screamed, startling the young criminal who proceeded to fall off his banana-yellow plastic chair onto the cold Formica tile.

"Get off that floor, you liar, I got you by the short hairs and now we are going to play."

The convict started to sweat profusely as he slowly crept back into his unforgiving chair. He understood he had been able to hide behind the language barrier, but that one word and his reaction had unfolded the true story.

Another victory for Dr. Sam Hubbard. He was a pro at observation. He was possibly the best there was. He wondered if he would be good enough to recognize one of the five true psychopaths lining his office walls if he met one on the street. Little could he imagine he would be getting an opportunity soon, and it would hit close to home.

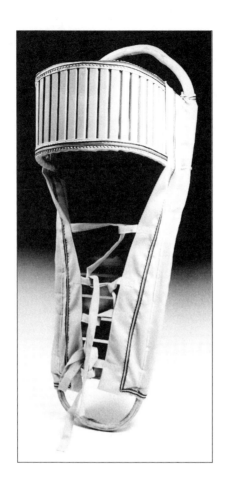

CHAPTER 10

A BLESSING WAY

It had been two months since Willy Bloom's birth, and the happy couple had been taking feeding shifts. Willy was a poor sleeper. Charles's own father Jack Bloom started laughing when Charles called him asking advice about his nocturnal problems. "Well son, you didn't sleep through the night until you were at least one. Your mother, god rest her soul, gave me the privilege of night duty just like you and I remember it well, even at 80. I wish you luck!"

Charles Bloom was actually looking forward to summer in Santa Fe. He would be forced to go and work at his gallery and leave Rachael to her own devices. Besides caring for the baby, she had to finish her big rug for Indian Market. She was the main headliner again for the August event.

This year, Bloom's Indian Market exhibit and sale would be a tribute to the Yellowhorse family. The show was entitled "Rachael and Willard Yellowhorse: A Retrospective." The hard part was finding some of Willard's work to exhibit and hopefully being allowed to sell it if loaned. Willard was Rachael's older brother, who had been dead for over 20 years. He died too young and his work was scarce. The average Willard Yellowhorse painting could sell for about $500K and nobody wanted to let go of their pieces, including Bloom. He owned a small but delicious abstract piece, which Willard had given him as a present for having had such a great opening one year. The back of the painting read: "Charles Bloom, the greatest art dealer an artist could have. I hope we grow old together." Not one time had Bloom read the inscription when it didn't bring tears to his eyes. Reading Willard's inscription made it still feel like yesterday when they both were young and the future still had no limits. His Yellowhorse wasn't for sale. Too many old feelings. The small painting was much more than a piece of art or money. It represented his own life's journey.

Bloom mailed his Yellowhorse retrospective invitations out in June, even though he didn't have a Willard Yellowhorse for sale. He hoped the card might turn up an available piece, someone hoping to take advantage of the show, and it did. One of his now elderly clients was potentially interested in selling his Yellowhorse drawing. Bloom remembered the piece well. It was large at 20 X 30 inches, and was executed by Willard during his second year showing at Bloom's. The drawing depicted multiple ghostlike images, highly abstracted with black holes filling the background. It was fully signed, Willard Yellowhorse, on the bottom right, which was a plus, making it much easier to sell than an artwork with just his initials, W.Y., which he often did on drawings.

Even better was the fact that the ghost drawing was a study for a large Yellowhorse painting which coincidentally was now in the permanent collection at the New Mexico Museum of Art in Santa Fe, a recent donation by a wealthy Dallas couple. The painting was hanging prominently in the museum's front entrance for all to see the generosity of Texas oil. Bloom was a big fan of Texans even if he was a diehard New Mexican.

The timing was perfect. It was quite possible someone would donate the funds to buy Bloom's consigned piece so it could hang next to the large oil painting, which was worth close to $1 million. Museums love to show how a drawing becomes an important painting, and this Yellowhorse fit the bill. Bloom figured he could get a tenth of the value of what the oil painting would be worth, so he told the potential consigner he would price it at $100K and take 20%. This was a low percentage for most art galleries, as many of the top dealers asked closer to 40%, but he wanted the Yellowhorse piece. The drawing would make his show, and besides if his old client got wind of the recent donation he would simply circumvent him and go directly to the museum. Considering the owner had only paid Bloom $3,500 originally, it would shameful if he didn't make something on the second go around, or at least that was how Bloom saw it.

The client finally committed to consign the work after Bloom promised to run a full-page ad in the best Santa Fe art guide. The book was the only one that was primarily content driven and actually was selective in whom they let advertise. It was called *Canyon Road Arts*, which was appropriate since Bloom's gallery was on Canyon Road.

It would be expensive, but the catalog brought the right people to his gallery and qualified his show by its inclusion in the book. The ad would be a two-page spread, with the left page describing the piece and its importance to the New Mexico Museum of Art's work and the right side a full-page illustration with the show dates. Bloom figured if he could hand the art book to the museum curator it might help sell the painting or a patron might independently bring it to the museum's attention.

With the one Yellowhorse piece for sale, plus his own painting, and another loaned piece for exhibit only, Bloom had enough for a show from the Willard side.

The Rachael branch of the family was presently looking like it would be mainly her old sculptures which she was originally known for, a few very early paintings which she thought were "not good" but Bloom insisted, and hopefully one large rug. Last year's Market show with Randal Begay had brought Rachael a lot of exposure and she could probably sell her current rug which was on the loom to an already interested Scottsdale doctor for what she got last year, $10K, but Bloom was hoping to hold out for more when he unveiled it during Indian Market. Then he'd call the doctor.

Bloom decided to also exhibit the last rug from Rachael's maternal grandmother, Ethel Sherman. It was a piece which Rachael had helped finish after Ethel's death. The rug was magnificent. Though only part Yellowhorse, it would add greatly to the rug side of the show. Rachael had titled the weaving "Generational" and it was not for sale, a special rug for Rachael. That piece was slated to be given to her first daughter, who she was now talking about having.

This additional family rhetoric was scaring the crap out of Bloom, who was just learning to cope with being a father and had still not committed to getting married. It was looking like the stars were aligning against him in this arena. He felt every bit a part of a complete family with Rachael and Willy, and couldn't figure out why the delicate fabric of his family needed to be screwed with by her wanting to get married. But it wasn't looking good for bachelorhood. Still, the retail season was starting up and he would soon be living apart from Rachael, staying at Brad Shriver's guesthouse. Selling was looking quite appealing.

It was July 1st. Bloom's bags were packed and he was getting ready to leave Toadlena in the morning just in time for the Fourth of July weekend. Bloom did not want to miss Santa Fe's annual migration of rich Texans up Canyon Road, their original home waters.

Then his plans changed suddenly.

Hastiin Johnson, Willy's godfather and a powerful medicine man, came to visit. Willy Randal Yellowhorse Bloom was named after Johnson's deceased grandson Randal Begay, and Johnson thought it was important that he have a role in young Willy's life, even if only for one trip as he realized his own life's flame was at the end of its wick. Johnson, who was 90, was still able to get around without assistance and insisted he could even ride his horse that had aged along with him, but it was a long drive from his comfortable hogan in Kayenta and one he worried about undertaking on his own. When Rachael offered to pick him up and arranged for him to stay in Sal Lito's cozy guesthouse, he agreed.

His first stop as he entered the Yellowhorse house after the long trip was not to the rest room as his body was suggesting, but directly to the newborn boy who was almost two months old. He shuffled over to make his first introduction. As he reached the boy, who was in a traditional cradleboard, it happened. Willy locked eyes with the old medicine man and without any prompting on Johnson's part, started smiling and then gurgled a little laugh.

The very first smile from any child warms a father's and mother's hearts, but in the Navajo world it also means a Blessing Way would be in order. The first person to see the smile, which has to be witnessed, has great meaning for the Diné. The person to whom the smile is directed is an indication that this person will be the one the child will most likely follow after.

Bloom—who saw the event, not knowing its importance to the Navajo—said to his guest, "Look, Willy Randal likes you! That's his first smile and laugh, you're so lucky." The old man started to laugh and sing an ancient song. He now realized why he had made the journey. Rachael, hearing the commotion and understanding the import, ran in from the porch where she was unloading the car and gave Hastiin Johnson a heartfelt hug. Understanding the implication of her son's choosing a powerful medicine man as his mentor, she was very proud.

"You're not going to Santa Fe this week, Bloom. Unpack your bags, no retail sales for you. We have more important things to tend to now. You'll be staying on Navajo time a little longer. You might as well take off the Santa Fe watch you put on this morning. Everything you were going to do or have me do, just got put on hold," Rachel announced.

For the first time since his son's birth, it felt like he was already married. Bloom wondered to himself, What the hell just happened?

Rachael picked up her son and with the old man still chanting, she started singing her own tune, lifting the boy's papoose to the sky with her every up beat in recognition of his first smile. Willy kept smiling and laughing. Santa Fe could wait.

CHAPTER 11

MORE THAN PAINT IN THE CAN

Organizing the Blessing Way was a big deal for Rachael Yellowhorse and an even bigger deal for Hastiin Johnson. The old medicine man knew his time on the fourth world was fading quickly, and to have the opportunity to be chosen by Willy as his life's mentor was a tremendous honor. Even though he was 90, Johnson had never been the one to see a first smile. He had been a busy man, an important social connector for his people, and many of those times he should have been home seeing his own children or grandchildren smile had been missed. The fact that Willy's middle name was Randal, named after Johnson's own now deceased grandson, made the experience even more special.

Hastiin Johnson would perform the Blessing Way ceremony himself and request to the *Diyin Diné'e* (Holy People) that Willy not be greedy but a generous individual, and always be helpful throughout his life. Secretly Hastiin Johnson hoped Willy would follow in his own footsteps and become a medicine man. Hastiin Johnson made a promise to live longer than he expected so he could show Willy the ways of the Diné.

Bloom could tell by Rachael's reaction that this ceremony would be much bigger than the Blessing Way that Willy had had when he was first born. That gathering was a small, intimate group. This event was taking on the feeling of something of critical importance in Rachael's life. Bloom may not have been married, but he had been around women, especially this woman, long enough to know that you got out of the way of a runaway freight train, which this was. The ceremony was to be paid for by the person who saw the smile, in this case Hastiin Johnson. Usually a party of this nature would be limited by money, so maybe 20 people would be invited. Not this one.

The old medicine man said he had been saving his money until the gods showed him what to do with what he had been given. The ceremony would be in two weeks, and much preparation had to be made. Hastiin Johnson brought Rachael a paint can with a red top. He pried the can open and looked intently at her and then speaking in Navajo put his hand into the can and pulled out a bundle of cash in a zip-locked bag marked in magic marker, $20K. It was obviously not the handwriting of a 90-year-old Navajo.

"Rachael, the gods have asked me to give you one of these packets for your child's smiling ceremony, which I have been blessed to perform. I ask you to use this as you see fit. It is all yours. I believe it is enough to get the kind of recognition for Willy and your family that you deserve." The old man handed the $20K packet to the young woman, who was shocked at the amount of money in her hand. Twenty thousand dollars would be three years' work for Hastiin Johnson at his prime, but he was old and the white man's money was only useful if it helped his people and Willy was now his special project.

"I don't know what to say, this is so much money! I will take all but 20% and spend it on Willy's ceremony. Four thousand I will put away for his college education. We will have the greatest smiling ceremony that Toadlena has ever seen!" She embraced the old man as tears rolled down both their faces. Willy, cooing in his papoose board, smiled the whole time as he looked intently at two of the important people in his life.

CHAPTER 12

MUTTON STEW AND FRY BREAD

The magnitude of the party Rachael was planning would require facilities and organization. Bloom only had two weeks to get it all together. He decided to ask Sal Lito if they could hold it at the Toadlena Trading Post. The huge numbers of people, many of them weavers, would be great for Sal's business, and he could invite a few special friends or clients of the post to see a real Blessing Way ceremony. Sal jumped at the opportunity, seeing no downside as Bloom would pay for it all. Sal figured he could take some credit and it wouldn't be on his nickel. He knew all about spending money on parties as he had done it many times in the past to celebrate the grandmother weavers.

The party was on. Bloom started to worry less about missing the first two weeks of July in Santa Fe. Yes, the opera season was open and the tourists were flooding in. But Brad Shriver was there to help Dr. J with anything he couldn't handle, and Shriver had gone ahead and started the annual "tourists say the dumbest things" board without him. He had a couple of good ones already. An older lady had wandered into Shriver's asking where Bloom's was, and did they have any good roses in stock. Brad explained that Bloom's was a contemporary Native art gallery, not a flower shop. She became quite indignant and huffed, "There should be a law against naming a gallery Bloom's. That should be reserved for flower stores!" The season was looking like it was going to be a doozey, whether Bloom was there or not.

In fact, being a slave to retail wasn't good for anybody. So Bloom invited Shriver to the Blessing Way party, hoping he would ditch a day of potential sales for this once-in-a-lifetime event. "I know it means being away from Santa Fe on a Saturday during peak season, but you won't regret coming to a real Indian party. Lots of free food, music, and a couple of hot-looking girls, I promise," Bloom cajoled. Shriver replied, "You had me at the food."

The drive was four hours in good weather from Santa Fe. Brad decided he could make it up and back in a day, as he wanted to only miss one day of work, unless of course Bloom's hot-girl prediction came true. Shriver was in, and Bloom decided he would close his "flower shop" for a couple of days and let Dr. James off to enjoy the special Blessing Way ceremony too. Bloom was on Indian time now. The retail money could wait.

Bloom knew that the retired anthropologist would get a kick out of seeing so many real live Indians and it would be good exposure to current Navajo culture. Many of Bloom's artists were Diné, and having a deeper understanding of the culture would make it easier to sell. Dr. James was thrilled. He was also hoping to see the petroglyphs that Bloom had showed him pictures of. Dr. James would stay in the 1948 guest trailer behind Rachael's house. Sleeping well might be hard since the woodpeckers' mating season was in full tilt and there was still no plastic owl on the roof to chase off the little jackhammer-like birds, but that should also appeal to Dr. James's scientific side.

Another person on Bloom's short list was Trevor Middleman, a textile curator from Austin, Texas, who oversaw the Navajo weavings collection in the Blanton Museum on the University of Texas campus. Rachael's last major rug was hanging there.

Hastiin Johnson also had Trevor on his list, one of only two *bilagaanas* he was inviting. Dr. Carson Riddly was the other. Johnson wanted to thank Trevor personally for his help with regards to his late grandson, Randal Begay. Randal also had a textile in the collection that Trevor curated. Trevor was thrilled to get to see the actual place where the weavings were made. He could hardly wait to meet a real medicine man and so many grandmother weavers. Trevor had worked with textiles his entire life and was an expert in the field but had never been to the Navajo Nation and knew it would provide a deeper understanding of the art form.

Dr. Carson Riddly finally was no longer the low man on the Navajo Clinic totem pole, having put in more than a year's worth of service, so he was able to arrange time off with coverage for his shift. He had become good friends with Hastiin Johnson and the old man had taken him under his wing, providing an understanding of what it meant to be a good Diné. Carson would of course come with his girlfriend Brenda Wildhorse, who wanted to invite a number of her relatives.

The most important person on Charles Bloom's list was his father, Jack Bloom. They had always been close and Bloom still used his father as a sounding board when things got tough. He cherished his days as a kid taking trips to Gallup, and it was probably seeds sown then that had grown into his career as a dealer in contemporary Native American art.

Dr. Bloom was a man who never strayed from his path in life, especially when it came to family or work. He was a renowned anthropologist, always looking to add to the world's database. Dr. Bloom and Dr. James had much in common, including that they were both anthropologists, both had taught at Eastern New Mexico University in Portales, and both loved petroglyphs. Dr. James in fact had replaced Bloom's father when he took an important position as the anthropology department head and graduate dean at N.M.S.U. in Las Cruces, a fact Bloom didn't even realize until after he had hired Dr. James to work for him.

Jack Bloom had been widowed from his wife for two years. It had been a storybook love affair from the start and had spawned a marriage that had lasted 52 years. The couple had been inseparable since their early twenties. Charles's father, now 80, was dealing with the aftermath of the deep loss of his lifelong partner. He was living in the same ranch-style home he and his wife had resided in for the past 25 years. The house was within walking distance of the university, so he could easily go over and spend time at the anthropology department. It was obvious to Charles that his father's heart would never really heal. The best he could hope for was for it to scar over.

Charles wondered if he too would be so distraught if Rachael would suddenly leave his life. Marriage was taking over his subconscious thoughts these days, especially when thinking of his own parents' successful marriage.

It was important for his father to be part of the festivities. The retired anthropologist would get a big kick out of seeing his only grandson and his son being embraced by the Navajo people. Bloom's father, after all, was one-eighth Cherokee and could relate to the event on a deeper level than most *bilagaanas*.

Jack Bloom responded that he was thrilled to be a part of his grandson's Blessing Way, and he would stay with Charles and Rachael in Preston's old room for the week. Preston—Willard Yellowhorse's only child who Rachael had raised—was on summer break from his first year at the University of Arizona. He had just gone to Alaska with his new Tlingit girlfriend, and there was no way he could get back in time. Rachael promised she would save some of Willy's salt crystals for him to touch, as it was important that her brother's son be included.

Jack Bloom was looking forward to seeing Dr. James again, and Bloom had a wonderful surprise for the two old professors, who were both important elements in his own life's balance: a field trip.

CHAPTER 13

THE BIG DAY

It was lucky the trading post was only a few miles away from Rachael's house, because they made what seemed like 100 trips during the two weeks preparing for the big day. Both knew everything had to be in place before the numerous guests started arriving.

Bloom had only invited one relative and a few close friends. But Hastiin Johnson and Rachael had no such governor. This was a party and they had the funds to pay for as many people as they could think to invite. There would be hundreds of Navajo well-wishers, many of whom would just show up for free food and music. The working number was 300 people, but Rachael knew the word was out about the big party and it was spreading like wildfire through the rez. In fact, 600 wouldn't be out of the realm of possibility.

Any weaver that wove in the Toadlena/Two Grey Hills style would make an appearance, a tribute to Rachael's mother and grandmother, who were master weavers. They would want to touch the rock salt that would pass from young Willy's hand. The smiling ceremony involves the medicine man passing the Navajo *ts'aa* ceremonial basket that holds natural rock salt. Once the baby's hands have held the salts, they are then passed to all the friends and relatives to help bind him to the people and ensure a good life. It was shaping up that Willy would have a lot of good wishes and a terrific life.

The day before the Blessing Way, Bloom decided to run to the post anytime his presence was requested. It turned out he made three round trips, which helped clear his mind to find his *hozho*, or balance, for the next day's ceremony. The added endorphin rush also allowed Bloom to soak in his environmental surroundings like never before. The incongruous utility poles that ran the course of the flat plains surrounding Rachael's home seemed that day to melt into the landscape. Bloom imagined that the electrified wires were giant sculptures that seemed to seek out distant Shiprock, the huge mountain obelisk which rose out of nowhere from the flat desert floor. Shiprock's imposing presence was sacred to the Diné and had always been a beacon of stability to the Yellowhorse family, its tip just visible from Rachael's home.

Overlooking the post's front door were the two prominent buttes that were the namesakes for the Toadlena/Two Grey Hills rug style. The Two Grey Hills formations had colors that seemed to change dramatically depending on the time of day and the cloud cover. On each of Bloom's three trips, the buttes appeared different in coloration: bright red, orange, and light brown. These geological outcroppings were becoming increasingly meaningful for Bloom. Their presence represented a focal point of stability and a sense of belonging.

The buildup for Willy's smiling ceremony was cementing this sense of belonging. He saw these buttes anew, forming a picturesque backdrop for the gathering he was helping to create. Bloom loved his Sangre de Cristo Mountains in Santa Fe, but these simple hills on the less-populated rez had a deeper meaning. These were now the life force of his world, living among the Diné. Bloom was at a crossroads in his life and was trying to navigate the correct direction forward.

His final run over to the post was to help string lights over the large tent that had been erected in the cottonwood tree-lined backyard. He stopped for a moment to have a Coke and ponder his life on the front porch of the Toadlena Trading Post. Its hundred-year-old entrance where the Navajos sometimes offered their morning prayers and its vista looking out onto old junipers and hogans comprised his new paradigm. Santa Fe seemed far away.

✳ ✳ ✳ ✳

The big day finally arrived. By 10 in the morning it was obvious they would need more lamb chops if they hoped to feed everyone. The inadequate parking lots were already filled and now vehicles were lining the deep, red-rutted dirt road. Trucks and cars well past their prime dotted the usually pristine Toadlena landscape, enlivening the old rock post as the ambiance of the 21st century collided with an ancient world.

The grandmothers strolled up the dirt road dressed in their best turquoise jewelry and velvet blouses as if the queens of the coronation had just arrived. All understood the importance of these matriarchs. These women held a special place for not only their ability to survive on a land that didn't give up resources easily, but also for the rugs they wove, the fabric of Navajo life. The many textiles produced over their weaving careers paid for all the pickups and children's tennis shoes that now filled the dirt parking lot and were running around the post. Their unrelenting commitment to Spiderwoman was not unlike Bloom's father's dedication to research. The difference was the grandmothers allowed an entire population to continue to thrive as a community.

The interior of the post that could handle 30 people comfortably was filled with 50, and another 300 lined the outside back patio with more streaming in by the minute. The smell of roasted corn, fry bread, and grilling lamb filled the fresh morning air. The unique aroma inside the post was one of wool and human sweat. Bloom tried to soak up the scents into his nasal memory so as to remember his son's day and a probable turning point in his own life direction.

Old Sal was smiling ear to ear as his post made sales of food, weaving supplies, and most importantly, rugs, all on Bloom's dollar. He had never been as happy with his selection of Bloom as a part-time employee as he was today. The bonus of the few *bilagaanas* who were invited was they all seemed to be deciding to bring home a memory—one of Sal's precious chocolate-and-white Navajo rugs.

Wilma George, one of Toadlena's master weavers, managed to finish an important new rug in time for Willy's Blessing Way. She walked in the door cuddling her latest monochromatic creation under her own dark brown skin. Sal couldn't help but smile, knowing the grandmother would ask a premium as her timing was perfect and they both knew it. She did, and he paid it happily. Not a moment too soon. Trevor Middleman purchased the monumental masterpiece for the Blanton Museum's textile collection in Austin, Texas. It was Sal's highlight of the day.

Trevor's highlight was that he got not only a picture of the weaver but one of him standing with her in front of the rug, which he planned to display in the museum next to the textile. The excitement of being in the presence of what he considered to be a superstar weaver made his knees weak. For Trevor, this weekend was more than Bloom's son's Blessing Way. It was also the Oscars of weaving and he was one of the special guests. He kept tracking down Bloom during the day's activities and thanking for his invitation to such a special event, emphasizing its impact on his life as it brought a deeper understanding of the weavings he loved so much.

Jack Bloom, who had spent decades discussing Native Americans in front of audiences of white students, for the first time got to experience what real Indian life meant. "My years of lecturing could have been so much better," he thought to himself, if he had only taken the time to find out more about the subject he cared so much about. Watching his own son interact with such ease among the Diné made him realize his child had a better grip on what Native life meant than he ever would. He couldn't stop grinning every time one of the grandmothers came up to Rachael, Willy, and his son to wish them the best and thank them for the festivities. Jack Bloom could see Charles was wiser than his fortysomething years, even if he didn't know it.

The medicine man Hastiin Johnson, dressed in his best cowboy shirt, was first in the greeting line of the honorees. He sat perfectly erect under a large green umbrella looking ever so much the king with the court paying homage. His back never hunched once during the two hours it took all the people to funnel through the little reception area.

Music filled the day, the pulse changing periodically depending on the type of band playing. There was a cowboy band with a hint of Indian undercurrents, followed by a rock band that all the young kids instantaneously started dancing to, and finally the Red Lake singers. The Red Lake group was four mature Navajo men whose distinctive voices seem to reflect life's rhythm on the rez, steady and slow. Their Navajo songs vibrated from low bass qualities to high soprano, with every other beat of their old drums.

There was a line of 50 people dancing, all in pairs, a long snakelike precession dancing in a Jackson's Chameleon fashion, each dancer's foot carefully placed before the next beat of the drum. The turquoise squash blossoms around all the women's necks added a second clinking noise to the steady drum rhythm. The dancing went on for nearly an hour as older couples dropped out and were immediately replaced by new couples.

After the dancing was complete and all the guests' bellies filled, the master of ceremonies, Hastiin Johnson, stood up next to Rachael, Bloom, and Willy, and began speaking. The crowd hushed immediately. Johnson's voice was strong like a young man's, but his wisdom was that of an old desert tortoise. Johnson told of the world of the Navajo as he saw it and why they were special to Mother Earth. Johnson thanked the special guests, including Trevor Middleman and Dr. Carson Riddly, telling of how the young doctor had once saved his life from a rattlesnake bite, clarifying for the audience that the snake who had caused his injuries had been a good spirit and that all animals were important to the Navajo. He pointed out it was Carson who had delivered Willy Randal into the world and recommended other expecting mothers use the doctor when they were going to deliver. Carson cringed and smiled weakly at the thought of the deluge of pregnant women that would undoubtedly soon be coming his way.

The old man's voice cracked slightly as he talked of his friendship with Bloom and his admiration for the *bilagaana* who had shown his heart was good and had extraordinary common sense (except for in his marriage duties). The old man talked of his long friendship with Rachael's grandfather who had passed away but how his presence

50

still ran through the veins of those he had touched, and how Rachael had the same spirit as her grandfather and this had passed to her son Willy, who with that spirit had chosen Johnson to host today's *Hozhooji*, or Blessing Way.

When he finished his accolades to the Yellowhorse-Bloom family, he turned to his audience and with a big sweeping motion of his arms told them in Diné he was here to help serve his community and if he did his job, the *Diyin Dine'e* (Holy People) would grant those pure of spirit their requests, and if not the evil among them would proliferate, and to never forget why the Navajo were placed on Mother Earth and to walk in beauty. Hastiin Johnson had the demeanor of a preacher talking to his flock. He then turned to Willy, whose eyes were large and transfixed on the old man.

Johnson started chanting the songs of spirit and wisdom to his young disciple, who would be a part of him from that day on. When he was finished singing, he took the ceremonial *ts'aa*, removed some little chunks of salts which he carried in his medicine pouch, and placed the salt crystals in Willy's hands and began singing again. Finally he finished, the crowd started to clap, and the small bits of the salt were passed around to add to Willy's power. Willy's smiling ceremony was completed, and he would be a good and generous person.

Bloom, mesmerized by the ceremony, realized he was now a part of the world of the Navajos. He beamed with inner satisfaction. He was also thrilled that Hastiin Johnson did not bring out any snakes as part of the ceremony. Bloom and snakes, unlike the old medicine man and snakes, did not get along.

CHAPTER 14

CLEAN UP

Bloom was exhausted from the two-week preparation and one-day blowout. The emotional stress had taken its toll. Every guest asked him at least once when he was going to make Rachael an honest woman. He could tell she was embarrassed by the constant talk of marriage, something she had stopped bringing up after Willy's birth. She figured Bloom would know when the time was right and she had stopped worrying about what others said. They were both happy, and happiness is a hard thing to find.

Five hundred-plus Navajos, no matter how much they respect Mother Earth, left a large amount of trash and human-related artifacts of the non-collectible variety. The morning after the Blessing Way was dedicated to filling Rachael's pickup truck with four loads of trash. Bloom muttered to himself, "Why didn't Hastiin Johnson mention that part of being a good person was throwing all the trash one produces into the nearest garbage can and not in the crock of the cottonwood trees five feet up?" Slowly the ground became visible again and all the popped balloons were retrieved from the numerous gnarly juniper limbs that had caught them.

The early afternoon was spent folding chairs and breaking down the wooden podium and huge tent that had been erected in case of rain. Sal would yell out periodically to Bloom and his small cleanup crew that they were doing a great job but to remember to return the surroundings to the way they had received them.

Sal himself chose to work inside the post, restocking his food shelves that were nearly empty. He could hardly wait for the next Yellowhorse-Bloom blowout, as this one was going to help him have his best month in two years. Bloom, on the other hand, wondered why a good businessman like himself hadn't at least negotiated part of any rug sales he brought in, like Trevor Middleman's purchase. Sal had charged Trevor $12,000. Just like the astute businesswoman Wilma George, Sal knew his timing was perfect and charged a premium for the opportunity to buy at such a historic event.

Trevor had taken his prized pictures and rug and headed back towards Albuquerque to catch a flight to Austin. He already knew exactly where the weaving would hang. Trevor did manage to stop for a quick tourist stop in Window Rock, an hour away from Toadlena over the mountain by the historic Crystal Trading Post.

Window Rock was named after a natural rock outcropping shaped like a window. Its red and white streaks of mineralization had been formed by deposits of water long gone. Attesting to the tenacious qualities of the Navajo, a town with little water was made the capital of the Navajo Nation. The Navajo Nation's museum located in Window Rock, Arizona, was currently featuring a show on Toadlena Two Grey Hills weavers, which Trevor found fascinating. Four of the weavers in his university collection were displayed in the exhibit. He had been told of the museum by Dr. Carson Riddly at the Blessing Way. Dr. Riddly and his Navajo girlfriend Brenda Wildhorse were contributors to the museum and helped support the permanent exhibit on the Navajo's greatest period of desperation and struggle, the Long Walk. Brenda's great-great-grandfather was one of the names on the treaty proclamation of 1868 that was displayed in the Long Walk gallery. The document had been signed by eleven Navajo tribal leaders, setting up a reservation on June 1, 1868. By signing the peace treaty, the Navajo people were finally freed from four years of internment in which 3,000 had died.

The highlight of the cleanup day for Bloom was returning home to find his father patiently waiting for him to finish his chores. Jack Bloom and Dr. James were sitting on the front porch in a Ford van seat that had become part of the outdoors furniture. It wasn't appropriate décor for most homes, but it worked on the rez.

The two old retired professors had talked all day, hatching a proposed research project they both relished the thought of. The proposal was simple. Go see, document, and publish a book about the sandstone wall of unknown petroglyphs in Hidden Canyon that Bloom promised to show them. The book would be a coffee-table publication for general consumption, not a scientific paper, a first for both men.

In the world of research the phrase *publish or perish* was the mantra. Pretty books of pictures did not really count, but they didn't care. They were retired. The final title of their proposed book was still under discussion but the subtitle would be something like *The Unknown Petroglyphs of Hidden Canyon.*

✳ ✳ ✳ ✳

At dawn the next morning, Bloom loaded them into the truck and took them to Hidden Canyon. On the drive over, they promised the canyon's secrecy would be protected. Infusing the location with a mysterious cloak-and-dagger aspect would give the book an edge. The two men had talked it over with Rachael, whose family along with the Manygoats clan had the rights to the land. Rachael thought it would be fine, and believed Susie Manygoats, the matriarch of the other family, would not care. Rachael didn't want any part of being involved with the project other than as a facilitator; her Navajo beliefs were too ingrained. The less exposure to the sacred wall of her long-ago enemies, the better.

Bloom agreed to be their guide and assist them in their project. His own belief system had no doubt been altered by his experiences with the Navajo, but his aesthetics told him it was still beautiful art and needed to be documented. After all, he was Jack Bloom's son.

Photographing the wall in the early morning would illuminate the petroglyphs perfectly before the overhanging rock shelf got in the way. Dr. James, who was an accomplished photographer, was going to photographically document the wall in its entirety, and Dr. Jack Bloom would make notes regarding the most prominent figures.

Bloom was excited to see his father get involved again with something besides his mother's memory. This was a great project and maybe even one that could bring his father some extra cash and recognition, and it couldn't hurt his own gallery. Free press was good press. The only downside was he had to have Bloom's closed one more day as his only employee frolicked on the Navajo rez instead of paying the light bill. Bloom tried to embrace Hastiin Johnson's words about being a good person and show enthusiasm for the project.

CHAPTER 15

A BOOK IS FORMED

Bloom parked as close as he could to the petroglyph wall, so the two elderly anthropologists didn't have too much of a trek. The compelling nature of the wall that had been decorated a thousand years ago was not lost on Bloom. It was as impressive a sight even the second time around: human graffiti from a long-lost culture. The beautiful symbols and animal/human figures were not unlike those he had seen spray painted on the Santa Fe Railroad cars that lined the railroad district. Images painted on a medium other than canvas didn't lose creativity and beauty, as far as Bloom was concerned.

The enormity of the wall and the human effort required to scale the massive cliff and meticulously chip away at the sandstone was monumental. Since water supplies were scarce, it all would have to be hand-carried, along with heavy stone tools to work on the wall.

These unknown Anasazi individuals were true artisans in every sense of the word. They must have suffered greatly to leave their mark for all time, a testimony to their gods, their belief system, and their need to express themselves. The largest figure on the long brown sandstone wall must have taken a huge effort. Its makers must have built ladders to work on the figure that floated 25 feet above the ground. His horns and pitchfork-like weapon had the universal effect of something powerful or maybe evil. His imagery was created for a reason by a people long gone, their only testimony to living in the harsh ancient world of the Southwest. If the two anthropologists had their way, these compelling images that had been lost to mankind for a thousand years would soon be available to the world, something their original makers could have never dreamed.

Jack Bloom understood all too well what the conditions were a thousand years ago. He had lectured about the Anasazi for decades. This masterpiece of the Anasazi world was made in a harsh environment by a people that rarely lived past 30. Little water or food, and dangers at every bend, yet these creative people carefully climbed up a slippery cliff using small, handhold holes chipped into walls, all in the pursuit of expressing themselves for eternity.

Seeing his father become emotional upon viewing the wall for the first time brought tears to Bloom's own eyes. He had rarely seen his father so moved. The last time was at his mother's funeral. But these tears were different for his father. Their stimulus was joy, not sadness.

The gods were shining on Bloom's exploration party today, as the unpredictable weather and light were perfect for capturing the moment. Both anthropologists were able to climb the tricky handholds and get to the rock platform almost 20 feet above the canyon floor. Jack Bloom, who had his cane with him, tossed the metal third leg up onto the rock ledge as if it was his lunch sack instead of his main force of pedal stability. Charles Bloom, who had enjoyed bouldering during his college years, felt a joie de vivre as he scampered up the sandstone handholds.

Once safely on the ledge, the two old men worked like the professional anthropologists they were. One photographed as the other yelled out measurements and descriptions that Bloom wrote down. He also recorded the event on his iPhone.

The team was efficient. By noon, the good light was gone and the wall had been documented for the 21st century. Soon the lost images would be transferred to paper and a digital format and distributed to all who had interest. Bloom, the consummate entrepreneur, could imagine developing a phone app called iPetroglyph. It would be a depositary for the world's petroglyphs all located on a smart phone. Unfortunately he didn't see any way he would ever be able to monetize such a herculean effort, though he did like the idea.

Having completed their duties as chroniclers, the group was free to explore the half-mile ledge of rock art. The ground was slick from the hundreds of thousands of hours of human usage a millennium ago. In a few places, large slabs of two- to three-inch thick sandstone plates had come loose and fallen off the wall onto the ledge floor. Their petroglyph images were now hidden, except to spiders and scorpions that could fit underneath the flat surface. The thin rock sheets that had not broken on impact resembled large sleds just waiting for someone to try a ride down the slippery canyon wall. Bloom wondered if it was possible to make the ride and the daredevil in him actually wanted to. He knew he now was a family man and such foolhardy tricks were ill advised, especially in such a remote part of the world.

Still, Charles remarked, "Dad, these rock sheets remind me of when I'd visit you in Las Cruces and we'd head to White Sands. Remember those laminated boards I'd use to surf down the slopes of white gypsum sand?"

"Son, those sand-dune rides were one thing. Sliding down these 150-pound slabs of rock off a 50-degree stone incline would be altogether another," Jack Bloom responded.

Charles let the thought pass like a cigarette craving. He knew it was bad for him. Instead he got busy unpacking the lunch that Rachel had packed for them: leftover lamb chops and baked beans, another good reason to get to Santa Fe soon. He was missing his green chile enchiladas. There was still lots of Blessing Way food in Rachael's refrigerator and she was not one to waste. They would eat lamb until it was all gone.

Sitting in the sunlight with his father was a time of clarity and reflection for Charles Bloom. His back faced the ancient past as he looked out on the future. His father was getting old and his time was limited. Charles wondered about his own life and what it had in store for him. If he could have seen the future sitting there peacefully on the ledge that day, Bloom would have been very afraid. A man of pure evil, a person the Navajo have no name for, was bearing down on his entire family and he would be making a visit very soon.

CHAPTER 16

SANTA FE

The retail season was in high gear by the time Bloom drove up to his neglected gallery in July 2012 one week after Dr. James had gotten back to work. Three weeks of opera season had already passed, though luckily he was in time for the annual Eight Northern Indian Pueblos Arts & Crafts Show. The exhibit and sale put on by the local northern pueblo tribal council was the second-largest Indian show each summer, and generally marked the start of the height of the selling season. The artisans were primarily pueblo potters, but some very good Navajo and Hopi artists also attended. It was the warm-up for the huge Indian Market weekend that was only a month away.

Historically for Bloom, this weekend would give him a nice monetary kick as his gallery specialized in Native artists and many customers coming in for the Eight Northern would also stop by Bloom's. Now that his gallery was also showing a few traditional artists, he was hoping for an even bigger weekend. His own newfound interest in traditional Native crafts made the weekend activities even more appealing.

For the first time in his career he wished he had something to show this weekend other than modern art. A rug or two would have been great. He cursed the fact that he hadn't asked old Sal Lito from Toadlena to consign him a couple of pieces for the summer. Next year he wouldn't make the same mistake. "Shit, that was stupid, another slick move by a professional art dealer," he muttered, reviewing how he had just been in the heart of Navajoland and didn't bring anything back with him other than some cold lamb chops. He knew everything about all the weaving families and could sell rugs with the best of them. Sal had eaten at least one lamb by himself at the Blessing Way festivities and the extra traffic had brought the post thousands of dollars. "No way would he have not given me a rug or two," Bloom shook his head as he walked through his gallery's 19th century low doorway wondering how he could have been so dense after so many years in the art business.

"Dr. J, how much money have you made me today?" Bloom asked. He had decided on the drive east to start calling Professor James "Dr. J" after the famous basketball player. It felt odd to call him by his first name "John" and "Dr. James" was too formal, so Dr. J it was.

"Dr. J, huh," the professor responded. "I don't know if I'm up to such a famous namesake, especially since there have been no real sales so far unless you call selling a book on petroglyphs making you money."

"How much was the book, and did I own it?"

"I'm afraid it was one of my books I consigned to the gallery. An early, less-scientific manuscript on Southwest rock art. Apparently it is now a collector's item, being out of print, and of course I signed it, which helped it sell. I got $100 so you made $40. It won't cover my salary for the day, but the day's not over and this weekend is the big Indian show out at San Ildefonso."

"Well Dr. J, it pays for the light bill this week, so keep up the good work. I'm back and plan to be in most every day straight through Indian Markup," Charles vowed, using the slang term gallery owners and locals use for Indian Market, the one time Native artists can actually get retail prices for their work, not having to wholesale them out to dealers.

"Great, Charles. I'll look forward to having company! It's been lonely around here. I see Mr. Shriver from time to time, but this back alley can be a little boring. I have managed to get a good running start on the new manuscript your father and I are working on. I think your Hidden Canyon must be one of the most unique finds in the last 20 years in rock art."

"Yeah, my dad has called me five times this week going on and on about how excited he is to be working again. He thinks the project will come together quickly. You're looking for publishers already?"

"In fact an old press I wrote for has agreed to give it a green light so now all we have to do is finish and start the book tour."

"No kidding, Dr. J, a book tour! That's fabulous. I hired a famous author. I hope it's in the winter when it's slow. Hate to lose you next summer."

"Apparently it's been fast tracked. Seems there is interest in the subject right now. I guess one of those New York designers came out with a handbag line using petroglyph images, so the publisher thinks the timing is perfect. So to answer the question, you're fine, we go in January. How's Rachael taking to the absence of your fatherly duties? She must be sad to see you go, with the new baby."

"You assume correctly. I will have been away from Willy for almost a month before she gets here. It seems weird to actually get to sleep eight hours tonight."

"I can't wait to see Willy again. He will have grown so by Market. She's bringing him, I'm assuming?"

"You assume correctly again, Doctor. I already miss his smiling face, just not at three in the morning."

"I remember those days, my boy. It seems so long ago, when I was in your shoes. It goes fast. Make sure you take advantage of every minute," the professor advised.

"I agree, Dr. J. I just have to come to grips with the whole marriage thing. I'm getting closer to the lifelong commitment. Maybe something will push me over the edge."

"Charles, something always does and usually it's a determined woman!"

Both men laughed because the fear of marriage is universal to the male species. Bloom was surprised he hadn't seen any petroglyphs depicting a woman with her finger pointing toward a cowering man.

CHAPTER 17

EIGHT NORTHERN DUST DAYS

For some reason anytime there is an outdoor Indian festival it rains, blows, or both. Today it was blowing. The monsoons in the Southwest typically run from early July through the first week in September. A large flow of moisture pushes up from the Gulf of Mexico and blankets the afternoon skies of Arizona, New Mexico, and Colorado with precious rain. Most anthropologists think that the demise of the Anasazi during the 1300 time frame was probably due to a severe drought. One year the monsoonal rains simply never showed up, and the people either starved or moved on. So far this summer was looking like a repeat of 1350.

No measurable rain since May 15th was not a good sign. Usually there were patches of snow on the Truchas Peaks of Northern New Mexico, but this year they were greenish/brown in color. One fire had already occurred and the outlook was looking bad. Santa Fe was in stage-four drought conditions. This meant little watering and all the great water-feature sculptures on Canyon Road were shut down. The usual lush gardens of Canyon Road were looking more like performance pieces done for dying plants, Charles Bloom thought as he drove down the street and headed for US Highway 84. He was going to take a brief gander at the Eight Northern Pueblos Show, then come back and sell, sell, sell.

The lack of rain plus strong winds with nothing to hold the dirt in place meant San Ildefonso's dirt lot was miserable, especially with the 30 mile-per-hour winds. Walking the rows of vendors on the sand-packed parking lot during the pueblo's busiest day of the year was painful. Bloom, who by this time in his life was a pro at flea markets and outdoor events in New Mexico, had borrowed a pair of Brad Shriver's old red ski goggles and wrapped a yellow bandana around his nose and mouth. He was almost unrecognizable and looked for all purposes like a kook or worse, but he also was breathing normally and didn't have any corneal abrasions, something he couldn't say for his Texas brethren.

Bloom saw three cowboy hats blow by, their overweight owners frantically chasing after them through the aisles of pots and jewelry. The local inhabitants found this hilarious and instead of trying to stop the Texas tumbleweeds, they simply lifted up their feet so the hats would continue down their paths back home. No mercy for those not from New Mexico and/or of Indian descent.

The market had a few good Navajo weavers, one of whom was so talented that Bloom told her if she didn't sell her rug and wanted to leave it through Indian Market, he would try to move it for her. She was skeptical at first until he explained he represented Rachael Yellowhorse, Ethel Sherman's granddaughter. He then brought up his new son Willy and his Blessing Way by Hastiin Johnson and her whole demeanor metamorphosed. He was no longer a *bilagaana*, but part of the extended Navajo family. Susie Manygoats had wanted to attend the event as she had been friends with the Shermans and would have come but she had to finish her rug and couldn't spare the day. Now Susie was in a dust storm trying to sell that same rug and wished she hadn't missed the Blessing Way.

This was the same Susie Manygoats whose family shared a common ancestral land border with Rachael's. Her grandson Frank Manygoats was also showing his reproduction rock art at the show, and Susie personally took Bloom over to meet him. Maybe Bloom would sell his work, too.

"Mr. Bloom, this here is Frank. Frank, say hi to Mr. Bloom. His wife is Rachael Yellowhorse. You know her. She used to run her grandmother's sheep in the canyon."

The wife phrase stuck in Bloom's throat, as he had not called Rachael that. He had said specifically "significant other."

"Hi, you want to buy some of my rock art? I make neat copies off an old site. None of these have been seen before, real private place," Frank offered. The old lady then jabbered Navajo at the young man, probably chastising him for not making small talk first and for getting down to business too fast. "I mean, nice to meet you, Mr. Bloom. You married one strong woman in Rachael. You live on the rez now?" Frank hastened to add.

Bloom immediately picked up on the grandmother's intentions for a more cordial conversation. "Yes Frank, I live over by Toadlena most of the time with my girlfriend, Rachael Yellowhorse. We just had a baby boy, Willy. His Blessing Way was last week."

"Oh, I heard about that from one of my neighbors who went, sounded like a big blowout. Sorry I missed it. Grandma couldn't go, had to finish the rug so it could get sandblasted. I heard that the Native Knights were there. I really wanted to hear them!"

"Yes they were, played for over an hour. Apparently they have a huge following. Rachael's ex high-school boyfriend is their lead singer."

"Yeah I know. His name is Johnny Badwater. He is very cool. Wish I had his pipes. If I did, I'm done picking rocks forever. Rachael must have asked Johnny a favor to come sing. They're pretty big now. Not a rez band no more."

"Maybe so. Well let's see what you got here, Frank," Bloom urged, wanting to move on from the ticklish subject of Rachael's very cool Navajo ex-boyfriend as he examined Frank's rock art.

"So Mr. Bloom, I make these from an old Nasazi picture wall. I take a thin piece of paper and lay it right over the old rock design, then I make a copy by gently rubbing a pencil over it. It's hard to keep the pencil tip sharp enough for the big ones, this is where lots of practice and plenty of pencils come in. Once I have copied the rock picture, I then take the tracing paper and put it on a flat piece of clean sandstone from the same area and chip out the design. I have to be really careful or the paper will tear. I get pretty close to what the old ones made. All the tourists think they are the real thing, but you can tell," Frank said, pointing to a chipped-out place. "All the chips I make are white. Real ones have a sandstone brown look, plus lots of wear at the edges. It's better for people to tell they are new so they don't think you're stealing nothing from gravesites. Most Navajos are not interested in even touching the old ones, much less stealing from them." Susie Manygoats nodded her head in agreement.

Frank held up a brown piece of paper with his signature on it for Bloom to see. "I sign a piece of paper for each rock art piece I make, telling what I see in the designs and kind of what they mean to me. I also sign each rock down low with a little goat symbol. That's my signature so nobody thinks they're old. Kind of insurance so I don't get in trouble with no Feds."

Bloom searched hard to find the goat that was barely visible as he looked through his dirty goggles. Indeed there was a small, finely carved goat in the very corner of each piece. "These are great. You won't believe me, but I recognize all of these images. I know the wall they come from."

"Really? How? I didn't know any *bilagaanas* knew the site. Oh, Rachael showed you, huh? She hates being around the old ones. She told me the place gives her the creeps. Surprised she brought you up there."

"Yes, you're right, she's not a fan. But she has shared it with me. Actually, two anthropologists are working on a book about the wall, too. It'll come out in January. Your grandmother knows about the project."

"Wow, that's a drag. Kind of ruins my whole, 'This is super special, no one has seen them before' angle I use to help sell my stuff," Frank lamented, giving his grandma a disappointed glance. Susie Manygoats looked down at her feet.

"It won't be unknown anymore," Bloom said, "but think of all the press we'll get with the book. Your family and Rachael's are the only ones with access, so it's not like people will get to see it in person, unless they want to pay for the privilege. They will still have to buy your pieces and now we can throw in a cool book showing the wall they came from."

"Does that mean you'll show my work in your gallery?" Frank asked.

"I will not only show your work, but I bet I can sell a bunch too. And you won't have to sit out here in the blowing sand."

"Count me in, Mr. Bloom."

Susie Manygoats chimed in, "OK, you two boys work out the details. I got to get back and sell my rug. I need a new set of tires." She walked off.

Bloom remarked, "I'm really impressed with this one image that looks kind like a devil. I've seen it in person and you nailed it. Making it a life-sized image must have been hard. It's terrific. You even got each of his little tattoo designs that fill his torso."

66

"That guy was tough. I don't how the ancient ones made him. I had to bring a six-foot ladder to trace the thing, and those guys didn't have no metal ladders back then. They had no nothing. Getting the ladder up the cliff was not easy. I had to tie a rope around it, climb up, then haul it up. When I was done I had to just toss it off the edge. Bent the frame bad. But it was worth it. The design came out good. I call him 'Fallen Man.' See how he bends a little at the top as if he is looking down on his clan of followers? He is so much bigger than the rest of the group and kind of mean looking. He must be a god or something. It was weird doing the sketch. I could feel his power, and my grandmother wouldn't let me bring the drawing in her house. She even had our booths here at market kept apart from each other so she don't have him looking down on her. She's real traditional and still don't like me messing around with the Nasazi stuff. Told me I better go get a sing after working on the 'Fallen Man.' I would love to leave that one with you in your gallery if I don't sell it here. It does make a great windbreak though."

The two men chuckled as they huddled behind the six-foot red sandstone petroglyph. It wasn't until that moment that Bloom remembered he looked like the Unabomber. He laughed some more at the thought of his appearance, yet he was still able to recruit a couple of new artists for the summer. It was obvious Navajos didn't judge people by their looks.

"OK, Frank, if you don't get it sold this weekend bring 'Fallen Man' and a few of the other bigger pieces in on Sunday after the fair closes. I'll stay till six and we can consign them. I take 50% of the price but I think your prices are too low so we will raise the retail up by 20%. That way you are only really giving me 30%. Sound fair?"

"Yes," Frank agreed. "That's a deal. Can't wait to see my stuff in a high-end Canyon Road gallery. I've made it to the big time!" The young man with the gorgeous waist-length silky black hair flapping in the wind couldn't help but give a spontaneous whoop of excitement. His enthusiasm made Bloom smile. He was enjoying retail again. It had been a while.

CHAPTER 18

FALLEN MAN

The appearance of the incredibly accurate petroglyph sculpture in the inventory room took old Dr. J off guard when he came in on Monday morning to get ready for the day's demanding schedule. Bloom, who was in the tiny office, heard his high-pitched voice wail through two thick adobe walls.

"Bloom, Bloom, what have you done, my boy!"

"Take it easy, Dr. J. You don't understand."

"I hope you're right, because if this is what I think it is, you've got a lot of explaining to do and not just to me but the authorities. I'm listening." Dr. James was using his stern professorial voice and talking to Bloom as if he had just caught his favorite student cheating on his final exam. He was no longer the employee.

Bloom thought maybe a little joke would be appropriate given Dr. J's admonishment. "See, I thought, Hell I'm a Native gallery with an Indian son and girlfriend. We are supposed to show the best in contemporary art by Native artists. Why not get back to the roots, the petroglyphs. They are very abstract in many respects. Remember this magnificent image? It's now been titled 'Fallen Man.' I should be able to get $3,500. You're an expert in this stuff. Does that seem a fair price for a petroglyph of this quality?"

"Charles, have you completely lost your mind? I have dedicated my whole life to studying and preserving this wonderful form of artwork and you are asking me what the price should be on this sacred object? I shudder to think of the press we will get," Dr. J exclaimed.

"Yeah, the press, that's a great idea. Think of how great it will be if you could write little stories about each of the images and then we will hit the buying public with my dad's and your slick coffee-table book. Buy a petroglyph and get a book free."

"God, there are more?" Dr. J roared.

"Oh yeah, I've got a whole bunch from a Navajo kid. His family, like Rachael's, raised sheep on that property for generations. He has access and is strong enough to haul them to the gallery. He brought the whole lot in last night."

"Bloom, you are in some serious trouble and you don't even seem to understand what it is you have done. This is heavy-duty federal offense stuff. Ancient petroglyphs coming off Indian lands!"

"Hum," Charles considered. "I'm pretty sure I'm just fine. How long you say you taught the anthropology course down at Eastern?"

"For 20 years, three major books, and 25 scientific publications. And what was supposed to be my first general public art book is looking now more like evidence against you at trial."

"Dr. J, take a closer look and give me your expert opinion." Bloom turned up the lights that had been at half-mast.

Now the old professor's weak eyes could see the petroglyph clearly for the first time. He realized it was not an original.

"You, Mr. Bloom, are a little shit, if I can call my distinguished employer such an undignified name," Dr. J responded, laughing as he said this, as with closer inspection and the better lighting the petroglyph was revealed to be an obviously excellent reproduction from Hidden Canyon's wall, and signed, to boot.

"Yes, as your boss, you can call me a shit because I am today. So how about you write some promo copy to go along with each piece that my newest artist, Frank Manygoats, has made? You can write your interpretation of the rock art to go along with the artist's statement."

"I would be happy to do so, my oh-so-gracious employer. I must say your 'Fallen Man' is quite the imposing fellow. Seeing it here in person all alone, it really does stand out. If you think Manygoats would give us permission, I would love to use this as the cover on the book, if your father concurs. 'Fallen Man' would be an impressive image and the name works. It's perfect. The one negative is I can't say much about the image since in all my years of research I have never seen this iconography produced on any other petroglyph. I don't know what the image is supposed to represent. I can say unequivocally that this image represents great power and whoever made this petroglyph was making a strong statement and was probably not someone you would want to screw with. A serious shaman, I'm sure."

Bloom and Dr. J would find out soon enough that certain powers can persist through the ages.

CHAPTER 19

THE AGGIES

Mo Bandgood always knew his calling. The banjo player from Lubbock, Texas, was born into a musical family in 1942. As a teen, he knew Buddy Holly.

Buddy Holly was the same age as Mo's oldest brother Larry, who was also interested in music. Buddy and Larry often would hang out together, and little brother Mo would tag along uninvited. Once while they were walking together Mo confessed to Buddy his love for music and that someday he was going to go to Hollywood to write and record hit songs. Buddy was impressed with the gumption of such a young budding musician, which he could relate to, as he too was following his own path, playing rockabilly songs that were unheard of in West Texas. He told Mo, "Don't ever let them tell you that you ain't good enough just because you come from Lubbock. Tell those L.A. boys that Buddy Holly said so."

Mo never forgot Buddy's words. Buddy's music influenced his own style as it had so many others in the rock world. Buddy died in a plane crash in Iowa the year before Mo graduated from high school in 1960. Holly's death made Mo even more determined to make music his career. Buddy would have wanted it that way.

Growing up in West Texas, Mo had a variety of musical opportunities as long as they were all country. Mo was named after his father's favorite comedy group, The Three Stooges. He suffered through his teenage years because of his odd name. Mo had a great personality and a gift for music but a weird first name by Texas standards. Every one called him Mow, emphasizing the W sound and drawing it out as if he had a business cutting lawns. At least he hadn't been named Curly.

Mo spent all his time composing songs and playing the forbidden rock-and-roll music that was gaining popularity even in Texas, thanks in part to Buddy Holly. Elvis was still considered to be extreme at this time, his wiggling hips not allowed on the "Ed Sullivan Show."

Mrs. Bandgood was an accordion player. She had hoped her sons would inherit her love of music and play in the city or church band. Mo, like his brother Larry, dreamed music, but he couldn't stand his mother's outdated instrument. It seemed to Mo all the old accordion players were missing teeth, which didn't sit well with his musical aesthetics. Besides, his brother Larry played accordion.

Mo's instrument was the banjo and he was a great picker, but he was even a better composer and could write anything and not just for banjo. He had over a hundred songs completed when he left for New Mexico State University.

N.M.S.U. is New Mexico's only state agricultural school. The smell of manure cloaks the campus grounds. Mo didn't care if he was called an Aggie or if it smelled of cow shit. He had picked this college in Las Cruces because of its faculty. Specifically, because of one well-known musician who had ended up in New Mexico due to his lung disease or consumption, as TB was called back then.

The musical professor who lured the budding Texas composer to the base of the Organ Mountains in southern New Mexico was the head of the music department at N.M.S.U. He was exceptionally trained and had taught at The Juilliard School in New York City. This remarkable musician, Dr. Robert Goldblatt, was ridiculously overqualified for an ag school known for its cattle breeders, not its flute players. But N.M.S.U. had something that New York never would have: the dry Chihuahuan Desert air. This climate was critical for Goldblatt, who would have died before age 40 if he remained back East. Goldblatt made a pack with god: "You make me well enough to enjoy music and I'll teach these cowboys some culture. Just give me a sign every so often and open a deli here, for Pete's sake." Goldblatt talked to god a lot like this. He had to have a sense of humor, being a New York Jew living in Las Cruces in the early sixties.

God's sign to Goldblatt was Mo Bandgood, who arrived on the campus in the fall of 1960.

His freshman year at New Mexico State University, Mo told Goldblatt his first career was going to be music and his second career was going to be television. The banjo player had only told one other person of his dreams, and he died in a plane crash in 1959: Buddy Holly. Mo knew Goldblatt would help mold his dreams into reality. It was simple. Mo wanted to be wealthy, and to do it writing music. Mo was very motivated to succeed. He had his whole life planned out: his next stop after getting his music degree at N.M.S.U. was going to be Los Angeles, where television shows were booming and live musicians needed.

By the end of Mo's freshman year, Dr. Goldblatt realized Mo truly was the sign he had been looking for, though he was surprised god had chosen a Texas-twanging banjo player from Lubbock. He had hoped the kosher deli would come first.

College life for Mo consisted of small gigs at local watering holes and writing music. He loved playing in front of a live audience, and in Las Cruces, he was a standout. Mo knew he was only average by big-city standards but not in southern New Mexico.

Mo's band was called Fire. It was named after the lead singer who had a shock of red hair and skin to match. The singer also went by Red, not surprisingly. The years of working out on the family farm had permanently damaged Red's skin, which always had a burnt appearance. Skin cancer was a given down the road for Red, unless he hit it big. Then alcoholism would win out, another family trait.

Fire was good. In fact, they cut one small record, a song written by their banjo player, Mo Bandgood. The record was OK, but the composition was great. Mo figured he would use the record as a jumping-off point in Los Angeles.

Besides Dr. Goldblatt, there was another influence on Mo's college life, a lovely, young English teacher who had just arrived in Las Cruces. Her widowed mother had retired to the warm weather of southwestern New Mexico so the dutiful Isabella Graves, a recent graduate from U.C.L.A., decided to teach at the local ag school for a while. Isabella's over-qualification was Mo's good fortune. She taught him English his senior year. Her unique perspective and vivacious personality inspired Mo to become a wordsmith with his music. Isabella Graves would only see Mo during '64, her first year of teaching, but her importance in his life was monumental. He would always be grateful for her guidance. It was her tutelage that shaped him into a true songwriter. Even more than Goldblatt's musical gifts, Graves inspired Mo's life course.

After four years, Mo was trained to be a competent professional composer anywhere. Dr. Goldblatt's sign from god had been fulfilled and Goldblatt was satisfied he had stayed in Las Cruces. He hoped his young protégé would apply to Juilliard for additional training, not in banjo plucking, which Goldblatt wasn't even sure was a real instrument, but music composition and theory, in which Mo was gifted. His mentor told Mo he would personally call the dean of admissions and make a case for his further development as a serious composer. But as Mo had done his whole life, he followed his heart, which was already set on Los Angeles. Movies and television. These would be his Juilliard. Unfortunately, Uncle Sam came calling first and he couldn't refuse that invitation.

CHAPTER 20

JOHNSON'S WAR

In 1964, Johnson's War was starting to look like it was going to be bad for any of those unlucky enough to end up in South Vietnam. There were 200 soldiers killed in 1964. The amount would escalate to ten times that in 1965. But already Mo could see the writing on that very deadly wall of war, so he decided a six-month reserve duty stint in 1964 would be his best bet. He'd use the time to write some antiwar songs. They were gaining in popularity. If you were a reservist you were safe from being pulled over to an active tour of duty, so six months it would be, then just the occasional reserves weekend afterwards. He graduated with a music degree in May 1964, and was an airman 1st class by July.

First stop of duty was Clovis, site of New Mexico's Cannon Air Force Base. The terrain in eastern New Mexico is not dissimilar to that in Lubbock, which is only two hours away. Clovis, a small town of 10,000 in the sixties, was flat with a few scraggly elm and poplar trees interspersed. You could always tell where humans had lived in this region, for if there was a tree standing it meant a house was not far away. If you were trying to find old house foundations, you only had to look at the horizon, which would be broken from its open lines by the occasional dying or dead elm tree.

The town's main sources of income were ranching and farming. The water table was not far below the caliche rock bed, and the farmers used the precious water resource with abandonment. Winter wheat, milo, and cotton farms were interspersed with cattle destined for slaughter in nearby Hereford, Texas.

The town's most famous individual at the time was Buddy Holly's first manager, Norman Petty, who had his studios in Clovis. Holly had recorded his early music in Clovis not far from Mo's new duty station. Holly had been dead for six years but was still influencing Mo's life. Mo figured being sent to Clovis was a sign that he was on the right path to becoming a professional musician. Like his former professor Goldblatt, Mo had become a believer in signs.

Military life is not generally conducive to those interested in the arts. Creativity is frowned upon. Rules, regulations, and rank are the order of the day, not E flats. Mo's job was to conduct the Cannon military band, an easy gig but one that allowed very little veering from the military songs provided. The military mainstays were "The Star-Spangled Banner" and "My Country 'Tis of Thee." But as luck would have it, the colonel in charge of the base happened to be a Buddy Holly fan and a friend of Norm Petty's. While Colonel Einke kept that relationship hidden from most, he shared it with Mo, and decreed that an occasional rockabilly song would be acceptable under two strict rules: never when any officers of higher rank were on base, and he always wanted to be present.

Mo and Colonel Einke became friends, which is exceptionally rare in the world of rank and power. Generally an airman is the next step from dog shit, but Col. Einke recognized Mo's gift and could not help but embrace his fellow Texan. Six months of duty flew by. Next step: California.

CHAPTER 21

FLY AWAY BIRDIE

Arriving in Los Angeles on the Santa Fe Railroad, still in his uniform, Airman Mo Bandgood's eyes were as bright as stars. He was amazed at seeing the famous Hollywood sign in the flesh. His face grinned so hard it left marks on his cheeks. He had memorized all the landmarks from maps at the base's library.

Mo's first stop was Capitol Records, a place Norm had recommended as being the best recording studio. It was easy to spot: a tall, round building not far from Universal Studios. It was impressive looking to the boy from Texas. The building had been the recording site for some of the greatest music of all time. Sinatra, the Beatles, Elvis, the Rolling Stones, and Mo's favorite, the Crickets, Buddy's old band.

After talking his way past the obtuse front guard, Mo's jaw dropped at the photographs inside. The walls were filled with images of those individuals who defined the realm of American music. Looking around the lobby in awe, Mo wondered if he too would have his image memorialized someday in one of the black-framed photographs, perhaps simply saying "Mo."

Mustering as much gumption as he could and smoothing down his uniform, Mo headed to the front desk where a fortysomething woman with a nametag that read "Ruth" was sitting. She guarded the entrance to stardom and Mo knew it.

Ruth had seen it all and was not impressed easily, though Sinatra was an exception. Her legs still got weak when he crowed, "Ruthhhh, how's my beautiful Ruthhhh today?" She understood how young girls could lose all their inhibitions and throw themselves at the gorgeous man. She would have, too.

"Hi Ruth, I'm here to introduce myself, as you and I will be seeing a lot of each other over the next 30 years," Mo beamed confidently.

Ruth, who normally wouldn't have lifted her head from her appointment book, was taken aback by such a forward introduction coming from such a young-sounding voice with a strong Texas twang.

"We will, will we?" she remarked, sizing up the wiry man carrying a beat-up banjo case.

"Yes, Ma'am, we will. You see, I've known since the day I told Buddy Holly that this was my destiny, that someday I would be standing in front of you at Capitol Records, starting my career. Today happens to be that day."

"You knew Buddy Holly? Buddy Holly who was killed in the airplane crash?" Ruth wanted to make quite sure they were talking about the same person, as it seemed highly unlikely. "Are you trying to pull the leg of a woman that does not have limber joints anymore?" Ruth was not the kind of woman you messed with. Her eyes were intensely peering through her green horn-rimmed glasses at the scrawny musician with the great bravado.

"Yes, Ma'am. I knew Buddy Holly. That's a fact and he's the one we're talking about. He and my brother Larry were fast friends, and Buddy encouraged me to follow my dreams. Recording at Capitol Records is one of those dreams. In fact, Buddy's exact words to me were 'not to let any of those L.A. people tell you you're not good enough just because you're from Lubbock.' Which of course I am, from Lubbock, Texas, if you haven't noticed from my slight accent." He winked at Ruth because it was clear he was a Texan, born and bred.

"Ruth, I've got a music composition degree and just got out of the air force where I was head conductor in the military band. More importantly, Norm Petty told me to come here first. I have an album that I wrote the music for and am looking to make a whole lot more." Mo failed to mention the record was cut at N.M.S.U. and that it was utilizing a small-time band, and it was more a single than an actual album.

"Impressive," she retorted. "What's your name, Mr. Banjo player?"

"Mo Bandgood, and it's a pleasure meeting you, Ms. Ruthhhh." The way he said Ruthhh reminded her of Sinatra. He didn't have the looks, but he definitely had the personality and her legs felt just the tiniest bit weak, bad joints and all.

Just as she was trying to figure out what to do with her Texan, the back door, which lead to the recording studios, flew open abruptly. It

78

shook the rows of gold records, sending some askew. A tall Englishman with a Beatles-like haircut loudly announced, "Ruth, I need some help back here. Can you spare the time please? Hate to take you from the desk, but it's a little crazy. I'm not kidding, either. I need help and I need it now. Can you get somebody to sub for you?"

"Hi, Mr. Flanders. I can do one better than help you. Mr. Bandgood here is free, and would be at your beck and call as long as you need him and he's a recorded musician. You are available, aren't you, Mr. Bandgood?"

"Yes, I am, as long as you need me. My name is Mo."

"Great, Mo," Flanders replied, "get a pass, then follow me. And bring that banjo if you can really play it. We may need you. You can play, right?"

"I'm very good and can sight-read anything," Mo assured, his confidence never wavering. Mo Bandgood was given a temporary sticky pass, which Ruth carefully stuck on his shirt. It read CAPITOL RECORDS, then underneath Mo Band Good, leaving a space in between Band and Good.

"Good, grab your instrument and come with me, young man. Today may be your lucky day. You should thank your guardian angel, Ruth, there," Flanders said as he hustled Mo back through the door. Ruth smiled and Mo gave her another wink.

Flanders and Mo squeezed into the back hall, which was also filled with record memorabilia. A mob of musicians was going in all directions, trying to determine which studio they were assigned to and meanwhile staring into the main studio, which had about 10 people in it, mostly dressed in vibrant primary colors, all with Beatles-like long hair. Mo's look couldn't have been more out of place, with his uniform and his short, military-cut hair. But he sensed what to do. He helped Flanders steer the throng of musicians down the hallway, then followed him into the main studio.

The studio was not particularly large, its brown wood paneling a stark contrast to the sea of color in the room. Flanders's need of help in here was apparent, as one of the guitar players seemed to be on some kind of a bad trip, wobbling back and forth in his black metal chair. The rest of the band members were chastising the inebriated individual. Mo soon enough realized Flanders was the manager of the band, which went by the name The Red Cardinals, not be confused with the early R and B band, The Cardinals. The five musicians were getting ready to cut their first major-label album, starting with their title song, "The Writing's on the Wall."

A heated discussion erupted on how to proceed.

"So what the fuck do we do here, Flan Man," said one exasperated band member. "We don't have a guitar player now that Mr. Dickhead here decided to down a 'shroom right before recording. Unfortunately he has a solo in this piece and we can't record it without him, and this song could be our biggest!"

Another of the band members chimed in, "How much are we spending again for this session? It's per hour, right?"

"OK boys, listen up. The Flan Man has a solution. Mr. Mo here," Flanders squinted at Mo's badge to make sure he got his name right. "He's a big fan of the band, says so right here." He tapped at the badge that said "Band Good." "He's ready to step in. Any chance we can make the solo a banjo? It might give kind of a Mamas & Papas feel, more folksy? You see how well they're doing with 'California Dreamin'.' We could capture a slightly different audience than we have. I'm sure Mr. Mo can work the song out, right?" Flanders looked at Mo for confirmation.

"No problem, Flan Man," Mo agreed. "Just give me what you got and I can compose it for banjo, see how it sounds."

The band members stared at each other and the incapacitated guitarist. One said, "This guy looks pretty square, Flan Man, but let's go for it, dude. Stick Mr. Fuckup Guitar Player in the sound room so he doesn't screw us up anymore. We'll have a banjo solo instead." The guitar player was roughly tossed into the adjacent sound room to enjoy his psychedelic high.

Mo pulled off his jacket, tossing it into a dark corner. He grabbed the sheet music. Humming it to himself, he took out his pencil and started writing furiously. This was the chance that he had been preparing for his entire life and he wasn't going to blow it. Mo had fate on his side, but he also knew how to capitalize on his fate. His mind was as one with the music. He rapidly turned the fairly weak song into his own new and improved composition, a Mamas and Papas-meets-The Crickets tune.

Months later, when The Red Cardinals' album was released, it contained their biggest hit to date, a song featuring the composition and banjo of Mr. Mo (as he was now referred to). The retitled song was called "Pickin' Your Heart Up in Pieces." Mo's name was on the sheet music as one of the composers, his first official California song. There would be many to follow. The hit sent the band in a new direction. When "Pickin'" went gold, Mo inscribed his gold record for the Capitol Records walls to read: "Without Ruth, I would be nowhere. Thanks and I love your legs.—Mr. Mo." Ruth hung the record directly behind her desk where no one could bump into it. She made sure everyone knew the story of Mo Band Good.

CHAPTER 22

JINGLE MAN

Mo's time in L.A. flew by. His remarkable break his first day in Hollywood at age 23 became legendary among those in the business. He became an urban legend, but for real. He and The Red Cardinals went on to cut two more albums together, which were successful by anyone's standards. However, Mo had plans beyond being a banjo player from Texas.

He spent his next 15 years in the business moving up the musical food chain, always intent on the ultimate goal: music composition for TV and film. He was now one of the few white sharks cruising the world of commercials. It was not the glamour of rock and roll, but it allowed his creative juices to flow continuously and the pay was startling for the boy from west Texas. He told one of his colleagues why he chose to concentrate on commercials instead of records: "800 jingles in three years, you do the math." The math was simple: lots of money.

It was the age of the big orchestras. Every commercial and the occasional movie script needed an original score, and they were willing to pay for the best and most efficient person in the industry, and that was Mo. He was known as the jingle man and could knock out three original compositions for three separate commercials in a single day. He ate, slept, and screwed music. His meals were served in Styrofoam containers and the women he slept with might as well have been too. Mo controlled the music jingles industry, which meant he was also a great connector for young actresses to get a foothold in the business.

Sex was never a problem, but maintaining a healthy relationship was. Success had seen to that. It was 1980 and you couldn't turn on a television channel without hearing at least one Mo composition playing. Toilet paper to hamburgers was Mo's calling and he loved what he did.

Depending on how much alcohol was consumed the night before, Mo's start time would vary, but he tried to be in his studio recording by 11 am. All the musicians in the business had a feel for Mo's circadian rhythm. Since a good number of them drank with him as well, they mostly knew when to be ready to begin their workday knocking out commercials.

A steady flow of musicians came through Mo's private studio, all experts at sight reading and getting the job done on time. They were Mo's personal orchestra. Time, like music, was money, and Mo was very efficient at his craft. The musical talent that hammered out the commercials was immense and Mo recognized it and respected what a great musician was capable of. Mo was a very good musician in his own right, but these guys were professionals and he never forgot they were the ones with the true god-given talents.

The part of the day Mo hated was when he had to deal with clients. Generally the agency that hired him took care of this, but occasionally the clients requested to talk to Mo. They wanted to be involved in how their money was spent. Some 200 composers in the world made 95% of the music and money in Hollywood, and Mo wanted his exorbitant piece of the musical pie. When he was forced to meet with an actual client, he made it simple. Big speakers, plenty of booze, and a lot of echo to the mix. It snowed them every time.

The music business in some respects never changes when it comes to drugs and alcohol. Drug abuse had given Mo his first big break in show business when the guitar player of The Red Cardinals was smashed in the sixties, but it also was taking a toll now on his own body which only had one setting: full tilt. It was stuck in that position all the time. The only activity he was religious about other than music composition was running. Mo figured he might drink too much and smoke some dope but he was going to keep his body in shape in spite of his lifestyle. Every morning he would run on Seal Beach, fighting off the effects of over-indulgence. One such run would change his life.

CHAPTER 23

YOU'RE WELCOME, I THINK

The day was magnificent, even by California's high standards. Mo had worked hard and downed too much tequila the night before, but he was enjoying his morning run. He had finally finished a project for a regional hamburger chain, Red Castle, and was trying to decide if he was happy with the outcome. The composition and lyrics were classic Mo. His hamburger song was playing repetitively in his head as he ran down the sliver of beach. The part of the song that his mind was currently stuck on was, "Our hamburgers are so cheap we're always in the red, Red Castle."

Mo loved the beat of the jingle but was unsure of its tag line. He had used heavy harmonica throughout the jingle. He employed his favorite harmonica player, Bobby "Blindman" Sanderson, who was one of his most gifted musicians. Almost all of Mo's songs used the Blindman. Blindman was not blind at all; in fact his vision was better than average, but when he was really wailing on the harmonica, he shut his eyes tight and didn't open them till he was satisfied. Blindman could make a hamburger feel soulful and that wasn't easy even with a Bandgood composition. Blindman had done his job and nailed the Red Castle tune but Mo was still worried that Joe America wouldn't understand the *in the red* bit. "Probably too sophisticated for most Americans. I might need to change it," he thought to himself.

The tune was playing in his head accompanied by images of sizzling meat when he caught whiff of a very non-burger smell on the beach. Then he saw what appeared to be a head bobbing in the ocean water between two gigantic bird-lined rocks.

The new image took a minute to sink in as his visual cortex was fixated on bouncing hamburgers, not floating corpses. When his mind finally reset, he realized his recording day was screwed. Not that he didn't feel bad for the dead person, but his two scheduled commercials would not occur today. It would cost him money and possibly a big client, plus he hadn't figured out the "in the red" dilemma. But what could he do? Ignore it?

Mo ran to the nearest phone and hesitantly called the police, describing the body floating in the ocean and its location. The police ordered him to go back and wait on the beach for them at the spot. Very few people run on Seal Beach, as it is only accessible at low tide unless you like running part of the beach in water, which Mo did. Today the beach was completely visible as the tide was at its lowest point, a perfect running day.

The morning, which had been so promising 30 minutes ago, now changed 180 degrees. The day would suck. The air, which had been filled with the enriching smells of salt water and blooming California ice plant, now took on a more ominous aroma, one of human putrification as the dead body washed closer to shore.

The sickening smell kept drifting across Mo's nostrils as he paced impatiently a short distant from the now very visible floater. Waiting for the police, he couldn't escape the smell. The hamburgers had vanished. The horrific scent of death was vaguely familiar, similar to snakeweed in full bloom, which filled the wide-open plains of west Texas every fall. Thinking about home and the yellow flowering plants gave Mo a new song thought: "Texas Snakeweed." He worked out the composition in his head until the police arrived. It was the only way he could pass time and keep his mind off his ruined, nonproductive day.

Mo had never dealt with the police. His life was one of routines and he was a good person who generally followed rules. He was now part of a dead body scenario. He had no idea what was involved or how much time would be required on his part. He had briefly considered running past the floating human cadaver, letting the red hamburgers continue their dance uninterrupted. He would have finished his run by now and would be getting cleaned up, ready for a busy, profitable day. But his Baptist west Texas upbringing would not allow such a thing. Instead, he'd already called his assistant instructing her to cancel his morning and early afternoon sessions. Now visions of yellow snakeweed flowers were bouncing in his mind. No money to be made with that. Finally the police showed up.

"Mr. Mo Bandgood. Is that correct, Bandgood?"

"Yes, but you can call me Mo, everyone else does."

"Mr. Bandgood, when did you notice the body and why were you on the beach?"

"I run on this beach as many mornings as the tide will let me. I come here because it's so peaceful and it's pretty close to my house. I saw the head bobbing in the water about an hour ago and figured it wasn't good so I stopped running and called you guys."

"You ever had any trouble yourself with the law? You're a musician, is that correct?"

Mo was taken aback by the somewhat accusatory tone Officer Brown was taking with him, as if musicians were all dope fiends. "Nope, no trouble. I'm a law-abiding citizen. In fact, this is the first time I have had any contact with the police in my entire life. You're breaking my police cherry, Officer Brown."

Brown was not amused and Mo could tell.

"You know this is serious stuff, Mr. Bandgood. This could be a criminal case you are now involved with. A murder, possibly. So far you are the only witness so you might want to take this interview a little more seriously. We don't like finding dead bodies in Seal Beach."

Mo was making a mental note so he would never forget today's conversation. He had been in the military and knew better than to volunteer for anything and by calling in the body he had just volunteered. He wouldn't make the same mistake twice. He wished he had been raised Protestant.

"Yes, Officer, I realize it's serious or I wouldn't have called you and ruined my morning's recording session. It has become a financial burden for me already and my guess is we're just starting the process."

Neither man was enjoying the other's company at this point.

A small crowd started to form atop the cliffs overlooking the scene where Mo was being interrogated and the body was being fished out. Mo was the only civilian down below. The rest of the gathering was divers and police. The area, which was now roped off with yellow tape, was working its way into Mo's subconscious snakeweed composition. Officer Brown continued to grill Mo about his past history and why again he chose Seal Beach when he lived miles away. Mo was starting to wonder if he should get a lawyer as he was getting nervous that Brown hated musicians and seemed like a bully.

As Mo finished responding to the cop's grilling, the decomposing body was dragged out directly next to his feet. In retrospect he suspected Officer Brown wanted to watch his reaction to see if there was more than an accidental finding by a runner. Brown got the response from Mo he was looking for.

The body had obviously been in the water for a while. The skin was coming off in sheets in places and the head was partially destroyed with a gray JELL-O-like substance oozing out of the open cranium. The eyes were open and covered in a milky film. One of the hands was partially gone. It appeared to have been eaten by something. And there were small crabs scurrying out of the open mouth. It was a horrible sight and one Mo had not been prepared for. He threw up all over the beach, confronted by the sight and the now very potent smell of death, not snakeweed after all. Officer Brown smiled with satisfaction.

CHAPTER 24

IT'S PERSONAL NOW

It was 1980 and a new chart had been added to Dr. Sam Hubbard's office wall. It required two large poster boards to fill in all the known data on a lunatic named Theodore Robert Bundy. Bundy had recently been sentenced in Utah for kidnapping and had been extradited to Colorado on murder charges. He had escaped from the Aspen County Courthouse, been recaptured, and was now apparently missing from the Glenwood Springs jail. The news had come over the wire today and an all-points bulletin had been issued for all surrounding states, including California. Bundy was from Washington State and it was thought he might try to make his way back home. The Washington authorities were looking into every active murder file in their state and Sam had added him to his wall as a possible link to murders in his own city and state. Sam knew serial killers, like migrating birds, didn't know state boundaries. Currently Sam's findings were consistent with the profile of a classic psychopath.

Bundy was a good student, a churchgoer, and even a Boy Scout. He thought his emotions instead of feeling them, and was looking very much like he might be an impressive serial killer. The latest entry in the ever-growing chart was made that morning. It read: "Bundy escapes second time in six months."

The phone call Sam received that morning would make Bundy's escape even more personal. It came from his older sister, Beth Sneadly. She was 12 years older than Sam. Her son Bill was only four years younger than Sam. The two boys had been close growing up, spending hours of playtime together as children.

"I've got some very bad news and I need your help," Beth sobbed, her voice cracking and barely recognizable. Sam was a professional when it came to human trauma and understood from the tone of her voice that she had probably experienced a severe trauma. Sam was an expert in these sorts of psychological catastrophes.

"Beth, tell me what's going on. Is it mom? Talk slowly, I'll take notes." Sam the ever-professional observer was well aware the next few sentences coming out of her mouth would affect him personally, but his training prevented him from flinching when it came to doing his job even when Beth was in distress.

"No Sammy, it's not mom. She's fine. It's Billy. He's been found dead in Southern California. His body was discovered this morning by a man running on Seal Beach. Apparently that's next to Long Beach. Billy's apartment was in Long Beach. The police officer said it looked like he'd been dead for a week. I've been trying to contact him and have been worried sick. He usually checks in with me every week." Beth began to cry again and Sam waited till she was composed enough to talk.

"Beth, tell me what you know and who is in charge. Is the case originating from L.A., Long Beach, or Seal Beach? I'll check into everything. I'll clear my schedule and be down there today."

Beth gave Sam the sketchy information she had, adding, "The police said Bill's death looked like an accident. He may have been drinking."

"How was Billy doing in general?" Sam asked. "Do you know if he was still getting counseling for the helicopter crash?"

Bill Sneadly had gone down in a helicopter crash near Tustin, California a couple of years before. All 12 passengers aboard had died, but Bill had walked away unscathed. It was a miracle that couldn't be explained. The remarkable survival had weighed heavily on the young seaman's mind. The Navy had discharged Bill not long after the wreck with a disability leave for intractable depression. Alcohol was Bill's drug of choice for his chronic melancholy.

"He was coping. No counseling. That stopped over a year ago," Beth replied. "He was drinking pretty heavy. He called me once last month obviously drunk. He was slurring his words and telling me how much he loved me." The thought of her now deceased son's love sent Beth back into a crying jag which lasted for a couple of minutes.

"OK, so he was drinking and living on the outskirts of Seal Beach. Any enemies or problems you know of? Any friends? Was he working?"

"No work. He lived off his disability check. I know he had a couple of friends but he didn't talk about them much and I never met them. I believe there was one of his old military buddies he would hang out with. He referred to him as a lifer. You know Bill could be hard-headed at times, but he was basically a nice kid who respected others. I can't imagine anyone wanting to hurt him. He may have just been drunk and fell off the edge of the cliff, it's possible. I don't know. Or maybe he committed suicide. He talked about it once after the accident."

"Let me handle the rest," Sam suggested. "I'll call as soon as I have talked with the police. I'm very sorry for your loss. You know I cared a great deal for your son. He was like my brother. If this is anything besides an accident, I'll find out, I promise you. No matter how long it takes." Sam hung up the phone, his hand visibility shaking. He had known of Bill's depression, yet had done nothing much to help. The psychological burden of Bill's death would be something Sam would have to deal with for years to come.

✸ ✸ ✸ ✸

Sam took the 3 pm flight out of Oakland and was in Seal Beach by 6 pm. He found a nice B&B and set up his temporary office. This was a homicide case as far as he was concerned until he was satisfied it was nothing more than a drunk slipping off a high slope. Sam had played sports with Bill and knew he was a gifted athlete. It was his athleticism that probably saved him during the helicopter crash. Bill had told him he jumped up as the helicopter hit the ground and rolled over the other sailors' bodies on impact. An athlete like that would have had to have been very drunk to fall off the edge of the cliff. Bill might have been depressed but he never seemed suicidal to Sam. Thinking on the possibilities of what could have happened caused the hair on the back of Sam's neck to stand on end. He was listening to his inner voice and it was saying things didn't add up.

A quick call to the police headquarters before he left had answered a few questions. The autopsy was scheduled for tomorrow and there were no suspects. Preliminary lab work showed Bill had a 2.2 alcohol level at the time of his death, way more than twice the normal limit for being drunk. An ethanol level of this magnitude would be consistent with someone stumbling off a cliff. However, if he had been drinking as heavily as his mother had reported, more than likely Bill had developed a high tolerance for ethanol and a 2.2 might have been a level which would not affect him like an average person. He could have easily been walking and talking the night he was killed. More answers were needed before this case could be closed as an accidental death.

A time of death was not established yet. There was severe damage secondary to water and predation. The body was in pretty bad shape. Everything was still attached to Bill's torso, but one hand was almost gone and the face was nearly unrecognizable. Identification had been established via military dental records and the ID he was carrying at the time of death.

The effects found on Bill's body included his billfold with $18, a Timex watch, a used wooden pencil, a half full package of Dentyne gum, and a dime. No notes or unusual items were seen with or in the body at forensic examination. For all purposes it looked as if he had fallen on his head on the way down the cliff and been killed on impact. His body had been lodged in a deep crevice at the water line, covered most of the time by the ocean water. The large blow had damaged his skull and it looked as if his cervical spine had been severed as well. If he were alive after the fall, he would have died shortly after from drowning. A large bruise to the sternum was found which could have been from another bounce off the rocks. Otherwise no unusual bruises or body artifacts were located. The body was fully clothed in long pants, windbreaker, short sleeve T-shirt underneath the jacket, athletic socks, briefs underwear, and low-top white Converse tennis shoes. No jewelry was found but Bill was not known for wearing any, either.

There was no sign anything had been stolen. The wallet still had money, his old military card, and a Texaco gas credit card. The wallet was in his back pocket, the dime in the front right, and the pencil in the left inside jacket pocket. The pencil had no identifying marks other than a common brand and it was a number two lead. Approximately ¼ of the pencil was gone so apparently it had been used, though it appeared new with no marks found on the pencil itself. It was sharpened. It seemed incongruent to Sam that a sharp pencil would be in a pocket. It seemed surprising it hadn't broken during the horrific fall, even when Bill had a significant sternal bruise not far from the inside jacket pocket. Still, Bill did have a 2.2 ethanol level so his carrying a sharp pencil was probably the least of his worries. The pencil not breaking could be just that, the luck of the fall, just like crashing in a helicopter and being the lone survivor.

The area on the beach where it was possible to run was limited and only completely accessible at low tide. There was a high sheer cliff above, with a significant drop-off of 80 feet. Most of the time the beach and rocks were covered by water. Accessing the beach required entering two miles south of where the body was found. Walking above the beach and reviewing where the body had been found gave Sam a sense of what was required for Bill's final plunge. It seemed hard to imagine that Bill just fell off. Bill would have had to try and go off the edge. There was only one spot where there wasn't some kind of retaining wall or fencing. It was hard to get to the water's edge from the cliff except for this small area. The one spot where it was possible to go over the edge to the crashing rocks below was not far from a frontage road. A car could have dumped a body there. That seemed more logical to Sam's analytical mind.

The ground in front of the drop zone was covered in ice plants and many did look like they had been trampled, but that was probably clumsy detective work vs. Bill stepping on them a week earlier.

It didn't make sense to Sam Hubbard: the idea that Bill simply walked over to the one spot where he could reach the water and then hurtled himself to a horrible death. It was implausible, unless he wanted to look over the edge for some reason and slipped on the blooming ice plants. It was feasible but seemed unlikely. If he were suicidal, would this be the way he would want to off himself? A man who had seen death at close range? He would have had to think what if it doesn't kill me? It would not be the way Bill would want to die. A bullet to the head maybe, but jumping off a cliff? No way. He had fallen from the sky before and lived. He wouldn't chance it again, not if he was intent on killing himself.

CHAPTER 25

SORRY, POLICE ONLY

Officer Dan Beinem had been assigned to the Bill Sneadly case. An accidental death secondary to alcohol, as Detective Beinem had already classified the case. The fact that the autopsy findings were still pending was only procedural in his mind. Seal Beach generally was a quiet beach city five miles from Long Beach, which was known for murders and rapes. The Seal Beach Police Department was proud of its clean little city. They were "not like our neighbor to the north," as Beinem told Hubbard. For the town to have two deaths a week apart was rare, but not unheard of.

The second murder, of Petty Officer Smith, had been turned over immediately to the military police to handle as he was on active duty. The Seal Beach Police Department was more than happy to oblige, as one death was enough to contend with. By making it a military problem it would not officially count against the Seal Beach statistics, something the police chief and mayor were keenly aware of.

Smith's death was a murder and most likely from some alcohol-related brawl. The two cases, as far as Officer Beinem was concerned, did not appear to be related. Beinem scheduled a meeting with Sam Hubbard to discuss the Sneadly case. Beinem had been briefed that Hubbard worked with the San Francisco Police Department and was its forensic psychologist and had been working with the state for the last eight years.

Officer Beinem was not a fan of shrinks, even ones that usually helped the cops. Too much mumbo jumbo as far as he was concerned.

Sam started the meeting cordially. "I'm glad you could meet with me. I was hoping you could enlighten me as to what we know so far regarding Mr. Sneadly's case?" He was trying to be as official and professional as possible, referring to his dead nephew as Sneadly instead of Bill.

"Well, looks pretty simple. Kid got drunk, maybe depressed, lost his footing or jumped. That cliff took another life at that same place five years ago. The fence in that one spot is gone. Kids keep knocking it down so they can sit over the edge and drink beer. Probably what happened is he slipped and fell. The rest of that area has been pretty well secured, but you probably know that already."

"Yes I walked it yesterday and today, both at high and low tide. I'm hoping the approximate time of death will be known soon and we can pinpoint what tide it was when he died. Might help."

"Yeah, we might know soon." Beinem didn't like the fact that this big-city shrink was trying to dictate the case. He wasn't a cop and he was out of his jurisdiction.

"Listen Officer," reasoned Sam, "I know this is your case, but this one is personal, as you know. The deceased was my nephew and there seem to me to be some possible irregularities in the findings. I just want to be sure if it is classified as an accidental death, that it really was."

"Sure, sure I understand, but we handle these kinds of things all the time and we're not small-town bumpkins. We will be sure of the cause of death and if it's not booze, I mean alcohol intoxication, so be it."

"Officer, if I can be of any service, if you have any suspects or witnesses you need my expertise with, I'm sure I can get clearance to help you. I'm here to help you and my sister get to the bottom of this, where ever that may take us."

"Fine. So far the bottom is an 80-foot cliff and if we find any other evidence, I'll let you know," Beinem concluded.

"Were there any other crimes that occurred around the same time as Mr. Sneadly's death?" Sam couldn't help asking.

"Nothing of significance. I'll let you know if anything turns up. I'll also let you know when the autopsy results come back. I've got another appointment, so I need to go. Thanks for stopping by." Detective Beinem had decided that the Smith murder was not related and he didn't need to let the shrink know about it or he would start stirring things up. More paper work and the military was in charge. Not his problem anymore. Just keep the Seal Beach homicide count to zero this year, like the last four years. The mayor's slogan after all was "tough on crime, so you can sleep at night," an important promise in a re-election year.

CHAPTER 26

ANOTHER CHART FOR THE OFFICE'S WALL

The funeral for Bill Sneadly was held near Beth's home in Marin County two weeks after the autopsy. Sam returned for the funeral. The final official coroner's report had been filed and the police had closed the case. The death certificate was signed off as accidental death secondary to head and neck trauma with alcohol consumption as a causative factor, plus a chest contusion. The coroner's report could not rule out the trauma occurring before falling down the cliff, but with the severity of the slope's elevation and the number of ragged rocks, and violent wave action, it was most consistent that his death was from the fall.

Sam had questioned the chest contusion, which was severe enough to have caused a sternal fracture, which would seem to indicate a blow directly to the sternum. There was no way to explain the unbroken pencil. No rock impressions were noted on the skin and there was no water ingestion or inhalation. Bill must have been dead upon hitting the water. The time of death was somewhere between 10 pm and 3 am, best that they could determine from pathogen colonization inside the body. The ocean water was at mid to high tide when Bill would have fallen in. If he had been mortally injured when he hit the water, but still breathing, he would have ingested and inhaled salt water. None was found.

Bill's liver was inflamed and had early fatty deposits consistent with significant long-term alcohol abuse. The 2.2 level, while twice the normal ethanol level, for a functional alcoholic like Bill would not have been incapacitating. "Maybe wobbly, but not wiped out," Sam wrote on his new chart, which he added next to his Ted Bundy chart, Bundy being still missing.

❋ ❋ ❋ ❋

Six months went by. Sam didn't give up even though the Seal Beach Police Department continued to be of little help, unless you call blocking Sam's additional attempts to reopen the case helpful.

Sam was able to track down the runner who had found the body, a Mo Bandgood, an L.A. music composer of some notoriety. His police record was clean, ex-military but he never knew Bill. Bandgood appeared to be just a Good Samaritan calling in a drowning. Nonetheless, Sam got Mo's number and arranged an interview. Sam explained his position with the San Francisco Criminal Justice system, and that he also happened to be the deceased's uncle and this was personal.

Sam found Mo to be very cordial on the phone. Mo answered all his questions directly and without hesitation. He even invited him down to a music session if he was ever in L.A. The years of working with deranged criminal minds had allowed Sam to pick through damaged goods, and Mo Bandgood didn't fit the bill. Sam was satisfied with his account of the findings but did express interest in seeing a commercial being shot someday. Everyone loves Hollywood.

Then came a breakthrough. After much legwork, Sam finally discovered the murder of Petty Officer Mat Smith on the same day and at the approximate same time as his nephew. The two deaths were only a few miles apart. That's as much as he could get out of the military police. Beth didn't know any P.O. Mat Smith and he was not as far as Sam could determine ever stationed with Bill in the Navy. The Smith case was a military one and they would not comment regarding any other findings and the Seal Beach Police Department just referred him back to the base commander. "Not our jurisdiction," Detective Beinem insisted.

Sam's own police department that he had worked with for eight years was also surprisingly of little help. They made some faint attempts but it was not their jurisdiction and frankly Sam was not a cop, not truly one of their own. He was a psychologist, not a detective, and they didn't care to make waves as those connections were saved for more important cases and Sam's requests didn't fit the bill. Even if it was Sam's nephew, it was probably an accident and Sam couldn't argue that point.

It was the "blue stonewall" that convinced Sam he had to take matters into his own hands. He would become a cop, a detective no less. He had made a promise to Beth. The San Francisco Police Chief who had worked with Sam for the last five years had promised Sam if he could pass the academy program and work as a rookie beat cop for one year, he would agree to let him have his own special department. He would be a detective specializing in mental cases. Not unlike what he did now, but with a badge. It would give him the power to help those who needed his voice, the Bills of the world. No longer was being a forensic psychologist good enough for Sam. He would be the only cop on the force who had the training to take down sick predators by force or through mental evaluation. It was personal now. He had seven charts, including one for Bill, none of which had been solved. No killer's name other than Bundy's and no one had been brought to justice, including Bundy.

The original Zodiac Murderer that had inspired Sam to get into the criminal mind would now be needed for additional motivation to help a 31-year-old, out-of-shape intellectual survive the rigors of the police academy. Bill's chart would be put on hold until Sam could break the code of silence and find out what the military police knew regarding Mat Smith's death. The two cases could easily be related. Their times of death would indicate so.

If Sam had only known about the used #2 pencil found on Smith, the connection would have been linked on Sam's charts without him ever becoming a cop, but the river of life had moved on. Missing the clue meant Sam had serious work ahead of him if hoped to solve the case and rein in a serial murderer. A mass murderer was probably gaining strength every year he remained free.

CHAPTER 27

RUN HARD, ROOKIE

Taking on a project as daunting as starting a new career in one's thirties that was also physically challenging required all of Sam's willpower. He knew he didn't have to do this to himself. He was happy enough in forensics; he liked being called Psychologist Hubbard and was relatively safe. He had a degree from Stanford, for god sakes.

Becoming a cop and going through a year as a rookie learning the ropes meant putting his life at risk every day. Whenever he had a possibly violent problem with a criminal patient as a psychologist, he had simply called in the police attendant and they handled it. Now he was going to be that person responsible for handling the violent situations and he wasn't sure he was up to the task. The physical stamina required was more than his present body could withstand and he realized that.

Sam took 60 days of sick leave and went on a strict workout routine, getting his almost-middle-aged body back in shape to try and pass the physical examination required of every police officer. Sam was overweight. His physique could have been worse but because he walked everywhere in San Francisco he did have some exercise stamina. However, walking around town and running with a 50-pound pack on his back were two different things. The daily routine of coffee and donuts became a distant memory. Surviving the police academy was now the order of the day. He owed it to Billy. Sam's new daily routine was divided into cardiovascular and weight training. Four hours in the morning and two in the afternoon. He halfway expected his body to rebel and break down before the two months of self-imposed boot camp was completed. It didn't.

Amazingly, his body responded to the challenge and he began to lose fat and replace it with muscle. The transformation was remarkable. In two months he went from Mr. Average to a respectable athlete, one who could compete with a room full of 20-year-olds.

The Police Academy is much like the military, except the drill sergeants are not as nice, or at least that was how Sam explained it to his psychologist friends. His mental health colleagues were horrified and perplexed as to why any academician in psychology would want to become a cop. They understood the role of cops and none of them wanted the physical and danger components that came along with the job, not to mention the shitty pay that went with it. They liked being respected for their brains and had no desire for the title detective.

Sam could relate to their bewilderment as he too wondered at times if this was the correct career move. As a person that deals with the human mind as a course of daily work, it is easy to over-analyze one's own feelings. It is much like a physician thinking about every missed heartbeat and worrying if it is a catastrophic dysrhythmia in the making. One tries not to over-think it. Sam had to work out his concerns for his extreme need for change. This forced him to further analyze his own complex mind.

He was stymied by the police not being able to help him with his nephew's death and his own remorse for not helping Bill with his depression. He had a fascination with serial killers, especially those that seemed to fit the definition of a psychopath. His office was filled with charts and images of dead people who had met with horrific endings. None of the serial homicides had been solved, and he had been working long enough in a criminal system in which he felt at least one of these cases should have been closed.

Sam had won major awards in high school in science. He had a Stanford degree yet had chosen a career path many would say was underachieving of what he should have accomplished. By becoming a cop he was insuring that the last half of his life would have increased stress, both physical and mental, with little else to expect in the form of positive gain other than maybe filling in one of his persistent murder charts. So why was he so resolved to follow this career which would lose him the designation of an intellectual and possessed one of the highest rates of alcoholism of any career he could possibly choose? Alcohol abuse was already something his family was highly susceptible to. Bill had proven that.

These were the thoughts he posed to himself while he was being tortured with the twentysomething recruits who knew no better. The questions would pop up at night before sleep, even though he was exhausted. These are hard questions for a man who also had never been married and by committing to this demanding police lifestyle would have an even harder time ever finding a spouse.

Living in San Francisco and being straight, he would have thought the odds would have been good for his finding a mate. At five-foot-ten, with a long, symmetrical face and warm cocoa eyes, Sam was a handsome professional man and it seemed logical a woman would want to marry him and share a life together. There had been opportunities but there was always some reason to step back, reevaluate, and avoid a permanent commitment. It was easier to be alone, he told himself, rationalizing, "No kids, pets, or a wife, eat what and when I want, a good lifestyle choice for me." But he knew it wasn't. What he truly wanted was something else, something deeper, someone to share memories with, not just charts of death and destruction on an off-white office wall.

Graduation day came. His sister Beth came down from Marin to watch Sam receive his diploma. It was during the ceremony that the clarity finally came as to why he had gone through such physical and mental abuse, not to mention a significant pay cut, to become a cop. He saw it in Beth's eyes. She was proud of her little brother and what he was doing, not only for her family but also for all the families like hers. The fact that he was not able to commit to a serious relationship with a woman was a minor fault in comparison. Sam had committed to helping those who were unable to help themselves. Sam Hubbard's life was one of those rare ones in which he gave of himself completely so others could prosper in safety. Seeking out the sick minds of the world that needed to be identified and physically stopped from hurting other innocent individuals was Sam's mission in life. Maybe his dedication to help others would lead to something more for Sam. Maybe it was the path he was forced to take to find true happiness or even love.

CHAPTER 28

AWFUL OLD FOR A ROOKIE

The first day on a job is stressful no matter who you are or what the work is. For Sam, who was an expert in identifying emotions, it was stress mixed with excitement. He had just turned 32 and was as old as many of the men in charge of the precinct. He knew his role as a rookie cop was only one year in duration, making it more like a long test to make sure the commitment was really there.

What Sam didn't know was Sergeant O'Brian, who he answered to, was privy to the deal the upper brass had made with Hubbard guaranteeing the rookie cop would become a detective after his year as a beat cop. The old-guard sergeant who had been on the force nearly 30 years wasn't a fan of the whole "you get to become a detective the day you turn one" deal. "You earn your detective shield. It's not just given to you for one measly year of police work," O'Brian told Officer Donahue, the weak-link cop he paired Hubbard with for his yearlong test. Sergeant O'Brian didn't mind Hubbard being a cop if that's what he wanted and he passed all the requirements. After all, Hubbard did graduate top in his class. But cutting in on the promotion line for detective didn't mesh well with his Irish upbringing. To O'Brian it was cheating, and he was going to make sure the rookie's time was not an easy one. Even if it was only a year, it would seem longer, a lot longer with Officer Donahue as his partner.

The first day, walking into the precinct and seeing his reflection in the washroom mirror was shocking to Sam. Before him was a trim, athletic-looking police officer, not Sam Hubbard the psychologist. It was the only time in his life he'd worn a uniform except as a Boy Scout. Sam's mind couldn't help but visualize Ted Bundy wearing a Boy Scout uniform as he stared in disbelief in the mirror. Sam had navigated around many of the pitfalls of his peer group. He'd avoided the draft by being in college and graduate school at the right times. So seeing himself in the blue uniform, his hat on perfectly straight, black polished shoes, and gold buttons in a straight line, seemed strange but felt good and right. Sam suddenly realized he was not alone in his mirror. Off to the far side was a bald, ruddy-faced man with grey eyes sunken deep into an oversized head. It was his new boss, Sergeant O'Brian.

"So we got a pretty boy here, do we? Glad to see you like spending work time admiring yourself in the men's restroom. Fun being a cop and getting to wear a pretty uniform and all? Kind of like Halloween, Officer Hubbard?"

"No, Sergeant O'Brian. I understand this is serious business and I'm being paid good taxpayer money to do a job and not spend time looking at my face. It's a pleasure to meet you, sir. You're a legend at this precinct. It will be an honor to work under your command."

Sergeant O'Brian's eyes eased just a bit, as he had not expected to like the straight-talking man who he had grown to despise on paper. "Yeah, yeah, enough kissing my ass, Hubbard, and don't call me sir, I work for a living. It's sergeant. Now you need to get your butt into roll call. I've got a full day planned for you, rookie. Hooked you up with a fine man. He's old like you, been around the block a time or two."

O'Brian had placed Hubbard with a notoriously slack cop who was close to retirement and hated to work any harder than he had to, not to mention that he was not a particularly reliable backup. O'Brian knew this guy would cause Hubbard grief from day one and would make Sam's workload twice as hard. He figured if he had Hubbard only for a year the precinct should get as much work out of him as humanly possible.

It didn't take a forensic psychology degree for Sam to figure out that Sergeant O'Brian had stuck him with a lazy partner who was a loose cannon and had a mean disposition. Not too different from many of the criminals he had diagnosed. What Sam decided to do was take on the added work and make the old alcoholic cop a case study for later when he actually was a detective. By using his bad situation as a sort of cop science project he would be able to cope with the man's incompetence. He figured with a little luck and subtle counseling he might even help the schmuck, though he had his doubts.

CHAPTER 29

WELCOME ABOARD

Six months passed on the job. Sam was slowly getting the hang of what it meant to be a cop on the streets of San Francisco in 1981. It was a hard and often thankless job. Sam was starting to understand the "blue code of silence": why police covered their own asses and didn't often want to help those who would possibly screw them. Even his worthless, disheveled partner would cover Sam's butt when push came to shove. It was unwritten and expected. If you couldn't understand the mentality it was going to be hard to survive as a cop. Sam realized why his superiors wanted him to experience the beat cop reality. Otherwise, he wouldn't have the stones to be a productive part of the force, as he discovered on day 200 on the job, when he learned what it meant to be a real cop. You know you're a cop when you are faced with a dangerous situation and don't lose your nerve even if it costs you dearly. On day 200, Sam found out he deserved to be one of the boys in blue.

During his eight years as a forensic pathologist, Sam had worked with numerous gang members and his testimony had put many of them in jail. He had always imagined what it must be like in the field and wondered how humans could be such animals. He found out.

Linn So Lee, a 20-year-old waitress who worked the evening shift at her father's Vietnamese restaurant, had gone missing. The distraught father had called the police the first hour she had not shown up for work. Linn So was a good girl who worked and went to college. She was never late, not once.

The standard police response was it would take 24 hours before a missing person alert could be issued. Mr. Lee was told if he wanted to find his daughter any sooner he should call all his relatives and start a private search party. In one day the cops could get involved. This is exactly what Mr. Lee did. He called everyone and asked them to call everyone they knew. Owning a popular restaurant meant a lot of people were involved.

Officer Hubbard got a call as he was just finishing his shift. The day had been a particularly easy one with no problems and they had finished early. The call was from his old interpreter, who asked for his help. For the first time as an officer, not a psychologist, he was needed. Sandra Grun needed help from the boys in blue who could turn up the heat to find her cousin's daughter before something horrible happened, if it already hadn't. She had been privy to many interrogations and had seen firsthand what man could do to his fellow human beings.

Sam knew the only way to get the backup he needed was to bribe his lackadaisical partner to help check out a couple of leads. Sam promised that he would buy Donahue the best meal in Chinatown and as much beer as he could drink if he would just give him a couple more hours. Donahue, who never worked a minute longer than he had to, realized that for maybe two hours of work he could stick Hubbard for at least a hundred bucks worth of food and drink. He agreed.

Sam knew that the worst Vietnamese gangs lived on the edge of Chinatown not far from Lee's restaurant so that's where the search would begin.

To get answers quickly required muscle, an asset with which Donahue was quite gifted. Mrs. Grun told Sam that one of his old clients had been on a tear and was out on bail. He should start with him. Sam was familiar with this particularly pathological person, Hung Lee Me. Sam's testimony had put him behind bars for a year, five years ago. Sam also remembered Me's residence, which was in the part of town where he wanted to start his search anyhow. Me's housing information was privileged, but a life was at stake. Sam would take his chances.

Sam and Donahue made a visit to Mr. Me's last known residence. Sam knocked on the door. No answer but he did hear movement from inside the apartment. An unauthorized door breakage by Officer Donahue found Mr. Me still resided at said residence and was also smoking what appeared to be a crack pipe that he was currently trying to dispose of. Mr. Me made a dash for the back door. Sam caught one of Me's legs as he almost escaped through the exit. Sam found out the hard way that he should have gotten both legs as Me started to relentlessly kick the shit out of Sam's hand with his steel-toed shoes. Sam held on, knowing this was the lead that could save Linn So Lee's life. Donahue was impressed with Sam's pain tolerance as he watched the tap dance on Sam's hands. After Donahue had

106

witnessed enough carnage on his stupid partner's swelling hands, he took all of his 250 pounds and rammed the half-open door nearly closed. The wooden door creaked as its wood fibers gave way at the same time as Me's fibula and tibia, which broke. Sam continued pulling on Me's now rubbery leg, which only gave minor resistance with its composition reduced to broken bones, damaged flesh, and weak muscle tissue, which somehow kept the lower portion of Me's leg from coming off completely into Sam's hands.

The singing in the rain routine on Sam's hands stopped. Donahue, who was laughing at this point, dragged the screaming Me back in by the broken leg and then placed the good leg in the door jam and held Me's foot down with his own oversized boot.

"OK Me, give it up, or ME is going to taking this good one off next...."

The brutalized Me knew Donahue was not screwing around, and he squealed, literally. Linn So Lee was down in the basement. Me had been her capturer and was coming up for a quick smoke before going back down to finish her off. Lee, who had been raped and beaten, was found handcuffed to a wall, semiconscious, a wall that had been used before by the looks of the finger marks and bloodstains.

Sam, who it turned out, had suffered four broken fingers during the altercation, gave all the credit for the bust to his overweight partner, who was also given a lifetime of free meals from Mr. Lee at his Vietnamese restaurant. Sam was now a member of the "blue wall" and proud to be a part of it.

After surviving having his hands pulverized and getting an unexpected two weeks of recovery from Sergeant O'Brian, Sam was back on the job. O'Brian knew it was Sam who had saved the girl and it was on his own time and nickel. O'Brian was proud of his rookie cop and was for the first time looking forward to his becoming a detective. He even told Donahue, "The force needs men like Hubbard, watch out for him. Next time don't let him break any bones."

When he signed up to become a cop, Sam had never expected to feel such a rush of adrenaline from tracking down and arresting bad guys. It was more fulfilling in some ways than mentally breaking a convict in a safe, controlled environment. Sam briefly toyed with the idea of staying on as a beat cop for an additional year just to get more experience under his belt. He decided he didn't know that his body could take it. He knew that he was forming the building blocks of being a good detective and wasn't sure a year's experience was enough time to learn his trade, but then again he had other assets. He still wondered if he would be able to identify a psychopathic killer if he stopped one, though.

CHAPTER 30

DETECTIVE WORK

The probation year as a beat cop finally passed. Officer Sam Hubbard went from being low man on the police totem pole to running his own department, albeit a department of one. His old office, which had sat vacant for the last year, had the glass lettering upgraded to add the word Detective, something he was very proud of. Sam figured he didn't have a family of his own so he would view the police department as his relatives.

Sergeant O'Brian made a special trip to see the new lettering and wish him good luck. He was impressed Sam could survive a year as a beat cop with a less than stellar partner to back him up and let him know how proud he was of the way Sam had handled himself. It was a heartfelt congratulation and in some ways Sam felt without the difficult initiation he wouldn't have been prepared for the challenges ahead.

Sam's new department was titled Forensic Investigation. The job was to use the combination of forensic psychology profiling along with good old detective work. This emerging field would balloon beyond recognition in the future with television programs filling the prime-time air waves with cases of unsolved murders, but in 1982 it was still in its infancy.

The goal of the department was to use psychological interrogation on particularly heinous or difficult crimes. Instead of just evaluating the mental state of a person, Sam was also now expected to go to the actual crime scene and look for answers that could be tied to the mental state of the person that committed the crime.

His own special interest in psychopathic serial killers had not waned and finally Sam had some good news to add to his very empty charts. Ted Bundy, who had been recaptured, was now allowing some in-person interviews. Sam, who had written in bold red letters CAPTURED on Bundy's chart, was on the list of individuals requesting a chance at the madman. The details of his nearly decade-long murdering spree were filtering out and names of victims and potential victims were filling up the once empty chart space quickly. Sam was trying to cross reference unsolved California murders to known victims of Bundy. Sam knew the chart was far from being taken off the wall, and would not be until Bundy had been fully evaluated. Psychopaths like him were never completely understood. Sam had put in his application when he was psychologist and updated it after becoming a detective. The good word came down the pipeline. He was approved and in line.

As he waited for his chance at Bundy, Sam decided to renew his efforts on the Bill Sneadly case. After all, Sam was now part of the inner circle of the fraternal brotherhood of police officers. He hoped he might get some additional information regarding the death of Mat Smith, as he was now Detective Hubbard.

Sam was shocked to learn the military police had actually closed the case, having found and convicted a fellow naval enlisted man. According to military records it was determined during the investigation that Petty Officer Smith was a closet homosexual. His lover, a young seaman named Robin Pettipoint, who Smith had recently jilted, had confessed to the murder. Seaman Pettipoint had a long history of unstable mental problems and probably should have never been allowed in the Navy to begin with. But the military was struggling with the draft no longer in place and so taking marginal candidates became the standard, although not queer ones, which it turned out Pettipoint was.

Seaman Pettipoint was presently housed in the Long Beach brig, having just been sentenced to serve 25 to life. Detective Hubbard was able to arrange a 20-minute meeting with Pettipoint to get his impressions of the man who confessed to Smith's murder. Sam had read the transcripts and now being a police officer could decode the unwritten police lingo, which he interpreted as Pettipoint was strong-armed to some extent into confessing.

The conversation he had with the sergeant of arms spoke volumes about how the Navy felt about convict Pettipoint: he was a murderer and queer. It seemed to Sam that the queer part was more frowned upon than the murderer aspect.

Sam, while not of the homosexual persuasion, had difficulty reconciling these types of prejudices, which he also saw to a lesser extent in the police force. Living 15 years in San Francisco had opened his viewpoint to the wide range of sexuality in the world. The fact that he was an unmarried, almost-middle-aged man himself, neat, good looking, with a professional degree, placed him in the eyes of most men he met at social settings as being possibly gay and Sam could have cared less, unless a woman was saying it. He still had hopes of finding a soul mate.

The brig at Long Beach was depressing, to say the least. The roof was low, the lights florescent, the furniture sterile in appearance and personal items nonexistent. The jail was more like a zoo filled with cages than a prison. It was obvious this was less a place of rehabilitation than one geared toward punitive purposes.

The person in charge of prisoner Pettipoint, a petty officer first-class whose white nametag read Blunt, got right to the point. "Convict Pettipoint is ready for you to talk to him, sir. If you need any detailed information regarding what he's reading, eating, who his visitors are, or his sleeping patterns, I have that available also," said Blunt.

"Thank you, Petty Officer Blunt. He is monitored that closely? You have everything he does charted?"

"Pretty much. We do it for all the inmates, but we take a special interest in the murderers of other sailors like Pettipoint. He's scheduled to be moved to Leavenworth in two weeks," Blunt revealed.

"That's in Kansas?" Sam questioned.

"Yes, sir. That's where all the convicts who are sentenced to 10 years and longer end up. He won't make a lot of friends there, I'm afraid." Blunt's face betrayed a smirk as he said this, knowing Pettipoint would probably be mistreated.

"If I could have the records on who Pettipoint has seen since he has been here, and also I would like to review his eating and sleep logs as well," Sam requested. Coming from a scientific background, Sam realized his subject's circadian rhythms of life might give him some insight into his psyche.

"Sure, not a problem. You will notice he has been on bread and water the last couple of weeks. Seaman Pettipoint has been in need of some attitude adjustment and his current diet is geared for that. Seems to be working well."

Sam was shocked that in the 20th century, prisoners could be treated so harshly. He hoped the man was not in such a bad mental state that Sam couldn't glean any useful information. Sam was led to a small cell with dark black bars and a huge antiquated lock where convict Pettipoint was sitting on a small iron cot that dated pre-WWII.

Pettipoint's face was gaunt and white. He had not seen the sun in some time. He looked to weigh in at a mere 140 pounds. Pettipoint jumped to attention as Petty Officer Blunt entered the room. His uniform was perfect and looked as if he had been working on it for hours. What struck Sam were Pettipoint's eyes. They were sunken inside his skull. It reminded Sam of the pictures of holocaust victims. Pettipoint was slight of build but not emaciated. It was more than a weight issue. It was much deeper than that.

"Thank you, Petty Officer Blunt," Sam said. "I would like to interview Seaman Pettipoint alone, so if you wouldn't mind giving us a minute."

"Fine, sir, but I will be just a few yards away if you need me for anything. Remember, you are not allowed to touch the prisoner."

"I understand. I'll let you know when we're done."

Sam began carefully. "Hello, Mr. Pettipoint, you have been briefed about who I am and why I'm here, correct?"

"Yes. You're wondering if I killed the other person that died the same night that Petty Officer Smith was killed," responded Pettipoint.

"Yes, that is correct," Sam concurred. "Can you tell me anything about your involvement in that case, if any?"

"Yes, sir. I probably was involved. I don't remember much of that night. I was very depressed about Smith and myself, and was very inebriated, and maybe I pushed the other guy off the cliff. Sorry I can't be of any more help than that. I wish I could be, sir."

"Let me ask you, do you remember actually killing Smith?" Sam questioned.

"No, sir, not in so much as a vivid memory. I do have images of wanting to kill him and I know I wanted him to be dead. Who else would want to hurt him, if it wasn't me, sir?"

Sam was stunned. This pathetic young man was facing 25 years of hard labor in the toughest prison environment known to man and he didn't even have a memory of the evening. Something was wrong with this picture. Sam's detective hat came off and he relied instead on mentally evaluating convict Pettipoint.

"Do you mind if I call you Robin instead of Pettipoint?" Sam asked.

"That's fine, sir. I'm not used to my name anymore. My family doesn't visit so I'm more of a number in here. Sounds weird even hearing it again. I don't know if that person is even alive anymore."

"Listen Robin, call me Sam, and you are most definitely alive. I have to tell you I have doubts that you killed Petty Officer Smith. Is it possible you are mistaken? Quite frankly, physically you don't look like you would have the strength to do what was done to him. Smith was a large man. Is it possible you are innocent?"

Robin, who had been staring at the floor, looked up and locked eyes with Sam. "Honestly, Sam, I don't know. I have racked my brains thinking about what happened and I know when I get mad I can be violent. You can ask my mom. She's seen me break plates and I put my fist through my bedroom door once. It feels like some big nightmare that I'm caught in and it doesn't seem like I have any options at this point. It's not like I'm really worth saving. I'm a homosexual, you know."

Robin Pettipoint had some serious mental issues, including having been brainwashed regarding his sexual orientation and self-worth. He was not Smith's killer, as far as Sam could tell, and if he was involved there must have been some other person or persons to help. He didn't have the physical or mental capabilities to pull off such a violent crime. He also wouldn't have been able to overpower Bill and throw him over a cliff, no matter how drunk Bill might have been.

113

"Robin," Sam sighed, "I think you need help. You have some fairly significant issues, but I can tell you I don't believe you're a murderer."

"Really, Sam, you don't? Why am I in prison then? They told me I did it."

"Honestly, I don't know why, but I hope to find out." Sam stood up and excused himself to review Robin's food and sleep habits, which were consistent with depression and mild starvation.

Next step was to try and get the case reopened and to update his nephew's chart, which he updated to read: "Smith's case not solved. Wrong person convicted."

CHAPTER 31

CASE CLOSED

The base commander was not happy to hear from Detective Hubbard, who was requesting all Pettipoint's records be reevaluated by an independent panel to see if the information that he had been convicted with was coerced, or worse, fabricated. He did not find Hubbard's accusations worthy of discussion. He sternly warned Hubbard that the prisoner Robin Pettipoint was convicted in a fair and impartial military trial by a group of his peers who found him guilty of all charges. The conviction was just, especially in light of the signed confession that was obtained from Pettipoint in his own hand admitting to all charges.

If Detective Hubbard had a problem with the court's findings, he would need to follow military protocol and submit his complaints to the Uniform Justice bureau for further review. As far as Sam's request for the transcripts of the trial and findings by the military police, he would take it under advisement, which was the polite way to say, "Fuck off, civilian."

All access to Pettipoint for future visits was cut off, so Sam started writing the first of many letters to the military Uniform Justice department requesting the case be reopened and Pettipoint have an independent psychological evaluation. He spelled out his own qualifications as a mental health expert and argued that in his professional opinion, Seaman Pettipoint was not mentally stable and his state of mind would not have allowed for a competent confession to be obtained. Pettipoint was sick and needed treatment, and a maximum security prison surrounded by real criminals was not the appropriate facility.

Sam felt badly for Pettipoint, who he knew was caught in some legal hell that would probably take years to unwind, if ever. Pettipoint's best hope was for Sam to try and find the actual killer, who may have been tied to his own nephew's death.

No common denominator had been shown between the two deaths other than Bill did appear to have at least been acquainted with Petty Officer Smith. This had been verified by a local bar owner in Seal Beach whose establishment both men frequented. It was unclear whether the men had been together the night they had died. No witness had been located to verify this either way. Sam would have to continue using his police ties to determine if any other connection between the two existed. He needed the complete file on Smith and up to this point no one was sharing.

CHAPTER 32

ZODIAC GETS A CHART ENTRY

It had been nearly 20 years since Sam's last entry on his Zodiac chart. The unchanging chart was now more a reminder of who he was and why he worked. The phone call he got one afternoon in the late 1980s revisited the case, and the person on the other end was a name that appeared on another of his charts, that of his nephew Bill Sneadly.

"Hi, Detective Hubbard. I was given your name as the person I should talk to about a project I'm working on. It's regarding the Zodiac Killer, the serial killer. I hear you're the guy who knows the details the best."

"Oh yes, the Zodiac, I know the case quite well," Sam agreed. "Let's just say it's a pet project of mine. How can I help you, Mr.?"

"I'm sorry, I should have introduced myself properly. I'm Mo Bandgood, a music composer. I'm working on a made-for-TV movie about the Zodiac, and I'm trying to do some background to get the feeling of the story the music should tell."

"Mo Bandgood...." Sam swiveled in his chair looking for that name he had written on Bill's chart so many years ago. "Are you the same fellow who likes to run along Seal Beach in the morning?"

Mo was silent on the other end, trying to figure out how this man knew his running habits. Not coming up with anything, Mo simply replied, "Yes. Have we met?"

"We have, Mo. It was before I got into law enforcement. I interviewed you regarding my nephew's death, Bill Sneadly. You found his body, remember?"

"Oh my god, sure, I remember that whole episode. It was really weird for me. Quite frankly, I have tried to put that event in some part of my brain that I don't visit, probably why I didn't recognize your name. Sorry."

"No problem. How have you been?" Sam asked.

"Well I'd like to say great, but it's been an interesting time in Hollywood for composers. Also I got married. It didn't stick but I lost a shitload of my commercial royalties. If you're not married, you might want to keep it that way," Mo advised.

Sam cringed because he really did want to get married or at least find a steady, interesting girlfriend.

"The divorce sucked," Mo continued, "but what really blows is what people refer to as progress. In my case, it's an instrument called the synthesizer. It literally cut my composing balls off. There used to be a time when things like originality and quality had meaning. Now it's about how cheap it can be done and avoiding paying scale to musicians. I used to ask my musician friends what they were recording. Now I ask them what school are they teaching at. It's not so much that I'm bitter, which I am, but it's more a sense of sadness knowing great music is not being composed because there is no market for quality. That's why when I do actually get a paying gig that has a throwback director who requests real, original music using profession musicians, I want to make sure I do a good job, thus the call. Wow, that felt good. I bet you weren't expecting my life story."

"No, but I enjoyed hearing it. Sometimes we all need to vent. I won't scare you with mine," Sam responded.

"So Sam, what was the final outcome of your nephew's death? Accident, right? That's what I remember reading in the paper."

"Officially, yes, accident. My own opinion, I'm not sure. It's an open case in my mind. Anything else you can add since our last conversation?"

"No not really, other than I thought the officer who interrogated me on the beach was a real dick. Officer Brown, I think it was. I doubt I said anything to you at the time as I was intimidated by the whole process and didn't want to make waves, but I'm older now and don't give a shit what people think about me or what I say, not like I did back then."

"I'll add that to Bill's chart. I'm still entering any information I might find out. I'll notate, 'Officer Brown (Dick).' Maybe that will make you feel better."

"Oddly Sam, it does."

"So, you're working on a Zodiac film? When is it due out?"

"We are shooting for a twentieth anniversary. The powers that be like the fact that it's still pertinent this many years later, and with the whole Bundy thing, the serial killer angle seems hot, so there you got it. I make my money because serial killers are all the rage."

"Well for me, they have never gone out of fashion. I'm happy to help however I can."

"Great," said Mo. "First of all, you will get a credit in the movie and a small honorarium. It's minimal, believe me. What I want to know from my end is the feeling of the time. What kind of pandemonium was going on in San Francisco? And how did you view Zodiac's mental status, being a shrink detective and all?"

"I'm actually not a shrink but a forensic psychologist," Sam clarified. "I'm not an M.D., although I do specialize in the criminal mind."

"Honestly, Doc, it doesn't matter what your initials are as long as you can give me the sense of this guy's mental state. I need to feel his derangement to really capture a mood for the movie. Can you do that?"

"Yes, I can. I have a very good feel for what type of person this man was or maybe is. We don't know if he's still out there, maybe even killing. Sure you want to do this movie score? You wouldn't want to piss off the Zodiac, would you?" Sam questioned, pulling Mo's emotional chain a bit.

"I'll take my chances with any serial killer finding me. I need the money. Did I mention I'm divorced? So tell me, what was Joe America feeling?"

"With regards to the mindset of the public, I was one of them and I can say it was compelling. In fact it helped me make up my mind as to what path to take in life. You might say without the Zodiac, I wouldn't be the person I am today."

"Shit that's great stuff, Doc. Keep going, I'm writing it all down. 'The Zodiac serial killer shaped my life.'"

The two men talked for over an hour and afterwards Sam looked at the Zodiac chart and wrote in "Made-for-TV movie." He then went to Bill's chart and made a little red diagram, a triangle with three phrases connecting to each other. The phrases were: "Zodiac movie composer Mo," "Found Bill's Body," "Me." A connection had been formed and Sam wondered if it was just an odd coincidence or if it had a deeper meaning.

CHAPTER 33

OPEN AND SHUT CASE

Sam's first call of the morning was a homicide, or at least it might be. It was 1991, and he had been heading the Forensic Investigation department for nine years. Today's subject of investigation was an 85-year-old woman who had been found by her maid, slumped over dead at her library table. The maid, who had worked for the deceased for 30 years, was surprised that her boss, a Mrs. Black, was at the table writing when she died. The maid reported that her employer rarely used the desk and of late had been in such poor health that she was having problems walking. Detective Hubbard was called in to investigate the death as a possible homicide as a favor to his chief. Apparently the chief's wife shared the same maid as Mrs. Black, and the maid was concerned there might be foul play.

Sam tried to approach the case as he would any other, even knowing it was probably a wild goose chase. Sam recognized the maid could know something even if it looked for all purposes like a simple case of old age. The deceased had been found sitting in a Stickley chair, her torso collapsed over a small Victorian desk. Her gray-haired head was laid sideways on a thick pad of white writing paper and her right hand was lying next to her head. There was a small amount of fluid that had accumulated on the paper, and a slightly used, sharpened #2 pencil was next to her face. There didn't appear to be any struggle and no unusual findings were seen. She was in her bedclothes. It simply looked like an elderly lady had gotten out of bed to write something and had died at her desk. But Sam had promised to investigate it, and investigate he would.

Mrs. Black's bed was only a few feet away. The bedding had been pulled back as if she had been in bed before going over to the desk. The television had been on, and there was a bottle of water next to the bed, the top off and the bottle half empty. The only unusual finding that Sam saw was that Mrs. Black's house slippers were still next to her bed and not on her feet. If she had gotten out of bed to go to the desk, one would expect her to wear the house slippers to keep her feet warm, especially being elderly with cold extremities. Sam knew the human mind is like a clock, it keeps its own time and habits, like compulsively wearing house slippers in the bedroom. This is done instinctually.

Sam decided he would do a complete work-up of the area, much to his partner's admonishment.

"Why the fuck you worrying about this old gal's death, Sammy?" His partner called him Sammy to irritate Sam when he thought Sam was being too thorough and wasting his time.

"You know good and well she died of natural causes," his partner insisted. "I've been a detective longer than you've been wiping your ass, and I'm telling you there ain't shit here. Just 'cause she forgot to put on her damn slippers doesn't mean anything. This is not some big psychological mystery, I know that's what you're thinking. Maybe her feet hurt, or she's so damn old she forgot how to get dressed, or how about her feet were hot and she didn't want no wool slippers. You're going to cost the department time and money, my friend. Take some notes and let's go catch an early lunch and sign off on this routine case so the chief can get his old lady off his back."

Sam basically ignored anything his partner said when it came to detailed detective work like the Black case. Yes, it could be an open and shut case, simply a nuisance call to appease the chief's demanding wife. But now that Sam was here, something was bothering him. So Sam followed his gut. His forensics mind told him that old ladies put their house shoes on when they walk around their bedroom.

A complete work-up was performed including an autopsy. The cause of death appeared to be myocardial infarction. In essence: a heart attack. There was ischemia not only in the heart tissue but in the pulmonary system as well. The pulmonary infarction was probably secondary to the circulatory collapse, but this was not certain. The heart itself was consistent with that of an elderly woman with fairly severe lipid atherosclerosis of the major cardiac arteries, including the left main coronary artery that is often called the widow maker. There were plenty of collateral vessels circulating around her heart which would indicate Mrs. Black had probably suffered from myocardial ischemia for years and her heart had adapted by producing and enlarging collateral vessels to deal with the insufficient oxygenation of the heart muscle.

Mrs. Black's brain showed some atrophy but no other findings and the atrophy was nonspecific and was probably early Alzheimer's.

The coroner's report found the cause of death to be natural causes secondary to heart disease.

Detective Hubbard decided to dig deeper even though the case was basically closed, his partner long ago putting his mark on the report. The shoes and something else didn't seem to fit the forensic findings of the personality of Mrs. Black. The maid insisted that Mrs. Black always wore her slippers upstairs as they were a gift from her late husband. She did write occasionally at her desk, but preferred phone contact these days, which is what bothered the maid most. Mrs. Black was well off, leaving an estate of almost $2 million and a house valued at just under a million. The sizable estate was handled by an attorney who had represented Mrs. Black's affairs for the last two years. According to the attorney, he had visited her at her home the week before her death, and he sent over the details of the estate for Sam to review. Sam had the city attorneys review the estate as well and they determined it to be straightforward in nature. No monkey business found.

Mrs. Black's attorney would be in charge of allocating funds to various charities, leaving the estate with a certain principal that was not to be touched. The charities would get yearly allocations depending on how much money the estate made from investments. The attorney would get compensated for his work and some small fees as needed to execute the will of the estate. Mrs. Black had left a little money to her maid and to her sometimes driver and there were no immediate relatives. No money was left to her attorney.

Sam figured he would interview the attorney just to make sure nothing seemed out of place. He would also follow up on the designated charities to make sure they too were above board, and if nothing else was found he would sign off on the case like his partner, telling the chief that in all good conscience it was not homicide.

He set up a meeting the following morning with Mrs. Black's attorney, a Mr. Fallon Scriber.

CHAPTER 34

BUSINESS AS USUAL

The business of law as it turned out was suited perfectly for Fallon's gifts, including killing. He had been practicing estate law in private practice for three years and had developed a small but well-heeled client base by 1991. It was limited in size because Fallon wanted it that way. Having few clients allowed him to allocate plenty of time for each. His goal was developing intimate relationships. For Fallon, a man of no real feelings, his idea of intimacy was building a house with veneer wood. It looked great but had no substance. Appearances were all that mattered to Fallon Scriber.

The clients that he chose to represent had to meet certain requirements: 1: total estate value of $2 million or greater. 2: No heirs or close lifelong friends. 3: At least 80 years or older. If the clients met those three prerequisites, they were added to his practice. Of course the clients never knew his screening process, which was uniquely psychopathic. Fallon thought of himself as a gardener. He sowed the seeds (clients), nurtured each plant carefully (plenty of time with them), and when he was in need of food or the vegetable was in danger of rotting he harvested (murdered).

Fallon's history of murder had changed since graduating from law school three years ago. Before becoming a lawyer, every individual that Fallon murdered was perceived as a threat to his welfare and they were violently disposed of. With his vegetable garden concept, this was a totally different kind of killing.

He liked the majority of individuals in his practice and they seemed to enjoy his company. It didn't bother him particularly when he needed to harvest, but killing for money was not the same as killing for a higher cause. It was simply a necessity. If he needed more money for something, the clients could provide the extra cash easier and faster by being dead. What Fallon was waiting for in his life was god to show him his calling. Fallon had been born with a special gift, a mind not filled with remorse or self-condemnation. He was the piranha of the human world and he needed to feed.

By working with elderly clients, occasionally Fallon would get a bonus he hadn't counted on. He already had two clients who had died of natural causes and it required nothing on his part other than being a decent lawyer, which he was.

Fallon encouraged his clients since they had no heirs to set up charities where his role would be to control the flow of money. Fallon would make his money by billing the charities to death. Every time the charity needed anything from the estate he would send them a bill for his minimal effort at an exorbitant hourly rate, which came out of the estate's funds. It was a license to steal and the charities couldn't do anything to stop him, not if they wanted their money.

So far he was handling three estates and was making nice monthly fees along with billing his living clients. There was minimal work involved. Fallon set the charitable trusts up in such a fashion that the principal would not be siphoned off too quickly. This assured him a retirement plan of sorts. No next of kin to kick him out of the cat seat. He would simply build up enough estates to where he would be set for life, billing each charity for his quarterly reports and sending out lawyerly advice they didn't need or want but had to pay for or risk his revenge.

As Fallon matured, he began to appreciate and refine his talents at manipulating people, the law, and his own emotions. He realized more deeply than ever his talent at taking another's life was given to him for a reason. A divine deity would appear to him at some point at which time he would then make his mark on the world. It was his destiny. The history books would know the name Fallon Scriber and they would idolize his brilliance and fear his wrath, which he felt was similar to being an angel. He was an anti-angel of sorts, doing harm but for a higher cause, a cause he was patiently waiting for his god to call.

Mrs. Black, whom he had killed, was a straightforward elimination. As always he left his signature pencil by her side. Her mind was starting to go. He discerned it in the questions she asked which he answered repetitively only to be asked the exact same question the next time they met or even during the same meeting. She was a charming, giving woman. Fallon thought she would have made a wonderful grandmother for someone as she aged, but life had chosen him instead.

Most likely if her mind had stayed intact he would have never killed her. Fallon recognized the fondness the old lady had for him. It was obvious in the way she looked at him and touched his hand when they talked. Though he wasn't able to feel any emotion like love, he tried to return what he thought the feelings must appear like, and the old lady ate it up.

Mrs. Black's love for Fallon would have ultimately meant she would leave her entire estate to him. All he had to do was wait for a natural death, which would probably come soon. But he couldn't chance her losing her marbles and the state getting involved. She had a longtime employee, a maid who was quite meddlesome and might have tried to get the old lady to leave her everything, so he decided it was time to harvest now.

Because of Fallon's access to Mrs. Black, killing was child's play. Less challenging than catching a trolley. He simply went to her home while her maid was off, knocked on the door, and she let him walk in. No cameras or alarms to contend with, no records of his presence.

The day he disposed of Mrs. Black he came dressed for work. Black clothes, a pair of gloves, and his special silver case of sharpened pencils. Fallon showed a rare display of emotion when he giggled out loud when Mrs. Black commented on how dapper he looked that day. "You look like Cary Grant in *To Catch a Thief*," she giggled. The irony stimulated Fallon's twisted mind. "No Mrs. Black, I'm more like Freddy Krueger, but I am a fan of Alfred Hitchcock movies." The old woman's comment would leave Fallon with fond memories of their last visit together.

Murdering without any sense of danger was boring, but leaving his subtle clue of a partially worn-down sharpened pencil turned his craft into a sport. He relished this part of the crime. It was like Tiger Woods pumping his fists after making an impossible putt. Fallon had left a pencil behind as his calling card at every murder he had ever committed and not once was it mentioned in the newspaper other than with his first victim, Willy Bellows, and that was only because he had left two pencils sticking out of his victim's neck. Fallon thought that the cops saw his pencils as nothing more than incidental artifacts, their subtlety like his own brilliant mind, too refined to be discovered. It gave Fallon a sense of added power. By engaging the cops each time, he viewed the police as his sworn enemies as they alone had the capability to try and bring him to justice. Every pencil was saying to the police, "I'm smarter than you. I'm giving you my last name, you idiots, and you still can't put it together."

Killing the old lady was simple. He sat next to her on the bed watching "Wheel of Fortune," her favorite game show. They discussed the weather and her arthritis, and then during a commercial he took a heavy pillow from her favorite sitting chair and slowly started to smother her. He could hear her muffled cries for help as he periodically lifted the pillow up a bit to help prolong her struggle. His demonic plan was methodical in its execution. The goal was to try and make her weak, elderly heart pump as hard as possible. He needed it to blow a gasket. Finally the stress of being slowly smothered to death led to her heart giving out. Fallon could feel the moment her body released its life force and he immediately removed the pillow so as to allow her lungs to aerate one last futile time so the coroner's findings would be consistent with a heart attack.

It was a masterful orchestration of evil and gave Fallon a feeling of accomplishment. He liked playing god. To take a life at will under whatever preconceived conditions you want was a wonderful feeling for Fallon, who rarely had such emotions. It invigorated him and he felt stronger. The downside was the added endorphin rush usually lead to a flare-up in his chronic dermatographia, which, like his pencils, was a constant reminder of his painful life.

After killing Mrs. Black, Fallon sat next to her bed and watched the conclusion of "Wheel" as Mrs. Black called it, laughing out loud when the show approved of his actions.

"Look at that, Mrs. Black, can you believe this one: 'Murder weapon.' I bet you could have gotten that one, and no, the answer isn't "P" for pillow though it should have been." Fallon believed the television was speaking directly to him, a clear sign he was on the right path.

Fallon finished his job by hauling the frail woman's body to the chair, staging her limbs as if she died while writing. He carefully opened her mouth so the saliva dripped on the paper and excitedly pulled out one of the sharpened pencils he had brought with him and left it next to her, his calling card. Fallon desperately wanted to leave a more definitive clue on the pencil itself to ratchet up the thrill of the chase, but the timing wasn't right. He would know when it was. Televisions were now talking to him. He would pay closer attention.

Fallon was surprised when Officer Sam Hubbard contacted him to find out additional details about Mrs. Black and her estate affairs. Fallon was smart. He had always made sure the estate documents Mrs. Black had signed were notarized and witnessed by a bank officer where the majority of the estate's money was held. If any questions were asked, the bank would look as culpable as anyone. Fallon knew how to slowly milk the estates over his lifetime and not try to strong-arm any clients into leaving it all to him. This distance would keep him safe from the cops.

Officer Hubbard's call was as exciting as it was concerning. "Finally maybe I have found an opponent worthy of my gifts. I will remember that name, Sam Hubbard, and do a little research. He might be the one I've been hoping for," Fallon thought, as he prepared for the meeting Sam had requested at Fallon's law office.

For his part, Sam was not expecting to find anything, but he was following up on the leads and this was a major one. Fallon was in charge of the estate. From everything Sam could tell, it was on the up and up. More than likely nothing would be found, but the slippers kept Sam's observational mind unsettled.

"Detective Hubbard," Fallon greeted Sam. "It's nice to make your acquaintance. How can I be of service to you today."

Sam tried to be keenly aware of initial interactions with any subject he was interrogating. Fallon's comments were unremarkable: he had a nice smile, strong handshake, looked him directly in the eye, and seemed normal. "Well, Mr. Scriber," Sam launched in.

Fallon interrupted, wanting to make Sam feel as comfortable with him as possible. "Please call me Fallon."

"Fallon, I'm doing some routine follow-up on the unexpected death of your client, Mrs. Black, just making sure her demise was as it appears to be, of natural causes."

"I had no idea there was any concern it was anything but natural?" Fallon put on a concerned look of astonishment, which Sam noticed as appropriate.

Sam explained, "The coroner has ruled her death as due to myocardial infarction, a heart attack, but I still have a couple of unanswered questions."

Fallon recognized that the officer had used a medical term to describe Mrs. Black's death. This was not something he would expect a cop to say, even a detective. He seemed more refined than the police officers he had observed in the elevators back in college. Fallon knew he had to be at the top of his game. Finally, a cop with brains, Fallon thought.

"What kind of unanswered questions? Maybe I can enlighten you?" Fallon offered. He secretly hoped Sam would bring up the pencil.

"Mrs. Black was found expired at her writing desk, but one thing keeps bothering me that maybe you can help me with. She didn't have her house slippers on. Any idea why? Didn't she normally wear them?" Sam was looking as intently at his subject now as if Fallon was one of his javelinas back in high school.

"Hum," Fallon stalled. "I guess I never noticed her footwear selection. When I would visit Mrs. Black at her home, which wasn't that common, it was usually for estate business. Let me think about it." Fallon was excited. He had a ready answer if the cop queried about the pencil, but he had completely forgotten about the damn slippers, a mistake on his part. The old lady loved those fucking shoes, she wore them everywhere, he thought to himself as he groped for an appropriate answer. Her late husband had given them to her, and the cop probably knew that. He was very smart. A worthy enemy and one Fallon would need to learn more about. Fallon's brain was in overdrive trying to work out the correct response.

"You know, Detective Hubbard, now that I think about it, I do remember her wearing them at least once before. I know she did have fairly severe arthritis. I'm pretty sure it was gout, as I remember. Maybe she didn't have them on because of that?" Fallon was brilliant. The old lady had gout and the most common joint involved was the big toe. If the detective didn't know it he would surely look it up.

"I hadn't considered that possibility," allowed Sam. "Thanks, you've been a great help. If you think of anything else please give me a call. Here are my office and home numbers. I'm the head of the forensic investigation department."

Fallon was thrilled. The cop was not only smart, he specialized in the deranged mind. Finally, a foe worth engaging. "It was a pleasure getting to meet you. If anything else comes to mind, I'll let you know."

Then Fallon impulsively decided to challenge his opponent on the spot to see what he was up against. He reached into his desk drawer and pulled out one of his pencils from his silver box and made a note on the back of Sam's card. He scrawled on the back, "Are you watching? The killer is right in front of you, dickweed."

Sam missed the cue. Fallon had served up a slow ball down the middle and Sam never saw it coming.

Fallon made his own internal mental note: a smart cop, but not observant enough to catch me. He put Sam's card in his wallet, a trophy of his superiority. He hoped they would meet again. If they did, it probably would not be under such pleasant circumstances.

The answer to the question Sam Hubbard had asked himself years ago—Would he be able to identify a psychopathic serial killer if he ever met one?—was no.

CHAPTER 35

INDIAN MARKUP

July 2012 turned out to be less than spectacular for art sales. In fact it was pretty weak. The Santa Fe Opera schedule was half over and it seemed this year's theatrical interludes were similar to that of the retail season. Unremarkable. Bloom wondered if it was the actual opera performances that were below par or in fact if it was just everyone's crappy attitude toward the entire bad economy and drought.

When the majority of the population was feeling the pinch on their pocketbooks, their outlook on life was just not the same. His Navajo influence had changed the way Bloom viewed his world. There was a spiritual component that he was now aware of. Bloom decided he would have a great Indian Market no matter what his finances were and he was glad he was saving money and time on not having to water his flower garden.

This year, Bloom had finally been asked to be a judge at Market. Ironically he still considered himself a contemporary painting dealer but the area he was asked to judge in was the textile division. "Two years in the rug business, I'm an expert. Twenty years as painting dealer and I'm still not worthy," Bloom thought to himself as he pondered whether to judge or not.

The problem for Bloom was his requested expertise was needed the same day as his Yellowhorse opening and the busiest retail day of the year. Finally he went with Hastiin Johnson's perspective on life and gave back to the community. He agreed to be a judge for Indian Market, even if it cost him some needed sales and cut it close on returning in time for his own opening. Bloom's perspective for August in Santa Fe for the first time in his life was not about the almighty dollar that he had strived so hard to acquire. He was more concerned with his core family. There was a lot to be thankful for. He had a new child, a loving significant other, two new gallery artists, and a father who was still with him despite his advanced age. All in all, not a bad year even if the sales sucked.

Market was less than two weeks away in mid-August and Bloom was starting to fret about the Willard Yellowhorse painting that was supposed to be in his show. Bloom had been very careful not to say a word to anyone about the consigned Yellowhorse drawing until it was safely in his gallery. Many a great art deal has been blown by mentioning something you're expecting and someone goes behind your back and poof, your surefire deal is gone.

It had taken a lot of years in retail to understand no deal is ever done until the money is in the bank for two weeks. Always keep your mouth shut or one of the Black Hat art dealers might descend.

Another week went by and finally the Yellowhorse drawing arrived. Packed inside was his precious consignment contract, which the client had signed. A sticky note was attached expressing embarrassment for being late sending the piece, but the client had been recovering from an unexpected hospital stay and had not been up to sending it as planned.

Bloom was very relieved as he had started to panic that his most important sales piece for the summer had gone south. He kept trying to think about Hastiin Johnson's words about the importance of family over material things, but you only get so many shots at Willard Yellowhorse paintings. He had even started fantasizing the client had changed his mind at the last minute or worse yet, sold it himself to the museum. Waiting for its arrival had been nerve-wracking.

There is a fine line when it comes to pushing a client too far to give you a great piece of art. You don't want to bug the person too much or they will sense your desperation and want to renegotiate the terms or even worse cancel the deal altogether. The added pressure from an overly anxious dealer may make the client feel they have been too hasty in selling. "After all, if an art dealer wants it so badly it must be better than we thought," the client might think, which could very well be right.

In the art business you get used to unexpected things happening. These usually come in the form of death or divorce, or occasionally both. Many a big deal falls apart as a husband suddenly decides he wants his secretary's ass more than a new painting hanging over the fireplace mantle and there goes the sale. Marriages fall apart, husbands and wives are forced to liquidate assets, and there's no money for art. "Another client out of the art world because their marriage failed, doomed from the start. After all, one in two ends in divorce," Bloom said to himself as he pondered how he hoped to never be in such a position.

The constant toll of ruined marriages and sub-sequential life destruction secondary to unsuccessful matrimony was something Bloom had witnessed up-close from more than 20 years working retail. This plethora of destroyed marriages that he had observed was likely the cause of his marriage phobia.

When Bloom really analyzed what he could lose in a divorce a truthful answer was "not much." He basically had only one valuable liquid asset, his little Yellowhorse painting, and Rachael would never ask for it no matter what. So really he had more to gain than she did. But so many of Bloom's secondary artworks came from divorced couples forced to liquidate their cherished pieces that this marriage trauma was always in the back of his mind, no matter how hard he tried to rationalize its absurdity.

Losing one's art collection due to dying even Bloom couldn't change. He knew this all too well, having had two of his artists murdered. Bloom realized it was important to live life fully. You just never knew when a piano (or a rock) might fall on your head. He was in his prime as an art dealer, but knew there would be a time when he too would downsize and need to find a place for his collection, assuming he had one. Now he had Willy in his life and somehow even though his son was only four months old and hadn't been around as long as most of the paintings on Bloom's gallery walls, he wanted the art to be part of Willy's inheritance. How to dispose of personal things was now clear for Bloom: Willy.

With the consigned Yellowhorse drawing firmly in hand, it was time to orchestrate the sale. Bloom's first call was to the director of the New Mexico Museum of Art, which owned and currently was featuring the painting that the drawing had been executed for.

The director, a lovely man in his late forties, scurried over during his lunch break to see the latest Yellowhorse. The art museum only had one piece by Willard and the thought of having a major painting and the drawing that preceded it was thrilling, especially since Willard Yellowhorse had trained in Santa Fe and there were so few of the artist's artworks available due to Willard's having died so young.

Bloom knew it was a sale even before the little man with the tortoise-shell glasses hurried through the door. He heard it on the phone when he called to offer the piece and now he could see it in the director's face. His glasses had extra-thick lenses that magnified his green irises. His eyes kept darting back and forth, looking for the drawing. He was frenetic, unusual for the mellow man who normally shuffled about, taking everything in on his own terms.

"Bloom, Bloom, thank you again for calling me. I got over here as fast as I could! So where is your little surprise? One of my patrons just gave me the latest copy of *Canyon Road Arts*. The piece sounds fabulous."

Bloom knew the game was over even though it was still the first inning. He could have had some fun with the academician if he wanted, telling him "sorry it just sold" and then watching the reaction, but today Bloom was all business. He needed the sale. He ushered Jackmo Peasly back into his tiny office to see the Yellowhorse drawing. A small halogen light had been strategically adjusted to illuminate the ghostly figures to their optimum eeriness.

"Magnificent, truly better than I had hoped! We have to get this for our collection, we just must," Peasly enthused.

Bloom loved museum people like Peasly, one, because they had the enthusiasm of a collector, and two, unlike a collector they didn't care about price. It was someone else's money; they just wanted the piece.

"I'm glad you like it. It's $100,000 firm, but you are getting first crack. It just arrived this morning and you are my first call. No one else has seen it, and I'm sure there will be plenty of my old clients who will be quite irritated with me when they find out I had a great Yellowhorse and didn't call them first, but because you have the painting in the museum it didn't seem right for you not to have first right of refusal."

"Oh, I'm sure it will sell fast, it's just terrific. His works are so rare and I can't tell you how happy I am to have this opportunity! I will need to make calls to my best donors and see if we can't come up with the money. When is your show's opening?" Peasly said, out of breath from excitement.

"A little less than a week, I'm afraid. So I will need to know on this very soon. I don't own the drawing. I'm selling it for one of my old clients who originally purchased it from me. His health is poor so I have to place it quickly. I would imagine it will sell at my opening on Friday. I'm sorry I can only give you till then. I will take it off hold at 5 pm Friday."

"That's fine, Friday it is. I'll pull out all the stops. We want this piece."

The museum world is known for taking months, even a year, to arrange the money or board approval to buy something. For many art dealers, museums are the last call because time is money, especially at Indian Markup, and sooner trumps later.

Bloom needed the $20K he would make in profit from the sale and couldn't afford to miss out on his best opportunity of the year to place the piece. As much as he hated to, he would push Peasly hard. Bloom knew the museum would buy it ultimately if enough time was allotted, but it was show time now and he was in Santa Fe for one reason: to sell.

CHAPTER 36

YOU SHOULD BE ASHAMED

Frank Manygoats's revival petroglyph artworks complemented Bloom's contemporary paintings beautifully. Bloom had placed "Fallen Man," the imposing six-foot devil figure, on the outside patio between Shriver's and Bloom's galleries. It was too big to keep inside Bloom's small gallery and if he put it out front it was just light enough that two strong men could steal it, though he wasn't really too worried.

Amazingly in Santa Fe, sculpture is rarely stolen or defaced—or at least that was the case until the recent recession. Even the criminals seem to enjoy art's addition to their world and they also inherently understand art pays the bills in Santa Fe. You hurt the galleries, you may cost a loved one a job.

The first week the "Fallen Man" sculpture was on display, over a dozen people complained that it wasn't ethical for a gallery to display ancient artifacts as decoration. The gallery owner should be ashamed. Bloom was finally forced to put a big sign in front of the rock art explaining it was a reproduction, "NOT AN ORIGINAL," in big, bright red letters. One lady from Tennessee after reading the sign asked Bloom, "Can you give me the location of the real Fallen Guy? I'd like to get my husband Billy Bob out there and see if he can jackhammer me one just like it." This of course flew to the top of his list of *Dumbest Things Said This Summer in Santa Fe*. Bloom didn't give the location, of course. He did take the woman's name as he figured she would buy a book once his dad and Dr. J finished their project, which would soon go to press.

Their publisher was trying to get the petroglyph handbag maker to sponsor the book tour, which was looking promising. Both the old professors were horrified but understood the economics of selling. The final draft of their book, which Bloom had previewed, was terrific. Even his father, a modest man who rarely accepted compliments, liked what he had produced and was proud of his accomplishment at age 80. He told Bloom, "I'm sorry your mother didn't get to see this. She would have loved it so, but she will be glad I stuck around to make a difference." Bloom was thrilled to see his father's happiness level return to almost normal. He scheduled a book signing featuring his dad for next May at Bloom's.

Because the book was going to come out during the worst selling months in Santa Fe, the winter/springtime, Bloom decided to promote early excerpts from the book with images and text next to Frank's pieces. Bloom also put the large words REPRODUCTION OF THE ORIGINALS above each rock art piece inside the gallery, so as not to spark the ire of any more tourists or a federal agent who might wonder what the gallery was doing selling rare artifacts.

Jack Bloom had decided he would spend the week before Indian Market 2012 helping his son in the gallery and pre-selling some of his books. He couldn't believe he would be earning money again, this time as an author. It had been nearly 15 years since he retired. Bloom was excited to have his father at his side witnessing what his son did for a living. Bloom had always felt his father wasn't pleased with his own decision to become an art dealer, that he should have aimed higher in life's career choices—research or medicine, not selling products. What Charles didn't know was his father couldn't have been any prouder. Charles would have to watch his own son grow up before he could understand how a father really feels.

No sooner had he arrived, then Jack Bloom did something completely out of character for a man on a retired professor's fixed income. He bought a piece of art. He had visited Santa Fe, the second-largest art market in the country, many times before and hadn't even sprung for a postcard. A big art purchase was completely out of character for the octogenarian. But Jack wanted to reward his son's hard work and he loved the piece, which immediately captivated him.

Jack admired what his son was able to do in a field that was so foreign to his own. Research and teaching in college are about as far away from retail selling as you can get. They are safe with a steady paycheck. The fact that his son had been so successful at something Jack couldn't imagine doing always seemed remarkable to the elderly Bloom. Jack's idea of negotiation was to buy a new car for the full listed price and then politely ask them to throw in a car wash and a tank of gas. Charles vividly remembered his father coming home with a brand new Pinto station wagon. He had traded in the family's 1967 Robin Egg Blue Mustang convertible as down payment. That was his father's idea of a good trade. When it came to buying his first piece of artwork it would not be any different.

"I found a piece of artwork I really love," his father announced.

"Dad, that's great. If you want me to take a look at it for you or help negotiate a price, I'm happy to."

"Not necessary. In fact I've already bought it."

Bloom cringed at the thought of his father buying a piece of artwork in Santa Fe without his help. There were areas in Santa Fe that were notorious for marking their prices up double, then coming down by half as if it were a good deal. He knew his father he would just say, "I'll take it." He was the pigeon these type of so-called art dealers preyed on.

"Really Dad, you've already paid for it? Which gallery was it in? I'd love to see it."

"It's in your garden. I don't know why but I just had to have it. They say art speaks to you, but until today I thought that was just a sales line. But this morning something really did have my name on it. The rock ark you have titled 'Fallen Man,' the piece Frank Manygoats made. It had such an impact on me that I couldn't imagine someone else taking it home."

"Wow, I'm blown away. I can't believe you bought that. It really is tremendous and with your new book if you ever want to resell the piece it should be a piece of cake."

The concept of reselling something you fell in love with was a foreign idea to Jack Bloom, but for his son it made good business sense. "I won't be reselling this ever. In fact you will get it when I die. If you want to sell it off then I guess that's fine, but for now it's heading south to Las Cruces. You can keep it through Indian Market, but I've already made plans. It's going in my living room where I can see it every day."

"Good for you! By the way, did you get Dr. J to give you a family and friends discount?"

"You do that?"

"Yes, believe it or not, art galleries including mine will work with you when it comes to buying art, especially in a recession."

"Oh, well, it's not necessary. The price was fair and I'm happy. Besides, Frank and you both get more money this way and I like that."

Charles had never been prouder of his father's horrible business skills than he was at that very moment.

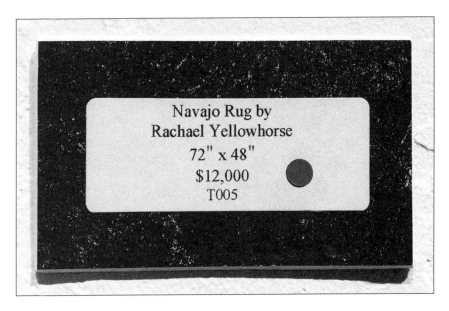

CHAPTER 37

RACHAEL AND WILLY

It was over a month since Bloom had seen his family and he was shocked at how much their being out of his life had affected him. Whenever his mind could wander, it inevitably drifted back to Rachael and Willy. The smiling ceremony had cemented a strong feeling for them both and he couldn't deny the fact that he was deeply in love.

The day Rachael was scheduled to arrive, Bloom repeatedly peered out his tiny bathroom window hoping for a glimpse of her Ford truck rolling up the gravel drive. He finally spotted her walking halfway down the alley with Willy on her back tucked into his Navajo cradleboard. There was a large chestnut-colored rug rolled under her arms. She had finished the weaving under the gun and Bloom was proud of her sizeable efforts. Being a mother with a newborn and weaving for the family's welfare was the Navajo way. Rachael seemed to take to it like all the previous women in her family.

Bloom had just finished hanging the Yellowhorse retrospective. He had left three bare spots: one for Ethel Sherman's rug, one for his small Willard painting, and one for Rachael's rug, all of which Rachael was bringing.

Used to low doorways, Rachael ducked reflexively to enter the gallery, making sure she didn't take Willy's head off in the process. When she saw Bloom, her eyes lit up for the first time that month.

Bloom, who acted more like a man in his twenties than his late forties, hurdled over his counter to give them both a big hug.

"So you finally came to help me! I thought you might have forgotten about my big show?" he joked, poking fun at Rachael's Indian clock, which always ran late.

"I did forget. I just got lonely so I thought I would come and see you and bring you my rug, which nearly killed me to finish. Remind me when that show is, anyway?"

"Right. It's in like three days! I thought we talked about it last night when you said you'd be coming today."

"Oh that's right, you know us Indians, no smoke signals and we will forget everything. Better if you *bilagaanas* put it in writing, you know, like one of those treaties you made us sign when we were in prison," Rachael jabbed back at her Anglo boyfriend, seeming not to ever forget the Long Walk and the fact that all *bilagaanas* want anything promised to be documented on paper.

"So let's see what you got there, my little Hiawatha," Bloom retorted, unrolling the piece, to which he would give first prize if it was entered at Market. He was glad it wasn't there because there would be calls of nepotism from the other weavers. Bloom's eyes got teary as he saw the magnificent brown-toned weaving. Rachael was truly gifted and Bloom's eye could recognize greatness. Her weaving was even better than last year's masterpiece. She was improving dramatically, which was hard to believe, considering how good she already was.

When Rachael saw Bloom's gut reaction to her weaving, she began to cry knowing how much this man cared about her. The two hugged in the middle of the gallery, oblivious to those around them, tears rolling down both their cheeks, Willy sound asleep in his cradleboard.

✳ ✳ ✳ ✳

The Yellowhorse show was small but tasty. Bloom couldn't believe it when *The New York Times* called asking for further details about the exhibit. He had sent his usual email press release to all the big-time publications, hoping for some little mention, but *The Times* was huge and for once the paper wasn't calling because one of his artists had been murdered.

The art section for the Sunday edition was going to run an article about Indian Market. They knew his opening would be over, but if the show was up for the remainder of the month they wanted to do a little profile. Willard Yellowhorse was a very recognizable name in the Big Apple.

Bloom emailed images of three pieces hopefully to be used for the article, the required Willard Yellowhorse which was their reason for calling, and also Rachael's work and just for fun the large image of "Fallen Man," mentioning Frank Manygoats's concurrent show of "recently made but historically inspired rock art."

❈ ❈ ❈ ❈

Friday, the day of his show opening, Bloom had to arrive at Market for the judging of Navajo textiles early. He knew the day was going to be brutal, as its start at 6 am followed the even earlier wake-up call Willy had given with his nonstop crying jag at 3 am. Bloom hoped his aesthetic sensibilities would kick into high gear once he started focusing on the artwork. Leaving his family sleeping, Bloom grabbed a Starbucks venti latte at DeVargas Mall on the way in to judge. It wasn't Rachael's stout cowboy coffee, but it still managed to hit the mark.

The judging process is give and take, with each judge jousting for his or her favorite piece. It was obvious that Bloom was more taken with the natural-colored rugs than his fellow judges, and the award for the best in the weaving category was not his favorite but he was satisfied he had done all he could. The winning weaving's background was red, a favorite color in Santa Fe galleries.

By the time Bloom arrived at his own gallery, it was a madhouse. It turned out Rachael had invited nearly every Navajo who was showing at Market, and Frank had done the same. A mixture of elderly grandmothers and young creative types had all jammed into the small gallery space, paying tribute to the Diné collection of artists.

It was so chaotic it was apparent no sales could be made even if somebody wanted to buy. Dr. J and his father were out front, standing by Jack's purchase, "Fallen Man," in deep discussion about their project, ignoring any potential customers, who honestly looked scarce. Rachael was holding Willy and standing in front of her rug with a group of older weavers who were all looking at and touching the piece, trying to figure out how good she really was compared to her grandmother Sherman. Bloom had priced the rug at $12K, and already sold it to the same Scottsdale physician who had wanted Rachael's piece last year during Indian Market. The doctor wasn't happy he was paying $2K more this year, but Bloom assured him it was well worth the extra as it was a tighter piece than last year. Her spinning was getting better. Bloom being the consummate salesman explained last year's piece ended up in the collection of a textile museum in Austin, Texas, and assured him that next year's piece would even be more expensive, which helped close the deal.

The grandmothers kept whispering to themselves and pointing at the tag, which had a prominent red dot next to the rug's price, meaning SOLD. Most of these ladies would not receive $12K for three years' worth of work, so to see a Navajo rug sell for so much was as exciting as it was discouraging.

Bloom's day was looking good. It became great when Peasly called to inform him that a donor had been located and they indeed would purchase his Willard Yellowhorse drawing. Bloom was ecstatic. This meant $20K in his pocket, another red dot, and a very successful show by anyone's standards.

If people see a gallery is doing well it makes them feel secure about doing business there and Bloom's could use a shot of positive karma after the last couple of years. The money would go a long way as Bloom's only regular bills were for food, electricity, gas, his cell phone, the gallery landline and website, maintaining the gallery itself (mostly paid for by Brad's rent on the adjoining space), and Dr. J's salary. Living at Rachael's cost nearly nothing. Willy would eventually drain a good bit, but because he was Native American he could use the I.H.S. for free medical care, which was huge. It looked as if Bloom's gallery was secure for at least one more year. As far as

Bloom was concerned, everything else was gravy. Bloom went out to sit with his father and Dr. J. It was an early happy hour and for once it really was happy.

That Sunday, as Indian Market was on its final day, *The New York Times* article came out and it mentioned not only the Yellowhorse retrospective but also Frank's (and now Jack Bloom's) impressive "Fallen Man" and blurbed the upcoming book tour. Bloom was thrilled and the phone and Internet sales were remarkable. It was almost as if there was no art recession. Bloom could have never imagined his including the "Fallen Man" image at the last minute would have such unexpected results. A lot of people read *The New York Times*.

CHAPTER 38

BOOK TOUR

The petroglyph book was released right on schedule in January 2013 and was gorgeous. Bloom had given his input on the cover design, which the publishers ignored and thankfully so. Theirs was much better.

The front cover was an oversized image of "Fallen Man" and the back cover a side shot of the long wall that looked like it went on forever. The beginning images on the wall were human handprints and halfway down was "Fallen Man" towering over his kingdom. Even in the distant shot he was an imposing fellow. The book was titled *Fallen Man,* then underneath the large bold red letters it read, *The Hidden Canyon of the Anasazi.* The author photographs were on the back just under the long wall shot. The book was extra-large, the kind that was difficult to fit into any kind of normal bookshelf but looked great on a coffee table.

Both men had made sure the book was not only beautiful but had accurate, relevant information regarding the different petroglyph images and the culture of the Anasazi. The sculpture "Fallen Man" had an entire page of text opposite the image, which was located in the center of the book as a glossy two-page foldout. The two anthropologists gave their interpretations and then Frank Manygoats was included offering his Navajo beliefs. Since the wall was also on Rachael Yellowhorse's property, she was asked if she wanted to write something about the figure. "Not going there, sorry," she quickly declined. Rachael was listed in the credits for her help, which was more publicity than she wanted when it came to Anasazi ruins.

A 10-city book-signing tour was arranged, including stops on both coasts at four fancy department stores featuring the very hip $1,500 petroglyph bags. The handbags were made of glossy red snake leather and embossed with an interlocking petroglyph design. An autographed book was included with each purse. The imagery on the purses was disconcerting to both the old anthropologists. It was far from historically correct. It was obvious some New York designer had taken huge liberties with the actual images to make them more arty. Charles Bloom, like a mother hen, repeatedly warned the men not to make derogatory remarks about the purses' petroglyph imagery when signing books at the department stores. The purses had helped co-brand with the publisher and allowed such an expensive book on rock art to be produced in the first place. Bloom added, "Without these purses you have a soft-cover book that fits in my back pocket, *capiche?*"

They both promised not to bring it up, but said if push came to shove they had to maintain their scientific ethics and would not lie. They might not elaborate on purses that cost more than Jack Bloom's first new car, but they also wouldn't compromise their credentials. Bloom understood, but couldn't resist offering examples of how he would handle certain awkward situations.

For instance, if they were asked: "Why do the purses show petroglyph humans carrying that look, for all purposes, like handbags? It seems farfetched."

Bloom's answer to the potential customer would be: "Humans have always had bags for objects, including medicine bundles for power and curing. These images are one interpretation of those actual events in early man's history."

What he didn't want the authors to say was: "Of course there were no handbags. These were just put on to sell product. They're totally false and any first grader would recognize this."

They both nodded their heads as Bloom gave the example, but he wasn't sure if it was because the two old professors understood his point or because they were agreeing with his first-grader analogy.

The book tour's schedule began on the West Coast, leaving the Eastern and Midwest stops till the weather was a little more forgiving. They would start in L.A., followed by Santa Barbara, San Francisco, Portland, and finally Seattle. There would be a month's pause for the old men to catch their breaths, and then they'd hit the South, the Midwest, and finally end up on the East Coast, with the mothership department store signing in New York occurring as the swan song.

The tour was timed to New York Fashion Week in February, as they had a whole line of petroglyph clothes coming out to go with the already incredibly hot handbags. Soon there would even be images of "Fallen Man" on hip $550 men's shoes prancing around the streets of New York. The men shuddered at the thought, but were also excited about the exposure the book was getting. They figured any press about rock art was better than the zero it had gotten in the past. So be it if they were to become the unexpected and precarious conduits of hipness.

CHAPTER 39

BOOM TO BUST

Mo Bandgood couldn't believe how fast the bottom had fallen out of the music industry. It was 2013 and he was now an antique by most Hollywood standards. A relic of a time when commercials had original musical compositions recorded by large well-trained orchestras. The world he understood was no longer.

Ruth, who'd been responsible for his big break into the world of music, was now residing in an assisted-care living facility as she was pushing 90. The record which he had inscribed to her was no longer behind the Capitol Records front desk, where a screamo band was the latest flavor. On one recent visit to the Capitol Records building he asked the pink-haired, multi-pierced girl who was sitting in Ruth's old chair about his gold record's whereabouts, which obviously confused her pink head. She was completely lost when Mo said it was by a famous sixties band, The Red Cardinals. Her blank look spoke volumes of his music and what the girl saw as hip. She replied, "You must mean Death to the Cardinal. Their platinum CD is down the right wall near the water cooler."

Mo didn't bother to correct her. Ruth had probably taken the gold album with her when she retired and as far as he was concerned it was in a better place. He loved music, it was his heart and soul, but the names and power brokers of his day had faded by the time Reagan left office. Everything was now electronically produced using computers. He longed for those idyllic old days, not to mention all the money.

His last 10 years had been spent between Branson and Vegas. He wasn't sure which was worse. Both required little thought and going back and forth was like driving a bus route through one-traffic-light towns. He was no longer arranging new music, but acting as he had at Cannon Air Force Base in 1965: a puppet conductor to uninspiring music.

Mo knew he had finally reached the breaking point when he conducted an hour-long program during his nightly Vegas act and could only remember his grocery list, which is what he had been thinking about the entire show.

So Mo had returned to Los Angeles and was trying to get back into creating music. He still made decent royalties off some of his early commercials. In fact Red Castle Hamburgers, now a national chain, had just re-released his old jingle. Finally people understood the term "being in the red." These phrases were everyday discussions in a recessionary world. The extra money from the playing of the commercial meant he could take time off from shit work and focus on some fun project to get his creative juices rolling again. His rejuvenated energy would not be decimated by Ms. Pink Hair. He wished there was a Viagra for creativity, but he would have to muster up the energy himself.

Reading *The New York Times'* Sunday issue a few months earlier had planted a seed in Mo's head, one he hoped might lead him in a new and unexpected direction. The article, which he had cut out and kept, featured an ominous red devil-looking image that was copied from a thousand-year-old petroglyph. The devil-looking figure had originated from an ancient Anasazi wall and had been carved as a reproduction by a Navajo man, Frank Manygoats. There was also a book coming out on the actual petroglyph site. *The Times* article predicted a book-tour schedule for the book's anthropologist authors, starting with an inaugural signing in Los Angeles.

Mo had taped the article to his refrigerator. When he moved back to L.A., the yellowing piece of paper came with him. The authors of the book would be in town tomorrow for their launch signing. He had an idea about capitalizing on the unique art form. He'd started seeing well-heeled women around Beverly Hills carrying the expensive handbags that had petroglyph designs, "petro bags" they were called. They all loved them. You don't do a thousand commercials without noticing trends and when something strikes a chord like the red Indian bags did, you had to act on it.

The book tour was launching in a huge multistory building in Santa Monica, a throwback to the golden age of bookstores when books were their only product, not lattes or Wi-Fi stations. The store specialized in expensive hardback books of quality, primarily about art and architecture, but anything that sophisticated minds could appreciate was available. It was a known hangout for stars and a must-see if visiting Santa Monica.

✴ ✴ ✴ ✴

The book signing for Dr. Bloom and Dr. James was a first for two men who were used to large crowds but of the student variety, mostly trying to slide by freshman anthropology, not fans of the petro bags. Seeing the line of sophisticated women waiting to meet them was astounding. They looked at each other and giggled. Who would have thought that two old guys from Eastern New Mexico University would ever end up as semi-celebrities in L.A.? It was mind-blowing and Jack wished his wife were here to see such a sight. He hoped she was looking down on him today, especially after he saw who was waiting patiently in line to get one of his books.

It was Diane Keaton, his wife's favorite actress and one of his as well. When he recognized her with her stylish black derby and white sash around a graceful, long neck he looked back over his shoulder to see if there was someone else behind them. "Maybe there are two book signings and she's at the wrong one," he whispered to Dr. J, but there weren't and she wasn't.

The long line snaked along and finally Keaton arrived at the front to have her book autographed by the professors. Both old men's hearts were racing like schoolboys in love. This was the first movie star they had ever talked to and they were at a loss for words. They simply said in unison, "Hi, how do you want it signed?" She leaned over the table close to them, pulled down her dark glasses, and smiling with her classic Keaton grin said, "To Di." She added, "I love the idea of what you guys have done. The images have such heart. It makes me want to reconsider the way I look at all art. Thanks for spending your lives studying these special people. I really appreciate all your work." The two emeritus professors who were now beet red didn't know how to answer the Oscar-winning star. They both just shook their heads vigorously so as to say thank you and then she was off. The two men decided they should have written popular books a long time ago. They loved being on book tour.

* * * *

The last person in line was Mo. He figured it would take the crowds two hours to work their way through and he wanted some face time. He had a proposition and he needed more time than the allotted two minutes per person at an author signing.

When Mo got up to the table, the two men were obviously getting tired but still into the process. They asked the obligatory, "How would you like us to sign it?"

Mo, who had been a showman in Hollywood now for more than 40 years, leaned over the table and looked the professors directly in the eyes and declared: "To Mo, the man who made us millionaires."

"I'm sorry I must have misunderstood what you wanted. I'm getting tired. Long day," Jack muttered as he turned up his hearing aid, obviously not understanding correctly what Mo had requested.

"I said, please write: 'To Mo, the man who made us millionaires.'"

The professors looked quizzically at each other, and then began to inscribe what the nutty L.A. man had instructed. After all it was Hollywood, movie stars and kooks all in the same day.

Jack then asked as he blew on the ink so as not to smudge his perfect signature, "Can I ask why you wanted us to sign your book in such a fashion?"

"I'm glad you asked, because if you have the time I believe with what I do and what you know, we can make a million dollars with your petroglyph studies. There is a whole market of people just waiting to enjoy what you have studied so intently, and I'm the guy who can make that happen."

Both men looked at Mo in complete amazement and replied simultaneously: "We're listening!"

Mo pulled up a large wooden reading chair and laid out his plan for fame and fortune for "Fallen Man."

CHAPTER 40

A NEW AGE

Mo was a fate kind of guy. Consider: the idea that had inspired Mo came from *The New York Times* article, a paper he only occasionally read. This led him to investigate petroglyphs and have the good fortune of being in L.A. at the same time as the two leading petroglyph authorities began their book tour there.

The way Mo looked at it, he had grown up when he did in Lubbock, Texas, in order to meet Buddy; had gone to New Mexico State to be taught and inspired by two gifted individuals, Dr. Goldblatt and Isabella Graves; and had made his way to California to find Ruth working the front desk at Capitol Records, and she had made his entry into Hollywood easy. Mo followed his instincts. When his intuition told him he needed to get back to get L.A. to get on track, he did. It was the place his career had started and that was certainly a good omen.

Mo understood the music industry, for good or for bad, had changed dramatically and if he still wanted to play in that world he needed to change with it. What Mo missed most was writing original music, but to be excited creatively he needed a visual stimulus. The last major score he had written was for a made-for-TV movie, *Zodiac*. Hollywood just wasn't interested in the Mo's of the world; computers ruled, not highly trained composers.

Seeing the photograph of the petroglyph in the newspaper made a connection spark in Mo's brain. He decided if he could juxtapose original music with compelling ancient images there would be a market. A man with a thousand commercials under his belt could see the unique marketability of compelling content in a visual and musical format that could be packaged on the Internet. Mo would jump into the 21st century.

Mo had already started writing a score from the single image he had seen. The music composition would be called "Red Man Writes," a similar sound to some of his best seventies song titles. It had the right feel for the jingle man. The book signing had been his opportunity to convince the other cogs in his music wheel that his idea was a worthy and potentially lucrative one.

The music score he would record the old-fashioned way with a full orchestra using all his old cronies, many of whom now only taught. He would use the *Fallen Man* book like a movie backdrop and fit the images with the score, which he had nearly finished.

The composition would be a 15-minute program and if done the way he envisioned, the commercial possibilities were limitless. He figured doctors' offices would be his first commercial venue. They could always use beautiful music and images flowing through their waiting room television screens. The remarkable photographs and soothing sounds of a hidden canyon wall in the otherwise sterile doctors' environments should be a no-brainer to sell. His arrangement would be so inspiring it would take the images of ancient man to a newer, higher plane, one the original artisans could have only dreamed about. They would have thought a god must have touched their minds.

The whole project could be compartmentalized and sold as snippets on the Internet, or could be bought by businesses for high volume use. If it worked well, Mo could see numerous types of music videos, not just petroglyphs but any soothing beautiful object could have music to accompany it. The greatest part of the whole plan was he would be composing again and his musician friends would have well-paying work, the first in a long time.

Mo laid out the whole idea to the two stunned anthropologists who probably would have done it for free. Both men saw it as a win, win situation. The more individuals who were touched by the images of early Southwest man, the more likely the field would stay alive and maybe have a renewed interest. When you dedicate your entire life to a specific field of study, you hate to think you are going the way of the typewriter or Polaroid film, just an interesting side note in the chain of human evolution.

For every person who was affected in a positive light by petroglyphs and their unique and gifted prehistoric makers, it would be the better for the New Mexico anthropologists' legacies. Plus the extra money wouldn't hurt. A deal was struck. Mo headed back into the studio. He would record "Red Man Writes."

CHAPTER 41

CAPITOL RECORDS ONCE MORE

The pink hair girl had been replaced with a bluish-tinted one when Mo entered to sign in to the studio for his midmorning rehearsal. He had bought five *Fallen Man* books and placed them around the studio so the musicians could understand what he was trying to achieve: art music in a way that was unique.

The orchestra of sight-reading musicians was the best in the business. There was Johnny Carson's old guitarist and the drummer for the Smothers brothers; each had been someone of note in the music field. Now most taught to survive.

The gathering took on the mood of a 40-year high-school reunion, the best of the best who no longer were needed in their field of choice, and all were thrilled to be getting a paycheck and working for Mo again.

The two professors even showed up to see the making of their book into a different form of art. Neither man had ever been in a recording studio. They were shocked how tiny the room was. There were 37 musicians crammed into a small studio in a semicircle facing the podium, where Mo would lead his vision for the composition. Mo thought it was ironic that he had gotten his start in rock and roll at Capitol, and his finishing act was now back there in rock-art. Each musician's stand had a freshly printed score of Mo's latest composition. The title was hand written by Mo in red ink on the upper right of each page: "Red Man Writes." Seeing his printed words made him feel young again. No more meaningless Vegas/Branson shows. This session for Mo gave his life purpose, the first in a long time.

The anthropologists were treated as semi-celebrities by the orchestra. Without their book, there was no inspiration for Mo's composition, and without his creativity to compose, none of the musicians would be making a good wage that day doing what they loved.

It was a festive gathering with donuts, coffee, and Mo's personality, which was as big as all of Texas. The time had come to record what he had seen in his head and he stepped up to the podium looking out at his audience of friends and colleagues and in his best Texas twang declared, "Not bad for a banjo player from Lubbock! I'm back, baby, and so are y'all!" pointing at his orchestra.

The bows of the violinists all hit their stands, the percussionists tingled their triangles as a sign of approval, and off they went. The session flew by, everyone in instant accord. It was just like it used to be, the creative energy amassing from so many talented individuals working together.

Mo had added another dimension to the program, and now he was glad he had. He had a videographer shoot the entire event. What he was creating musically should be captured for posterity's sake, even if just for his own personal gratification. Of course he hoped that the film might find an audience. The footage he recorded at Capitol Records would later be edited with footage shot at the actual petroglyph site. Both anthropologists, along with Bloom and Frank Manygoats, had agreed to take Mo and his cameraman up to the Hidden Canyon site. The plan was to capture the canyon in the early spring and then do a second CD once summer arrived, showing a different kind of light and how environmental changes could affect not only the canyon but the artists who had created it.

One of Mo's old buddies, Billy "Fleck" Robertson, a veteran of Hollywood, had worked last with Mo on the television movie *Zodiac*. His job was to capture the moment, from the anthropologists' faces of amazement today to Mo's own triumph.

Fleck was a one-man tornado when filming, touching down periodically throughout the room. His eye was honed from years of horror movies and lately porno flicks. Times were tough. He was as thrilled as the rest of the crew to be working on a creative job with someone he respected. It had been a long time, and it was nice that his subjects were wearing clothes.

The session went off without a hitch. The musicians who sight-read the score for the first time played it as if it had been their childhood lullabies. Professionals of any field can do this, even ones who only ply their trade occasionally in the computer age of digital music.

All of Mo's energy and focus was now directed to "Red Man Writes." He planned to have the finished project in doctors' offices in less than a month. He had presold the concept before ever shooting a single frame. Using his old commercial connections, he had met with the head of the largest HMO in California, who had agreed to play the track continuously on his network's screens in between drug commercials and preventive care snips. The idea was that the soothing imagery and music would give the consumer time to better focus once the paid advertisements appeared.

Much to the amazement of Dr. J and Dr. Bloom, they would eventually make more money in a week with Mo's project than they made altogether on the *Fallen Man* book. Both men loved California. Being from the remote state of New Mexico, California had the reputation of being full of nuts and squirrels. The anthropologists didn't see this side of the state, just the opposite. They loved the feeling that was present at Capitol Records. Such a family of gifted individuals. Little did they know, however, that along with the success that would soon be coming their way, one of California's biggest nuts would soon be visiting as well, and he was hungry for souls.

CHAPTER 42

AND ACTION

It was early March 2013. Mo and Fleck were headed up to meet Dr. J, Dr. Bloom, Frank Manygoats, and Charles Bloom in Navajoland. The storyboard that Mo had commissioned called for Fleck to record Mo's first impressions as he arrived at the remote Navajo Reservation. Day one was to get B-roll of the reservation and watch Mo's reaction seeing New Mexico's landscape in person for the first time.

The soon-to-be fans of "Red Man Writes" would not be disappointed. Mo's eyes told the story of his own amazement at the stark land of the Diné. Growing up in Lubbock, he was used to no trees and flat areas, but this was nothing like Texas. It was a foreign country. The dirt was gray, copper, yellow, and red. He recognized one bizarrely shaped mound as an image from the movie *Planet of the Apes*. No mistaking such a dire-looking landscape, yet so beautiful.

As Fleck followed him with his floating camera, Mo couldn't control the emotions he was feeling. "I knew this was right! Look at what Mother Nature can do. How Americans cannot know about such a unbelievable place amazes me," he told Fleck, camera recording.

With a sweeping motion of his arm, Mo directed the audience to the barren, beautiful plain behind him, looking directly into the camera, Fleck capturing a close-up of Mo's emotional face. "America," Mo continued, "this land has motivated me to create my own sense of beauty. The Navajo Reservation should be included in those 'Places not to Miss' books." It was great stuff, and Mo and Fleck both knew it.

Bloom, Rachael, and Willy met the crew and anthropologists at the 100-year-old Toadlena Trading Post. Again, Mo went off on an emotional tear. The natural sandstone rocks that the building was built from couldn't have been better imagery for the film. Sal Lito was thrilled at the coverage and spent time introducing them to some of his grandmother weavers who he had invited in for the occasion.

Mo was convinced what he had done with the petroglyph series could easily be translated to other Native art forms. Weavings were now high on his list. His creative juices threw together bars of music in his head as Sal showed him the natural-colored weavings. No more grocery lists in his mind, he was creating again and he was thrilled.

After the B-roll was in the can, it was to time to film sit-down interviews at the Trading Post, to interview Mo about his impressions, and to get a real Navajo meal.

Rachael was making her mother's recipe of mutton stew for that night's meal. Mutton stew is a staple of the Navajo diet and for good reason: there are a lot of sheep. The stew called for lamb, potatoes, celery, carrots, and a variety of local herbs, which was the family recipe part. It was important that the meat had as much fat on it as possible to make the stew have the required taste. Rachael knew she had the correct portion of fat when the entire surface of each bowl was shimmering like a mirror. Too little fat and it was a pond with its ice breaking in the spring. Perfection was required of Rachael's stew each and every time. Like with her rugs, attention to detail mattered.

The dinner and stew were a hit and Fleck captured it all on tape for the documentary. Rachael, while having a great evening, begged off being interviewed about the canyon. Her Navajo aesthetic continued to avoid the Nasazi ruins in person or on film.

Day two would be visiting the actual petroglyph site. This meant the entire group would need to get to Hidden Canyon at sunrise. The skies were threatening intermittent snow, so it was going to be a dicey day for filming but hopefully the gods would be with them.

The small house was filled to the brim with people, all of whom were spending the night (excluding Frank, who was at his grandmother's hogan). Bloom Sr. got Willy's room, who moved in with Rachael and Bloom Jr. Mo and Fleck took the living room/kitchen. Dr. J got the 1948 trailer behind the hogan. Dr. J felt lucky to have the space all to himself. He had stayed there in the summer. However, what he found in March was an entirely different environment. The trailer's outside carcass had been breached in numerous places, no doubt by woodpeckers, and the only way to stay warm from the night's air would be to sleep clad in a hat, long johns, and woolen socks. He could see his breath. He felt a little less lucky as he unpacked.

Mo could hardly wait and his excitement was contagious to all. He had come up with an original score of music from a small photograph in *The New York Times*, and soon he would experience it in all its grandeur and raw beauty, not to mention coldness. The success of the doctors' office screenings of Mo's composition would soon be a hit. Everyone would make money and receive great exposure. Little did the party realize though that the exposure they sought would soon change the way they viewed Hidden Canyon forever.

CHAPTER 43

COUGAR COUNTRY

The crew had eaten and was dressed and out the door by 5 am. The sun would not bless the front of Rachael's home for another hour. To get to Hidden Canyon required four-wheel drive or horseback. Today was by vehicle, which was much faster, especially if you're lugging camera equipment.

To find the entrance to the canyon required local knowledge which Frank, Rachael, and Bloom all had. Hidden Canyon was bordered by Frank's property on one side and Rachael's on the other. Today, Frank was leading the charge as one wrong turn would mean they would miss the crucial morning light and ruin a day of filming. Rachael had warned Bloom on his way out the door, "Get my truck stuck or worse, get really lost, and it will take us a day to find you, and you've got kid duty tonight. No cell phone service out there, never." Rachael still looked at Bloom as a *bilagaana* when it came to some aspects of the rez.

Most petroglyph sites have southern exposure to catch the winter sun's precious heat. Hidden Canyon faced more southeast, so when the sun rose, its rays illuminated the canyon wall's rock art like a door slowly opening. The camera shot had to be planned perfectly because sunlight would race across the wall's face, making timing essential to get the best movement of the light.

There were two inches of snow on the ground at Hidden Canyon and except for scattered animal tracks there was no sign of human life. People never visited Hidden Canyon. In the dark, the great petroglyph repository wasn't visible. The team decided to use a two-camera shot once they got up on the ledge. As soon as the sun's first rays hit the long canyon wall, Mo would climb up the steep incline using the ancient hand holes. Frank warned Mo right before he started his ascent, "When you get up top, Mr. Mo, check for any cougar tracks. There used to be an old cat that liked that ledge. According to Rachael's grandfather, she once used a rabbit stick to thump a lion in the head that got too close to her grandmother's sheep. No one messed with those sheep, she was fearless when it came to protecting what was hers." Then Frank turned to Bloom and ribbed him, "You don't want to mess with Rachael, huh Bloom." Bloom shook his head violently in agreement, not wanting to use speech as his throat, face, and mouth were freezing in the pre-sun March air.

Mo wondered if Frank shouldn't reach the petroglyph floor first, being an Indian and all. "Hey Fleck, don't you think it's a better shot if the Navajo kid goes up first, you know, we play on the whole Red Man concept?"

Fleck took his eye away from the camera for a moment to look directly at his hesitant star, and assured him: "There are no cougars, Mo. Remember, this is about your inspiration. You have to go first. This is the money shot."

Finally the sun broke, no flurries, and it was perfect for filming. The crew broke into action. Mo slowly worked his way up the 20-foot cliff to breach the landing area to the massive rock-art wall mausoleum. As he reached the top, the first light hit the far edge of the cliff face and slowly started creeping along, illuminating each new image with the sun's steady gravitational pull.

Mo had memorized the images from the book by Dr. J and Dr. Bloom. But nothing prepared him for the incredible beauty of man's creativity accomplished in such a harsh environment. The desert's high elevation and cold wind accelerated Mo's heart rate and respiration. His adrenaline rush was pulsating with every beat of the jingle man's heart. Mo knew he was on film and wanted to give a good show, but he had never in his wildest dreams expected the spontaneous emotional reaction he was experiencing. He totally forgot about cougar tracks as he saw human creativity in its most primitive state.

Tears ran down his chapped red checks. There was a power that was palatable in this sacred place. For some reason this wall had called Mo to come, record, and share his vision for what art and music could be. It was as if he was part of a bigger plan.

As he caught his breath he tried to take in the enormity of the sandstone outcropping. The large overhang's roof that had protected it for a millennium was covered in soot from generations of human fires as they toiled away at the rock surface making their mark of existence. The roof was 20 feet above the ledge and looking up Mo could see the great fissures that somehow remained intact, protecting the great museum of ancient man.

Snow was minimal on the ledge as the natural cave-like structure kept the majority of the elements out, except for cougars of course. Halfway down the wall was the six-foot "Fallen Man," his tall torso bending over his subjects and ominous tattoo-like decorations filling his body's midsection. Looking at him closely revealed the intensity of his eyes, which couldn't be adequately reproduced in photography. His horns graduated to fine tips that still retained a red mineral paint outline, emphasizing his power. To his side was a long three-pronged spear also tipped in red coloration, possibly representing a bloody conqueror's weapon. He was certainly the guardian of the wall. At least that was how Mo saw it and he said so on camera.

The rest of the party snaked their way up the cliff and took turns being interviewed about their thoughts as to why this place was so special. Bloom felt a little uneasy filming at the place Rachael wouldn't visit, her Navajo considerations affecting him more than he would like to admit. Bloom had great respect for Rachael's belief system, but the evil *chindi* spirits of a people a thousand years long gone was a hard concept for him to wrap his head around.

Bloom snuck off as the others inspected the long, immense wall. He had his eyes focused not on rock art, but on the large flat sandstone-looking sled that lay on the ledge floor. He secretly wanted to ride it down the cliff. The snow covering the ledge's edge would be perfect, one good push and away she goes.

Looking over his shoulders at the rest of the group still expounding on the religious nature of the site, Bloom lifted the back end of the slab to see if he could move it closer. It was heavy but not unmanageable, and it slid forward. He quietly pushed a portion over the cliff's edge. He could actually do it. Bloom pondered what the response would be if he did such a crazy, dangerous, and somewhat sacrilegious stunt. He knew that the downward-facing side was covered in unseen petroglyphs as the sandstone slab had cleaved off the picture wall probably due to some underlying water seepage. When carefully turned over, the images might be as spectacular if not more so.

Riding down the sled of petroglyphs more than likely would erase a portion of the hidden rock art, as the high friction of stone on stone contact couldn't be good for them. He knew all this but the deep urge to try the black-diamond run still remained. Maybe when he was older or had something he needed to prove to himself he would sneak back up and take the ride of his life, but not today when there was a crew filming a high-def documentary on the spiritual nature of the unnamed petroglyphs of Hidden Canyon.

CHAPTER 44

DOCTOR'S VISIT

Law had been a great choice for Fallon. He was entering in his 25th year of practice and was doing better than he ever imagined. The poor white boy from Oakland who had killed a rival at 14 was now for all outward appearances a model citizen, a pillar of the community.

The numerous charities Fallon was involved with as a secondary pursuit to killing off his elder clients were impressive. One charity, a nonprofit mental health clinic, had put Fallon on the board in the hope that he would stop billing them so aggressively, which was eating into their marginal budget, but Fallon actually increased his fees once on the board as he found more legal actions the charity required. Fallon thought it was hilarious that he was on a board for helping mentally deranged individuals since he had killed many people and knew this would be considered a serious mental disorder, even if it did feel normal to him.

The eliminating of clients had stopped five years ago. He was making enough money and his reputation had grown to the point that murder wasn't necessary. Fallon just waited now for them to die of natural causes and he would take over and add another golden calf to his portfolio. Not killing was emotionally upsetting. Fallon liked the feeling of power he got after taking a life. The euphoria lasted for months. He still could get pleasure by reliving his past conquests in his mind. Sometimes he would return to the crime scenes, which helped accentuate the feelings, though nothing was as fulfilling as a fresh kill.

Fallon was still waiting for a sign from god as to what his real mission on earth would be. It was early 2013 and he had just turned 54. Why was he given the power of life and death if it wasn't for a higher purpose? It couldn't be just for killing old ladies to make more money. He had been very patient. A sign must be coming soon. He watched television waiting for "Wheel of Fortune" or another show to speak to him again. Fallon had even gone as far as to purchase Mrs. Black's expensive apartment when it came on the market and to watch television each night in her old bedroom in case this was part of the master plan.

Fallon's skin disorder, dermatographia, had never abated even though all the doctors he had seen told him it would fade as he aged. If anything, it was worse. Anything touching his skin caused him discomfort. He had grown out a beard years ago, as shaving was a torture he could do without. A woman's touch was no longer appealing. The intense pain that inevitably occurred when she would stroke his arms or back was not enough pleasure to counteract the intense skin welts. Even masturbation was problematic. It was easier to be celibate and wait for his orders.

His doctor's visit today was to start a new series of allergy shots that would hopefully sensitize him to any possible allergens found in the San Francisco area. Fallon thought maybe a different environment besides the cold moist air of the Bay City would help, but he had visited many cities and none relieved his condition.

Fallon had resigned himself to the fact that he had a disability that god had burdened him with. For others with the same malady it was a minor inconvenience, but the intensity of his ailment was more like a slow water torture he could not turn off. He had no other option than to try and cope and hope the doctors could come up with a cure or at least a treatment plan. He was beginning to think maybe he needed to start killing doctors to see if this would somehow counterbalance his condition.

As it turned out, today's physician did have the answer to his debilitating chronic disease, but it didn't come in the form of an ointment or cream.

Fallon was lounging in an overstuffed chair at his dermatologist's waiting room watching a commercial for Accutane. The annoying acne medicine spiel was blasting on the overhead television monitor when his life changed. The change was precipitated by the sweet sound of a clarinet followed by a French horn. Fallon focused on the monitor intently, which five seconds ago had shown a teenaged face full of pimples and now was filled with a red sandstone cliff. Then words appeared in white letters outlined in blood red: *Red Man Writes.* The words brought instant anxiety to a man who usually felt nothing. His skin erupted in goose bumps and he instinctually grabbed his abdomen where Willy had scarred him permanently 40 years ago playing the torture game of Red Man Writes.

What could this mean? Fallon's mind was spinning as his eyes remained transfixed on the monitor's Anasazi petroglyphs that gently changed with each bar of music. The petroglyph imagery was taking on some kind of existential meaning to the man who was still stuck on the show's title. The tape ended and a few names flashed for credits, lasting a second, and then another commercial was blaring, this time for the acne scarred, trying to sell some cream for those who hadn't been smart enough to use the Accutane from the first infomercial.

Fallon was stunned. He didn't know what to say or do. How could a tape playing images of petroglyphs with the exact same title as his childhood nightmare be showing in his doctor's office as he waited to be treated for that same vicious malady? He sat up in the brown soft chair and concentrated on his life.

Then it hit him just like one of the kids had with their knife-like fingernails. Fallon jumped out of the chair and without caring who heard him, exclaimed out loud, "This is the sign! Today is the day I have been waiting for, for so long. God, you're speaking to me! This is 'Wheel of Fortune' all over again, and I'm paying attention!"

Fallon's calling had finally arrived and it was in between two infomercials. The other patients were in shock, staring at the obviously deranged man who was standing looking intently at the television monitor as if it would talk back to him.

Fallon went to the front desk and explained to the receptionist he would no longer need the doctor's services anymore as he had found a cure and thanked her for her excellent television programming. He then asked the confused front desk girl how he could obtain a copy of that great "Red Man Writes" video he had just watched. She handed him one of Mo's business cards.

The card was vertically oriented, featuring an image of a devil-looking person with a pitchfork-like spear in his hand. The website was www.FallenManMusic.com and it had an L.A. address. Looking at the image and the website's name gave Fallon goose bumps for the second time in his life, a sure sign for the man who had ice water running through his veins.

Fallon quizzed the receptionist about the video, hoping she might have additional insight. All she knew was the product was recently released and was playing in many doctors' offices. "Go to the website, it's very well done. All the images in the video are detailed, especially that devil-looking guy. I think they call him 'Fallen Man,'" she said.

Thanking the girl, card in hand, Fallon walked out of the office excited he had finally found why god had cursed him with dermatographia. It was so he would be in that doctor's office to see "Red Man Writes." God had warned him it was coming when he was 14 and again at Mrs. Black's. It was now time to act.

The long time since his last kill had given Fallon the maturity to implement his exceptional gift of controlling his emotions. Fallon had a quest to follow. It was to destroy all those involved in spreading the word of "Fallen Man," the precursor to all those afflicted with dermatographia. "Fallen Man" was the original devil who spawned his skin ailment and he must be destroyed. His secrets lay somewhere in the desert Southwest. Even in the flash of time the "Fallen Man" image was on the screen he saw the deity's torso was covered in welts like his. The devil had entered the 21st century and was trying to spread its malady to the world through the propaganda being played in the skin healers' offices. The children who had tortured him playing Red Man Writes on his body were the devil's disciples. He had already killed one of the strongest proselytizers, Willy Bellows, but now he was being asked to stop the source.

Fallon had to contain the infection and destroy the maker of the film and those who were spreading the lies. His Holy Grail was "Fallen Man," the source of his relentless pain. He would find and eliminate all those who radiated from the source. It had to be, otherwise why would he have been named Fallon Scriber?

CHAPTER 45

GOING INTO BATTLE

A new invigoration filled Fallon's soul. He had to prepare himself for the battle with his ultimate protagonist, "Fallen Man." His days as a lawyer were over. He was now a soldier in the war against early man's darkest foes, the original source of his skin disease. Fallon knew nothing about the images other than that they were called petroglyphs and occurred throughout the ancient West.

The website Fallon visited was a wealth of information, a shopping list of sorts with names of individuals who would do harm if not stopped. Like his own battle with the police where he had left sacred pencils as clues, the website www.FallenManMusic.com had been given to him as a clue. The website recommended a specific book on petroglyphs titled *Fallen Man: The Hidden Canyon of the Anasazi*. Fallon found a signed copy by the authors of the book at a nearby store. Apparently the two disciples had just made an appearance, another sign in Fallon's eyes that they were taunting him in his own city.

The canyon was located somewhere in New Mexico on Navajoland. Fallon found out that the Navajo or Diné generally tried to avoid the old ruins as they were made by their ancient enemies, the Anasazi that the Navajos call Nasazi. He was impressed with how savvy the Navajos must be to understand the danger of "Fallen Man." He assumed his silver pencil box that was made by a Navajo was preordained, why else would it have his initials. God knew he would be heading to Navajoland someday to find and destroy the Anasazi warrior "Fallen Man." The box was his Excalibur. Further research from Wikipedia confirmed Fallon's assumption: skin diseases were much less common in Native Americans. Wikipedia pointed to higher melanin levels in Native American skin, but of course the contributors didn't have the insight Fallon had regarding the devil "Fallen Man." Once he had eliminated his sworn enemy, the Wikipedia page must be corrected.

It was clear that Native cultures, especially those of the Navajo, must have passed down through generations the evil power of these ancient petroglyphs. It was like in Bali. The one village of people who did not get wiped out by the tsunami ran into the mountains when they saw the fish flapping on the beach. They knew it was a sign their ancestors had warned them about and they remembered to run into the hills for survival.

In the bible of *Fallen Man* (as Fallon was now referring to the petroglyph coffee-table book) there was one prominent Navajo disciple who made petroglyph reproduction sculptures, a Frank Manygoats. It was on his land where the great beast's figure resided. Fallon figured Manygoats must have been seduced over time by the evil one and had been turned to the dark side. He would need to be eliminated. Those who were helping to spread the word of the devil's bible (now also available on CD) were all listed, making it easy for Fallon to compile his own list:

1) Mo Bandgood, probably the leader or at least a very important person in the devil's religion
2) Isabella Graves, listed as a mentor to Bandgood, so probably a high priestess
3) Dr. Jack Bloom, anthropologist, a priest of knowledge
4) Dr. John James, anthropologist, a priest of knowledge
5) Frank Manygoats, a disciple and traitor to the Navajo
6) Charles Bloom, son of the priest and acknowledged benefactor
7) Rachael Yellowhorse, girlfriend of Charles and also co-owner of the site, benefactor and traitor
8) Willy Yellowhorse Bloom, only descendant of Bloom and Yellowhorse, a powerful combination of priest, benefactor, and traitor, and most likely the heir apparent

Seeing in the bible an acknowledgement to Willy confirmed in Fallon's mind that he was on god's path. The other Willy he had destroyed had initiated the so-called game of Red Man Writes. He had mistakenly thought he had extinguished the torturous game by killing Willy Bellows, but Willy had been reborn in another more powerful form.

Fallon decide he would need to make his calling card reflect his newly enlightened thinking. No longer was leaving a plain pencil enough. He needed all the forces of evil to pursue him as he pursued evil himself. Each yellow pencil would be engraved so it was obvious why these demons had been eliminated. A wood-burning drill was purchased and as with the rock art he sought, the pencils were embedded with small letters that he pecked out of the soft wood. A box of 12 pencils was purchased. Each pencil was methodically labeled: "Live by the sword, die by the sword." These replaced all the pencils in his silver case.

While only eight individuals were on Fallon's list, at least 10 pencils would be needed and a couple of spares were a good idea. It would be necessary to use two pencils for Willy, who would be killed as the previously Willy had been once before in Oakland. And a pencil was saved for a person not on the list, Fallon's archenemy who he'd never forgotten. Detective Sam Houston Hubbard would be disposed of after Fallon had finished his battle at Hidden Canyon.

CHAPTER 46

FROG HUNTING

The next two weeks were spent developing a plan. If Fallon was successfully going to eliminate his now sworn enemies, he had to be prepared to overcome "Fallen Man." Quests are not meant to be easy and Scriber didn't expect anything less than total destruction.

He needed a weapon, a spear similar to his rock nemesis. Finding a pitchfork that could be implemented for taking lives took a little research. After many failed attempts at locating one, he finally found online just what he was searching for. Google was a useful instrument in helping locate his weapon of death.

Scriber found if he played the music of "Red Man Writes," which he had downloaded, it helped him focus on the task at hand. The weapon turned out to be a gig for spearing frogs. It had three sharp prongs and its shape was identical to his beloved Sun Devils' logo, another sign. The three razor-sharp stainless steel daggers were about five inches in length and each tip had a barb that prevented the intended victim from pulling away as the metal hooks would catch the underlying muscles it had been driven into. Called the "portable frogger," it even had a telescoping handle, making the compressed size something that could fit inside a coat pocket. Very handy if you don't want your enemy to see what's coming. He ordered a half-dozen froggers.

His law practice had to be put on autopilot. It would implode sometime in the near future, but Fallon would be gone. It wouldn't take long for the charities to figure out he had blown town with their funds, but for now it had to look like he was on extended vacation.

Fallon knew he would not come back once he left a path of destruction that even his clumsy foes, the cops, would be able to follow. He put all the charities' funds which were not scheduled to be realized anytime soon into an overseas bank account under the name Willy Hubbard. Willy in honor of his first and soon to be most important kill, and Hubbard the one cop who had ever come close to catching him with Mrs. Black, 22 years ago. Detective Sam Hubbard was part of god's overall plan as he had already been touched by Fallon's handiwork, with the death of his nephew Bill Sneadly, a connection Fallon had discovered after researching Hubbard online.

Fallon had waited his entire life in anticipation of his calling. Now it was clear. He destroyed the paper trails he had accumulated, including law files, notes, photographs, and his ad hoc biography on Hubbard. He left on his coffee table a single book. It was the *Fallen Man* bible, into which he placed a pencil in the center binding, marking the location of the two-page illustration of "Fallen Man." "A clue for those smart enough to look, maybe Hubbard will figure it out," Scriber thought. Scriber had followed Hubbard's career closely: he had been decorated by the city for solving a particularly heinous crime spree in Chinatown and was considered to be one of the top detectives in the country, one of the few who was also a forensic psychologist. He also had the rare distinction of interviewing Ted Bundy before his execution. Fallon idolized Bundy, a fellow creature like himself. The thought that a man who had gotten into Bundy's head might soon be tracking him was exhilarating.

Fallon loved outwitting those who were supposedly able to understand a so-called damaged mind. He had already gone up against Hubbard and won. Now it was time to up the ante. Start killing again and he would begin right here in his hometown and it would be a brutal crime, one that would catch Hubbard's attention.

To effectively battle an enemy you need them as close as possible. Fallon decided there was only one way to engage his rock nemesis. An image of "Fallen Man" had to be reproduced and it must be placed on his own skin. "Fallen Man" was the reason for Scriber's life struggle. He saw his own chalkboard-like skin as the ancient wall in New Mexico.

Fallon enlarged an image from the book showing "Fallen Man" and made a rudimentary tracing that he took to an off-the-beaten-track tattoo parlor called Just Tattoos. Apparently the establishment didn't do piercings, only tattoos. Fallon called ahead on a public phone making an appointment under the name Sam Hubbard. He explained he would pay in cash and only had a limited time frame to get the tattoo done so it had to be accomplished in one sitting. He would pay double the normal cost, but wanted the last half of the evening reserved for him alone. He explained he had a skin disorder so he only wanted the tattoo artist around, no one else. This was not a problem at Just Tattoos as it was a one-man store, the recession eliminating any hopes of growth. Apparently those seeking tattoos didn't have money during downturns in the economy.

Fallon, going by Sam Hubbard, took two shots of Jim Beam to blunt the unimaginable pain he was about to self-inflict, and began his quest to the Holy Grail.

The tattoo shop owner went by Meat. This was not a nickname but his legal name. He wanted a single-word name as he felt his distinctive body of artwork was worthy of such a title, like Picasso, Madonna or Tiger. He was special and the large bloody sirloin steaks inked on his two bulging biceps proved it.

Meat was an imposing individual: 245 pounds, shaven bald, with an array of ink designs throughout his torso. Besides his steaks, there were serpents, women, and cryptic references to his life as a tattoo artist. He had been working at his trade for years and had hundreds of examples of his work lining the tiny store walls. A large neon sign glared out the second-story window in bold red letters: We Use Sterile Technique, a reference to those who worried about AIDS. Fallon didn't care. He knew his path. AIDS was not in the cards for him. Walking up the two flights of stairs to get to the out-of-the-way business Fallon felt a rush of power. The quest had begun. His life was finally starting.

✹ ✹ ✹ ✹

"So, Man, you sure you want this special tattoo? Looks cool but might take a couple of hard hours grinding. Your skin up for that kind of abuse? How about a small real devil? I know that tat like the back of my hand. I can knock it out in 25 minutes tops." Meat didn't relish the thought of having to be an artist today. He was hoping to be just a technician and get out fast even if he was being paid double.

"No. As I said on the phone, I want this particular image and I want it here." Sam aka Fallon Scriber lifted his shirt, revealing Willy's still very present lower abdominal scars.

"Those are some bad-looking marks. I'll try to incorporate them into the tattoo, cover 'em up a bit."

"No, don't touch them. They are reminders. I need them. Keep the tattoo in between the scars, it's very important. Also as I explained, I have a skin problem so try to keep from touching me except where you're tattooing, otherwise it will be more painful for me than it should. And I would appreciate it if you could pull down the window shade. I would like a little less light during the procedure."

"Cool, Man, no problem, you're the boss. Keep it a little dark and no touching the scars or you, unless absolutely necessary." Meat took the tracing, laid it on Fallon's abdomen and with a sharpie drew out the image.

Instantaneously Fallon's skin began to welt and turn violently red around the fading black sharpie marks.

"Wow, Man, you were not kidding. That is some wild covering you have there. I've been inking for 20 years and I've seen some sensitive skin before, but not like that. There's some long medical name, right? It's like dermata something, right?"

"I have severe dermatographia."

"OK, I'll be careful. I know this shit's got to hurt."

"Meat, you don't know the half of it."

Meat began torturing Fallon, the first time in his life that he willingly endured someone drawing on his skin. He turned up his iPod, which he had brought to help with the pain and set it to repeatedly play "Red Man Writes."

Finally after nearly two hours of intense work, Meat was happy with his finished product. He took a hand mirror and handed it to Fallon, who was still lying down in his chair. His body was drenched in sweat, his skin on fire like he had never felt before. He had almost passed out twice and was extremely nauseated. The intense skin stimulation had affected his entire hormonal system, not just his abdomen, which looked like one giant red welt.

"What do you think, Sam? I like this better than I thought I would. I'm going to use this image again, much better than the standard devil, but I'll have to make it lots smaller for the average Joe. Not many people would want it this big."

"No Meat, you will never use this image again." Fallon got up and dried his hair and cleaned the mirror of fingerprints with a nearby towel. He looked as if he had just stepped out of the shower. Quietly, Fallon walked over to his coat and pulled out his pocket gig and un-telescoped it with one quick flip of the wrist, hiding it from Meat's view.

"Listen, Man, you may have paid me double and brought in the picture, but once it's on your belly I own it. It's my art, not yours. If you don't want me to reproduce it, then you better get it off now." Meat didn't take kindly to anyone telling him what he could or could not do in his own shop.

"Fuck you, Meat," and with that Fallon like a Spanish matador turned around, gig exposed and stuck it directly into Meat's beefy neck, Fallon's first victim of the quest. Meat was shocked. The pain was intense but nothing compared to seeing the dangling gig, with blood spurting in all directions, which had also pierced his tracheal voice box, a direct hit. Meat tried to scream but could only manage a high-pitched gurgling squeak as the blood spurted out of two separate sides of his quickly enlarging neck.

Meat tried in vain to extract the spear, which had penetrated numerous layers of muscle, fascia, and fat, but the small frog barbs had done their jobs too well. No amount of jumping or pulling could remove the deadly prongs from their intended target. Meat realized his life would be over in just a few short minutes. Intense anger seized Meat and he wanted to make sure he did not die alone. The bastard with the fucked-up skin who had just mortally wounded him would come along on his ride down to hell.

He lunged at Fallon, the gig hanging from his neck like a Popsicle stick in JELL-O. Fallon, his Navy training still remarkably intact, perfectly executed a tripping maneuver that swept Meat's wobbly legs from underneath him, blood flying everywhere. Meat fell head first onto the gig, hitting the ground hard. Meat's own mass pushed the spear further in. Before the metal telescoping pole bent under his massive weight—the aluminum spear made for frogs, not Meat—it released his body to the ground, quivering like a fish that just hit a boat deck. He literally was dead Meat.

Fallon, whose own skin was still on fire, the red-inked massive welts covered in his own blood, reviewed the outcome and remarked with a smirk of satisfaction, "Looks like we will have fresh Meat tonight." Then he extracted his first inscribed pencil from its silver box and positioned it in his victim's open mouth. No missing this one. Fallon took the towel he had just dried himself with and cleaned the spurts of Meat's blood off him and then wiped the gig of any fingerprints. He removed the tattoo machine's needle and placed all his bloody gauzes and water into a bottle and back into a large carry bag he had brought. As he walked out, Fallon whispered, "No DNA matching, the cops have to use detective skills to catch me. Let the games begin."

CHAPTER 47

THEY FOUND WHAT!

The *San Francisco Examiner* had a small paragraph under "local news" on Meat's violent demise. The newspaper detailed the gig to the neck and gave a brief history of his checkered past, including his five years at Folsom Prison. The police had no leads and were waiting for forensic results. The pencil was not mentioned nor that Meat's last appointment of the day happened to have the exact same name as San Francisco's only forensic psychologist detective.

Sam had just sat down to work on yesterday's paperwork when the call came in.

"Hi Sam, this is your good old buddy Buckley here. Do I have a case for you. Get a new chart ready, because you will like this one." Buckley, who had worked with Sam Hubbard for 10 years, knew Sam as well as anyone could.

Buckley, like most of the precinct police department, followed Sam's penchant for serial killers. Sam's wall charts were legendary and about to outgrow his new office. Buckley knew this case was a compelling one. Sam's name was in the deceased's appointment book as his last client of the day, and more importantly a clue had purposely been left by the killer: a pencil with a cryptic message.

This was not a random case of violence as the paper made it sound. Buckley knew Sam had a yellowing chart with the words PENCIL FOUND in big, bold letters. That unusual fact had been underlined by Sam at least 20 times over various years in multicolored pens, which seemed odd to Buckley considering the word was *pencil*.

As soon as he finished talking with Buckley, Sam dropped everything he had been working on. Maybe this would prove a connection to his nephew Bill's death? Before he bolted out of his office to look at the case himself, Sam grabbed a red magic marker and circled the word *pencil* for good luck.

The preliminary crime report had just been finished. As soon as Sam entered the room, he began peppering the attending officer for all the details.

Meat's autopsy was underway and toxicology wouldn't be out for two days. Sam pored over the images of the dead man's mouth holding the pencil and microscopic close-ups of the inscription. The pencil was of a typical variety, like what was found in Bill's back pocket, and as with Bill, the pencil was partially used and sharpened. The difference was this pencil was left by someone trying to make a bold statement. He killed his victim viciously and placed the pencil in Meat's mouth where it would not be missed, a calling card. The murderer was reaching out to Sam by using his name to make the tattoo appointment. He must have known about Sam's interest in pencils.

Sam hoped that Bill's death might be somehow tied into Meat's, even if that had been more than 30 years ago. The unanswered question was if there were other deaths where a suspicious pencil had been found at the crime scene in the last three decades? If this was the same person, there could be dozens. It was time to revisit the case of Petty Officer Mat Smith. The naval seaman Robin Pettipoint who had been convicted of Smith's death had been dead for nearly 30 years. He had committed suicide his first week at Leavenworth and all access to the files of Smith and Pettipoint was cut off; "no need to know" was the command order. Now Sam had a reason to know. He knew there would be hoops to jump through but he was ready, no matter what the political cost. This was why he had joined the force. As soon as everything was known about the latest homicide victim, Sam would go after Smith's sequestered records. Meat's case at the precinct station was now referred to as The Pencil Murder.

Nearly a week went by before Meat's lab and autopsy results were available. The cause of death was exsanguinations. Both carotid arteries had been lacerated. It took less than seven minutes for him to bleed out. No drugs or alcohol were found in the deceased's tissues, including his brain, according to the forensic reports. The victim was probably not threatened by the assailant as the murder weapon had to be implemented at a close range unless it was thrown, which was highly unlikely, but possible. If it was thrown, then the murderer had some special talents or was very good at gigging frogs.

There were no defensive wounds seen, which would corroborate the assumption that Meat felt comfortable with the situation before the attack. Most likely the murderer had gotten a free tattoo, executed a premeditated murder, and was savvy enough to take anything that might have contained his DNA. It was possible that the gig was lying around Meat's office and something went bad and the client simple speared him, but this didn't seem likely as the pencil's cryptic message had to have been put on ahead of time, as it was left purposely as a clue.

The last client before Sam's name in Meat's appointment log was identified and interviewcd. It was a male in his early 20s who got a skull and cross bones on his right arm. He paid cash but amazingly had gotten a receipt. The man played in a band and figured he might be able to write off the tattoo for his profession. He was the lead singer of a screamo band, The Raging Hot Heads. The man's story checked out as did his alibi. After he left the parlor, he was screaming in front of 100 people at the same approximate time as Meat's death.

So whoever used the name Sam Hubbard for the appointment was the killer. There were no tattoo books nor money missing as far as could be determined.

Meat was a generalist when it came to his artwork in tattoos. He was well enough liked in the neighborhood and had not been in trouble with the law in years. He paid taxes and wasn't on drugs.

At the crime scene, there were no other interesting findings other than that it was a very violent ending for Meat. The blood splatter was consistent with Meat having run a little ways with the gig impelled in his neck, but no real signs of struggle. The seven-inch pencil was a common variety found at any corner drug store; the writing was etched in carefully with a wood-burning tool. The words were spelled correctly and neatly. Handwriting experts were analyzing the script. The killer, besides being neat, was obviously smart, not leaving any fingerprint or DNA findings, and was challenging the cops, specifically Sam, by leaving his pencil calling card. The killer was mostly likely a man.

The message "live by the sword, die by the sword" was such a vague reference it could mean anything. More information or bodies would likely be needed before this case would be solved. Sam felt this was the work of a very disturbed cold-blooded killer, possibly a serial killer. He was also convinced the pencil found at his nephew's death was connected. But he still needed more evidence. It was possible that the man's name in Meat's log was really Sam Hubbard and it wasn't directed at him, but Sam's psychological voice said coincidences are rare. The killer was reaching out. Hopefully, something had been missed at Mat Smith's death. Robin Pettipoint, the young seaman convicted of the crime, clearly in Sam's mind was not the killer. So that case was still wide open and unsolved. Sam needed additional information that he was about to receive. It would come from, of all places, someone already on one of his charts.

CHAPTER 48

LOVE TO RUN

So far, 2013 was proving that life was at one of its high-water marks again for Mo Bandgood. He had gone through many gyrations throughout his unique life and this was one of the good stages. He was happy and making music once more. More importantly, he had been able to employ his old friends and come up with a unique 21st century approach to music and art.

He had already finished his second composition, which was inspired by Navajo weavings—those rugs he had seen while visiting the trading post in New Mexico. He had worked with Bloom to obtain images of both antique and new Navajo textiles along with a few historic photographs of weavers. The new piece was titled "Spiderwoman Lives" and was a reference to the mythology of the Diné and how they learned to start weaving. The music was scheduled to be recorded next week and he was paying to have a Navajo singer fly in. Mo would overlay Navajo chanting on top of his own "Spiderwoman Lives" composition.

Mo was especially excited today as he was going to meet a lawyer who had seen his "Red Man Writes" video at a doctor's office and was possibly interested in investing in his company, Fallen Man Music. The meeting was scheduled for the mid-morning, which gave Mo time for his daily run, which was more like a slow jog since he'd hit 70, but Mo was feeling reinvigorated these days. They would meet at Mo's house to review "Spiderwoman Lives." Mo couldn't believe his good fortune: that a serious investor had found him. He was glad he had taken the time to send out his company cards to so many doctors' offices. He realized that there was a slim chance anyone would ask for one, but it was all about building the brand of his product, something he knew about.

If all went well today, Mo would have the potential client come in next week, meet a real Navajo singer, and watch a live professional orchestra perform an original score, which he knew would hook the investor. How could it not? Mo wouldn't even need booze to snow this client, like in the old days. Just great music.

Mo was really looking forward to discussing his whole concept in greater detail. He did have a nondisclosure form for the lawyer to sign, just in case he was trying to poach his concept. After all, he was a lawyer and Mo had worked with plenty of bad ones in Hollywood. Mo had explained to him in advance that he would need to have the disclosure signed to meet, and the lawyer had no problems. Mo had looked the fellow up online. The man had a few listings on the Web. He apparently was a lawyer in business for 25 years, nothing out of the ordinary, and was on a mental health charities board of directors. Mo thought about it all as he jogged. Then he showered, dressed, and was having his first cup of coffee when the doorbell rang. Mo's visitor was right on time, 11 am sharp.

Fallon Scriber was dressed in a black business suit. Short, cropped salt and pepper hair, a neatly trimmed grey mustache and beard, carrying a briefcase, and for all purposes looked like a typical businessman. Skipping all the perfunctory small talk, Fallon got right down to business. God was speaking directly to him now.

"Thanks for having me over, Mo. I'm excited about your latest project and I would like to hear more about what drove you in this direction in the first place. The Fallen Man composition seems very unique. How did you come up with it?"

"I hate to be a drag, but could I have you sign the nondisclosure, before I go into details? I'm sure you understand. You're welcome to take time and read it first," Mo demurred.

"Not necessary, Mo. I'm a straight shooter as you'll soon find out and I'm not going to tell a soul. Hand it over." Fallon signed the paper with just a perfunctory glance. "So how did the project come to you?"

Mo recounted seeing the photograph in *The Times* and meeting the two anthropologists at their book signing. Then Mo uttered a sentence that triggered Fallon to change personalities: "I believe it was destiny for me to read that paper that day, some sort of sign that I had to do this project."

The words *destiny* and *sign* sealed Mo's fate. The lawyer decided that the jingle man who had done a thousand commercials would never live to see "Spiderwoman Lives" recorded or his musicians play for him again. Fallon stood up directly in front of Mo, not saying a word.

He took off his jacket, carefully laid it down, and then slowly unbuttoned his white starched shirt.

The stunned Mo didn't know what to say or do.

Then the strange lawyer pulled his shirt open and yelled: "Mo Bandgood, I am your destiny and here is your sign!" Fallon revealed the "Fallen Man" tattoo, which was still red and irritated on Fallon's defective skin.

Mo knew he was in deep shit. This man was mentally deranged. He had the "Fallen Man" petroglyph tattooed on his entire chest and abdomen. The man's eyes had that insane Jack Nicholson look.

Horrified, Mo tried to bolt behind a chair, but Fallon was too athletic and took Mo down with two punches, in his solar plexus and right temple. Fallon jumped on top of Mo, putting all his weight on top of his neck, "Fallen Man" staring down on Mo like the angle of death.

Fallon began to speak in a monotone, out-of-body type of voice: "You and I are bound by the "Fallen Man." I for good, you for evil. Mr. Bandgood, you and I have crossed paths before, only you didn't know it. Remember Bill Sneadly, the man whose body you found long ago on Seal Beach?"

Mo was terrified now, as he knew poor Bill had ended up dead, probably at the hands of this murdering lunatic and he was likely next. Mo shook his head yes. The blood was having a hard time getting to his brain from Fallon's continued pressure. Mo couldn't speak; he was about to pass out.

"He was killed and thrown off the cliff by god's hand!" Fallon declared. "God knew you and I would meet again, and Bill was my calling card. You should never have done the work of "Fallen Man." It's a shame you became possessed by the dark side as I'm a fan of your composition, but your 'Red Man Writes' title sucks!"

With that, Fallon applied additional pressure with his thighs and the lights went out for Mo Bandgood.

Considering Mo taken care of for the moment, Fallon found Mo's latest musical composition, "Spiderwoman Lives." Fallon took the sharp pencil he had brought with him and scratched out the word

Lives and replaced it with *Dies,* and then left the pencil and another clue, an old business card he had been carrying in his wallet for 20 years. Then he loaded Mo's body into the trunk of his car.

CHAPTER 49

IS THIS HEAVEN

The first thought that came into Mo's conscious state was a sound and it was music. As Mo tried desperately to open his eyes, he recognized the music was his own "Red Man Writes."

Mo's mind was hazy, wrestling to get a grip on what had happened and where he was. "Am I in heaven?" Mo said out loud in a dry, raspy voice as his mind started to clear. His eyes were now responding to visual stimulus.

He looked around the room, which was dark, still unsure if he was dead or alive until a light was clicked on. He was most definitely alive and Mo wasn't sure that was a good thing, considering his company.

The deranged man who had choked him was before him in his underwear, the large imposing figure of "Fallen Man" again glaring back at him from Fallon's abdomen and chest.

"No Mr. Mo, this is far from heaven, closer to hell I'd say," Fallon grinned at the pathetic wishful thinking of his naive captive. "Thought you were dead, did you? Not yet anyway. I do love your new look though, red becomes you." Mo's face was marked with splotches of petechial hemorrhages from being choked. Fallon laughed at Mo's predicament.

Mo tried to speak, but this time his throat wouldn't cooperate. He was feeling intense pain in his neck where a 200-pound lunatic had rested. He also realized his hands were bound and he was tied to a metal chair. His mind was foggy as if he had been drugged, which he had, and his bruised body ached from being contorted in the trunk of Fallon's car for hours.

"Here's how things stand for you, Mo, as I bet you're wondering, why me? Well Mo you are the disciple of a devil, whether you realize it or not, and I have a quest to stop that demon from hurting those of us on this earth who must battle our skin on a daily basis. You can't even begin to imagine my life. What it feels like not to ever sit in a chair comfortably or lie in a bed without my skin aching," Fallon explained.

"Thanks to your 'Fallen Man''s powers, I have been trapped in my own hell as long as I can remember. But now you have the opportunity to help me fight the devil you have canonized in your music and film. Death can come in many forms, Mr. Mo. Some are not nice, in fact, so incredibly painful it's hard even to comprehend. Do you want to find out what kind of person can kill a 14-year-old with pencils inserted into his neck?"

All Mo could muster was, "No."

"Good," responded Fallon, "because I am that man. You and I won't have to go down the road of me removing your teeth one at a time or eating your eyes while you are still living. Let's chat, shall we." Fallon was playing with one of his froggers, telescoping the handle in and out as he looked down at his captive. He wanted all the information Mo knew.

Mo was afraid not to divulge it in its entirety. It was obvious Fallon was capable of doing what he threatened. Mo's eyes told him it was true and the contraption Fallon was toying with was scary as shit.

So Mo started spewing information, including about the site where "Fallen Man" was located and the details of who knew the place and how it was accessed. Mo told Fallon about everyone who had helped him develop the tape and about those names listed in the *Fallen Man* petroglyph book. Where the authors resided and as much personal information about them as possible. Mo explained who Rachael, Charles, and Willy were. Fallon seemed to take great interest in Willy. It gave Mo chills watching Fallon's reaction as he described the boy whose father and grandfather had such prominent roles in bringing "Fallen Man" to the world's attention.

Mo's hands were untied and he was ordered to draw a detailed map of the location of the petroglyph, and list who had access to the remote site. Mo's cell phone numbers were meticulously copied, and notes were taken on anyone of interest in his database of contacts.

The final interrogation was about Isabella, whose name had been shown as "a special thanks to my mentor, Isabella Graves, the best English teacher a student could ever have," in the credits of "Red Man Writes." Mo explained he had not seen her in decades and only talked with her occasionally. He had sent her a *Fallen Man* book and one of his CDs, but had not heard back from her. He did have her address in his phone. It was in Las Cruces and it was current as far as he knew. Mo also told Fallon, even at the risk of angering him, that she had absolutely nothing to do with the project. It was just an innocent thank you to someone who had helped him in college, nothing more. Isabella didn't even know about his project and might hate petroglyphs for all he knew.

Fallon didn't seem to care about Mo's excuses, but he did love her last name. It was catchy, Fallon thought: "Graves, I like that."

After Mo had revealed everything he could possibly think of, his capturer stopped the interrogation and seemed satisfied. Fallon surprised Mo by turning human again.

"OK, Mo, that's good. I can tell you have given me everything I need to follow my quest. Now I will show compassion," Fallon announced. He untied Mo and let him go to the bathroom.

Mo was thankful to relieve himself, as the coffee he had consumed so many hours ago had filled his bladder to the point of breaking. He guessed he was in Fallon's home. But where? He reluctantly returned to the living room to find Fallon had brought him a turkey sandwich garnished with a pickle, chips, and glass of milk.

Mo was afraid not to eat what was handed to him, even if it was poisoned or drugged. He knew he was screwed, anyway. Maybe Fallon was so crazy he would simply feed him and let him go free. The answer, Mo would find out shortly, was not a chance.

CHAPTER 50

BIG BUCKS

Charles Bloom received a text on his phone, which was a delight to see considering it was the worst part of the retail season—late March 2013—and no one bought anything in Santa Fe or Toadlena during this unpredictable weather month.

Early spring was a time of fixing things, whether on the rez or in Santa Fe. Roofs that needed to be patched, trees that needed trimming, and if there was enough money, better frames changed out on expensive paintings that hadn't sold.

Today's text from Mo was heaven sent. It read: "Hi, Mo here, going out of town for a few days. Wanted you to know about a big spender who will be calling you. A petroglyph lover named Fallon Scriber will be contacting you about seeing the Hidden Canyon site. He wants to meet all involved with the project. Offered $20K to see it. He's giving me $10K to set it up. Hope you can make it work, I could use the extra money."

Bloom reread the note three times. $20K to show someone a petroglyph site? It was amazing. That was the same amount he had made selling the Yellowhorse during Indian Market, and this would require only a little coordination on his part since he was already on the rez. He enjoyed visiting the site anyway, even when it was cold. March was a drain on the checking account, so this was a no brainer. Everyone would make good money.

He wrote back to Mo: "GREAT! Look forward to hearing from him. Give me a call at your earliest convenience. Love to hear the details."

Mo (really Fallon) wrote back immediately: "Catching a plane. Out of contact for a couple of days, but will holler soon. Scriber seems like a stand-up guy and for real. Could even want to invest in 'Spiderwoman Lives.' Good luck. I'll check in periodically."

Bloom didn't know why Mo was going out of town as he had a singer from Red Lake coming to L.A this week. The "Spiderwoman Lives" recording was booked for Friday and today was Sunday. But Mo was from Hollywood, and it was not a place Bloom figured he would ever understand. Like the Navajos, L.A. musicians had their own time schedules.

The call came one hour later.

"Mr. Bloom, my name is Fallon Scriber. Hope it's OK to call your cell. Mo Bandgood said it would be fine. Did he give you a heads-up I was going to call?"

"Yes he did. Mo said you would be interested in seeing the Hidden Canyon petroglyph site in person?"

"Very interested, indeed. I loved the petroglyph book you were involved with and Mo's musical composition was so inspiring I told him I had to visit the site in person and meet all the people who have enriched my life in such a meaningful way. Do you think it's possible to arrange? I'm a busy man so my hectic schedule will only allow me to see it on short notice. Say, in two days? But I am willing to pay handsomely for your efforts to make it happen," Fallon promised.

"Mo mentioned you'd pay $20K to see the site, and he would get another $10K separately. Does that sound about right?" Bloom verified.

"That is correct, Mr. Bloom, and I will also pay for the participants' travel expenses. I'm sure some of the authors will have to travel and it may be expensive to get to the site, especially with such little advance warning." Fallon knew exactly where Dr. J and Dr. Bloom lived and doubted it would be any problem, but the added incentive of expenses seemed a good way to seal the deal.

"It sounds like it should be very doable. Who exactly would you like to have there?" Bloom asked, taking notes.

"I'm interested in meeting Mr. Manygoats and seeing his work in person. The two authors, of course. Yourself. Love to have the opportunity to meet your wife and newborn. Mo told me you were a new father. Willy, right?"

"Yes, that's correct. Having a newborn is lots of fun, except for the lost sleep. Love to have you try Rachael's mutton stew, it's the best on the rez."

"Maybe she and Willy would like to join us at the site?"

"I'm afraid Rachael has a problem with Anasazi sites, so I doubt I can convince her to tag along. This way it gives her time to get a home-cooked Navajo dinner prepared, no extra charge. I'll make the calls and get right back with you," Bloom arranged.

Fallon made sure Bloom had his cell number and hung up.

Mo was in the same room with the smiling Fallon, his mouth duct taped over, listing to the entire conversation. Mo tried to concentrate on not throwing up and not listening, as it was he who had just inadvertently set his friends up for their likely deaths.

CHAPTER 51

IT'S A GO

Bloom called his dad and Dr. J to see if they would be up to coming to Toadlena on short notice. Any excuse for the anthropologists to see petroglyphs and get paid to talk about them was like being given money to eat ice cream. His father was planning to come up next week anyways, so he would just come up a little early. Dr. J was thrilled to get out of the cold no-sales days of Santa Fe with his boss's permission.

Frank lived only a short ways from the site and started whooping an Indian chant when Bloom told him he would get $5,000 to guide the small expedition to his petroglyph site, plus maybe sell a few of his sculptures. He was definitely in.

Rachael was less than pleased about more people visiting the site, but she couldn't argue with the money.

Bloom notified Fallon that it was a go, requesting half down and not refundable in case something came up. Bloom was a businessman and understood shit happened and he wanted to make sure he could deliver on what he had promised the other participants. Bloom gave Fallon his wiring information and the stranger told him $10K would be in his bank account tomorrow.

Fallon wire-transferred the funds from his overseas account. "The price for doing god's will," he told himself as he did his deal with the devil's minion. Thanks to Mo, Fallon already had a detailed map to Bloom's world, including pertinent landmarks, so he could visualize his trip in advance.

Bloom recommended meeting at the gas station at the turn off at 491 and N-19, the road to Toadlena.

Fallon told Bloom he would be there in two days at 10 am. Fallon requested that no other persons come along, as it was a special treat for himself and he only wanted those close to the project to be included.

Bloom agreed to Fallon's terms, which seemed a bit odd, but so was paying $30K to view a wall of rock art he could view anytime in a $50 book.

What Bloom didn't know was Fallon Scriber would be leaving San Francisco tonight, heading in advance to the GPS coordinates Mo had noted during filming, which were now in the hands of a psychopathic killer who was planning a surprise welcome for his Hidden Canyon guides, one they could never imagine.

✳ ✳ ✳ ✳

Mo Bandgood watched anxiously as Fallon got ready to leave for New Mexico. It was a sickening feeling watching him pack his bags. As Fallon offered a blow-by-blow of each item he packed, Mo realized his own demise was coming and soon.

"You see Mo, I have to completely destroy your devil's nest and all those disciples it has spawned. They must be killed in quick fashion, left to rot on the desert floor. See this?" Fallon asked, holding up a large, skin-colored tube in each hand. "This my friend is some powerful explosive material. I can assure you of this as I was a specialist in bomb-making material back in the day at Seal Beach Weapons Station. Ring any bells? This shit in my hand here is very hard to acquire. The Feds don't want bad guys like me to have any. I can't understand why?" Fallon grinned as he rolled the sticks between his palms, and then slowly waved them in front of Mo's nose so he could see and smell the material was real. "It's called C4 and used properly can bring down a huge overhang just like the one so brilliantly captured in your 'Red Man Writes.'"

Mo got spontaneous shivers throughout his body. Fallon not only was planning to eliminate a whole group of innocent people, he was going to take out one of the most pristine archeological sites in North America. Mo couldn't say anything. He just prayed his own death would be quick.

Fallon placed a large, clear plastic sheet on his own bed, tucking it in around the edges. He then had Mo strip and handcuffed Mo's feet and hands to the bed. Mo looked for all purposes like he would be crucified naked in some ritualistic way.

"I bet you were wondering why I was so kind as to feed you, huh?" Fallon taunted.

Mo didn't say a word, afraid of irritating his torturer and not wanting to hear the answer. He wished for a musical composition to fill his mind, but it was blank, nothing but Fallon's voice making its way through.

"Well, it wasn't because I'm a good person, I hate to say. No, I needed your stomach and intestines to be working, digesting all that food. I am giving you a chance to live, but it will be up to your old buddy Sam Hubbard, remember him? He interviewed you when I killed Bill."

Mo remembered Sam and hoped Fallon didn't know about the Zodiac film connection. What was it Mo had told Sam about not worrying that any serial killers would be coming around looking for him? Boy, did he regret that now.

"I'm going to send Sam another clue and if he's smart enough and lucky, he will find you in time. If not, or if he's too busy to give a shit, you will die and it will be uncomfortable, very uncomfortable, I'm afraid. You, Mo, will get a rare opportunity to feel what it's like to be me. Chronic pain is not fun. It takes a special person to be able to cope with this kind of torture. Now Mo, from this point on you need to be very still because if you wiggle around more than likely one of two things will happen: you will blow up or I will hit something which will kill you and old Sam will never get the opportunity to help you, understand?"

Mo nodded yes.

Fallon unraveled more duct tape, covering Mo's eyes to match his mouth.

"Got to do this, Mo. Otherwise you will see what I'm going to do and you'll flinch, kind of like the doctor sticking you with a needle but mine's a tad larger."

Mo shuddered at what must be coming. Finally he was able to muster up a song in his head. It was the Red Castle jingle. He hummed it, knowing red was in his future.

Fallon removed a pencil from its silver shrine, then sharpened it for good measure.

The noise of the electric motor grinding made Mo hum louder, suspecting his final moment was upon him.

"Mo, if you're going to hum, it might as well be something good, a favorite Doors song of mine. I remember hearing it the day I killed Willy. It brings back one of the few good memories I have of childhood." Fallon hit "play" on his CD set to "Riders On The Storm" and sang along in a high-pitched falsetto to the lyrics of what also used to be one of Mo's favorite songs by The Doors.

After Fallon stopped his rendition, Mo knew what was coming wouldn't be good.

Then, as if he was a surgeon, Fallon palpated the left lower quadrant of Mo's abdomen. When he was satisfied, he admired the sharpened pencil, warning his captive, "Don't wiggle like a toad, or you'll wish you hadn't, Mo." Fallon then caressed the pencil with his long pink tongue. After he was satisfied with the amount of saliva, he plunged the yellow stick directly into Mo's abdomen, leaving it stuck halfway inside Mo like a thermometer stuck in a turkey waiting to be roasted.

Mo screamed at the intense guttural pain, the ample duct tape dulling the sound of his agony, his tears not allowed to flow down his cheeks either. His whole body began shivering, sweat forming small rivulets on the plastic sheet underneath it.

"Good boy, you hardly moved, very impressive. So here's what happens now. Try to concentrate or you may miss something important," Fallon ordered. "I'm going on a trip and not coming back. If Hubbard can figure out you're here in time, you might live and can help finger me, wouldn't that be fun? But if not you will die of one of three things: infection, dehydration, or you will simply blow up. I would keep my movement to a minimum if I were you, unless you want to blow up, which toward the end might be a good choice. My guess is infection will get you because I just inoculated the pencil and you had a nice big meal. You may not be a big fan of the War Channel but I learned the most interesting fact about deaths. Did you know most of the soldiers who died during the Civil War died from complications that were secondary to gunshots to the abdomen?

They died from infection, not the actual gunshot. Fascinating, huh? I always wanted to see if it was true. Sorry I can't stick around to find out, but my guess is you will end up on YouTube. Everyone else does. I'll watch it there."

Fallon, smiling at Mo's pitiful position, eyed the pencil which was bouncing up and down with each fast breath Mo took. With one mighty yank, Fallon pulled it back out of Mo's abdominal cavity. Another round of moaning came bellowing out of Mo. The pencil had done its job. Fallon then retrieved an envelope from his desk that he had preaddressed to Sam Hubbard. Mo's pencil was Sam's next clue. The inscription read: "Live by the sword, die by the sword," and on the other side, Fallon carved in something extra, the words "Isabella Graves." To seal the envelope, Fallon wiped the edge with Mo's sweat, a little DNA gift.

"OK, I'll drop this in the mail on my way out. I hope Detective Hubbard is up for the task, assuming the post office doesn't lose it!" Fallon concluded with his own Doors-inspired twisted song: "I'm a killer on the road/Mo your time is ticking down/Hope you can survive/Don't know if there's a will/It's up to Hubbard to persevere/Or your death is very near/I'm the killer of your fear."

As Mo imagined his probable murderer leaving him to die of his own infected fluids he thought, "Wish he had used FedEx." Even in facing death, Mo had a sense of humor. He hoped he got to tell the story someday.

Fallon rented a four-wheel-drive truck for his trip, heeding Mo's description of the rez's rocky unpaved roads. In two days there would be no more "Fallen Man" or its disciples. Plenty alert as he planned his strategy, Fallon drove straight through the night into New Mexico, headed for Gallup.

Mo Bandgood remained trapped in Fallon Scriber's San Francisco house almost 400 miles from his own Los Angeles home. His primary hope was a letter sent to Detective Hubbard by U.S. Postal. The clock was ticking and so was the bomb.

CHAPTER 52

MAIL FOR YOU

Sam Hubbard was looking forward to finally reviewing the entire military records of the murder case of Petty Officer Smith. It had required Sam's calling the mayor and his captain, but he made it happen. He had just used up 20 years of political capital for a man named Meat. He was expecting a courier's package at any moment with Smith's entire file. Sam was quickly going through the morning mail, hoping it might be mixed in when he saw the envelope.

No return address, postmark was San Francisco, and it looked like it had something in it. Sam's talents of observation had grown legendary over the years and seeing the odd-looking letter made him stop. He instinctively picked it up gingerly from the sides and held it up to the light. Inside was a shortened pencil and it was sharpened.

Sam knew this was from the killer or someone very close to Meat's case. He grabbed a set of gloves and headed down to the forensic lab, nearly knocking over his boss on his way.

"Hey, Hubbard, any luck on your Pencil Killer?"

"I think he just sent me something! I'm heading down to the lab right now to open this up—looks like a pencil."

"Holy shit Sam, get going. Let me know what you find. Be careful. Make sure it isn't filled with anthrax."

The envelope was X-rayed first. The contents appeared to be a single pencil. No powder was seen. The envelope was gently steamed open to save any fingerprint or DNA evidence that might be present. Inside was an ordinary pencil, on one side streaked with what appeared to be blood and the words Isabella Graves. Because Graves was capitalized, Sam assumed it was someone's name but it also could be pointing to someone named Isabella or even a real grave. A murderer sending a clue with the word Graves on it was not good. The pencil was the same length as the one found in Meat's mouth.

The rest of the pencil's verbiage was identical to Meat's. It was obviously from the killer. The envelope and note were sent for dusting using a procedure called superglue heating. Basically, superglue is vaporized in a controlled lab setting and it binds with anything on paper. This method can detect organic prints that regular methods could easily miss.

The name Isabella Graves was entered into Sam's national database, with 15 names matching. Surprisingly, a large number of Isabella Graveses lived in the United States. Six of them had addresses west of the Mississippi: three in California, two in Idaho, and one New Mexico. Sam figured if the killer's clue was a proper name, it was most likely someone from the West as he figured the killer was based in California, or at least had been in California. Being a detective means sometimes making assumptions and going on hunches. His gut told him California. He would call each one and see if any might have a connection to Meat, San Francisco, or Seal Beach, as Sam was still convinced there was a tie-in. He also would ask if anyone had sent them a pencil recently or if the word *pencil* meant anything special to them or "live by the sword, die by the sword."

Before he could start making his calls, a courier brought over what he had been waiting to see for 30 years: Mat Smith's murder case file, marked "confidential."

Holding the file in his hand, Sam wondered if it would give an answer or if it would prove just another dead end, one that he had pinned so much hope on for too many years. He was much more skeptical now than when he was a rookie cop. Realizing most leads went nowhere was part of the process. Sam had made a promise to his big sister Beth to find out what happened to Billy and he also owed it to Pettipoint, as he knew he wasn't the killer, just a screwed-up kid whose only crime was being gay in a hostile military environment.

The answer didn't take long. It was on page two under "contents of pockets." It read: a quarter, one billfold containing $35, a new chap stick, and a yellow partially used number-two pencil.

There it was, the connection. It was overlooked and never brought out at trial. Not one time was the word *pencil* ever mentioned even though a dead body was found not a mile up the street with a similarly shortened #2 yellow pencil.

They were clearly connected. Was it related to Meat's case? It had to be. Sam's name was all over the Bill Sneadly case, one he had been discussing for years with his peers, and when Sam had interviewed Bundy there was a series of articles in the paper on "The Man Who Hunts the Hunters." Numerous photos of Sam were taken with his famous charts. It was time to revisit everyone who had a hand in the Smith case and see if the new pencil finding would make some kind of sense, especially in light of the cryptic message on Meat's pencil and the one that had just arrived with Isabella Graves' name.

Sam Hubbard retreated to his office and began calling Isabella Graveses as he stared at Bill's chart with the word *Pencil* that had been underlined and circled over many years. He added the words *Short, Sharpened Pencil* to Mat Smith's chart and circled that for emphasis. Sam knew from experience his best chance to solve this puzzle would be to figure out why the killer felt strongly about leaving pencils and why shortened ones? The killer was also on a tear so this would be Sam's best chance to stop him. If he had killed 30 years ago it was possible he went in spurts and this was one of those. Something had set him off again. He had all the makings of a true psychopath, unstopped for decades.

Sam was able to get hold of two of the California Graveses. Neither woman had any previous connection to his key phrases or the murder sites. The remaining California Graves was not at home. Sam left a message to have her call as soon as she got his message, leaving both his office and cell number. He then called his New Mexico Isabella Graves, who lived in Las Cruces.

"Hello, may I speak to Isabella Graves, please."

"This is she." The voice was gentle, with a well-heeled timber and perfect diction. He liked her immediately.

"Hi, Mrs. Graves. I'm sorry to bother you but my name is Detective Sam Hubbard. I work for the San Francisco Police Department and I'm investigating a recent murder. A note was sent from a murder suspect with the name Isabella Graves. I'm trying to find a connection, so I'm literally calling all the Isabella Graveses in the country. Would you have any connection to a tattoo artist named Meat in San Francisco?"

"Meat? That's a person's name, Meat?"

"Correct. He was a rather colorful individual. His legal name was Meat."

"No, I don't know a Meat, and in fact I don't know anyone with a tattoo for that matter. I can't think of anyone who I even know in San Francisco."

"Does the phrase 'live by the sword, die by the sword' mean anything particular to you?"

"I've taught college English since 1964, and an occasional bible study class. It's from the Gospel of Matthew, verse 26:52."

"Anyone you know that might have used that verse when they talked with you?

"No, not that I can think of...."

"How about Seal Beach. Anyone you know there?"

"I do have a friend who used to live in Seal Beach. Now he's in Los Angeles."

"Who, if I might ask, do you know in Los Angeles, Mrs. Graves?"

"It's Ms. Graves, actually. His name is Mo Bandgood, a talented musician and writer. In fact, he just sent me a CD he completed in which he mentioned me as his inspiration. Quite touching, considering I haven't talked with him in years."

Sam's mouth dropped open. He quickly swiveled his chair around and focused his eyes on the triangle he had drawn so many years ago from Bill Sneadly to the Zodiac Killer to him. The triangle had just expanded.

CHAPTER 53

FALLING DOWN DAY

Rachael fixed a large breakfast for the boys, knowing today was going to be busy as they showed the big-shot tourist around, a guy named Fallon Scriber. Fresh salted bacon, home-cooked biscuits, and plenty of red-eye gravy (a Bloom family recipe) to fill everyone to the gills. Frank had joined the party and they would all go in Rachael's new red expanded-cab Ford pickup, another truck bought by the grace of Spiderwoman's gifts. The four-wheel-drive gas guzzler could fit five comfortably, which was good since they didn't know if Mr. Scriber had a four-wheel-drive vehicle or not. He would need one where they were going, especially since there were a fresh couple of inches of spring snow this morning.

Dr. J, who had gotten his usual trailer digs, had arrived better prepared this time with extra clothes and a wool hat for his trailer hotel. He was glad he had. One particularly large hole in the trailer's facade had allowed snow to accumulate near his head. Jack Bloom, who was limping badly after the long book tour, had gotten Willy's room again. The cold morning was getting to his sore hip and today would be tough walking. But all the men were excited, as they each would have an additional $5K after today, assuming Scriber showed up. If not, they would split the $10K deposit he had wired in. Either way, easy money. Unheard of in retail.

With bellies full and spirits high, the men gathered up their jackets, scarves, and gloves. Charles kissed Rachael and Willy goodbye. He told Rachael he would call once he got back into cell range and was heading home. "Have the stew waiting," he cheerfully tossed out.

Rachael tossed back, "Remember, those ghosts are still alive out in that *chindi* village. I know you think I'm full of shit and Frank blows it off, but remember what I tell you."

She gently kissed him on the cheek and gave him a pat on the butt. "Don't slip. It's icy today. I don't want you following off that ledge."

With that, the boys were off to earn their easy paycheck.

✱ ✱ ✱ ✱

Fallon Scriber was anxiously waiting at the Minimart gas station at the intersection of U.S. Highway 491 and Navajo Route N-19, due north of Gallup. No other Anglos seemed to be within miles and the foreign nature of the reservation bothered Fallon. He felt the same tension in his gut as he had growing up in Oakland without a real family.

Bloom had said he would tie a red bandana on his antenna so Fallon would be able to recognize the truck. What Bloom didn't know was Fallon had already visited the petroglyph wall yesterday and knew the route. He had taken care of everything; the rest was in his god's hands.

Bloom pulled into the parking lot and immediately discerned the non-native's truck—no bumper stickers, gun rack, or dents, obviously a rental. Bloom pulled up and cracked his window, trying not to lose too much heat.

"Hi, you must be Mr. Scriber. We are the tribe to take you into Hidden Canyon. You want to follow us or hop in?" Bloom could hear Mo Bandgood's "Red Men Writes" playing in Scriber's truck. Wow, this guy was a real fan.

"Nice to meet you, tribe," Fallon greeted them, making a large swooping sign with his arm as if he was some great chief. "I'll just follow. My truck is nice and warm, and it looks a little crowded in your vehicle."

"Fair enough. Make sure you keep it in four-wheel when we get off pavement. It will take about 40 minutes or so to get there. No cell coverage, so if you need to call anyone, now's the time. No bathrooms, either."

"I'm all set, can't wait to see the 'Fallen Man.' I'm ready whenever you are." Fallon rolled his window up and shadowed the red truck as it slowly pulled out of the parking lot, trying not to skid on the late spring snow. Fallon wasn't kidding when he said, "Ready when you are." He was very ready for today's agenda. In just a few hours, his prophecy would be fulfilled.

CHAPTER 54

NO TIME

The connecting pattern that formed on Sam's charts featured Mo Bandgood smack in the middle. The CD Isabella had received was Mo's latest project, something called "Red Man Writes." Sam tried calling Mo three times, but there was no answer. He left messages.

Sam downloaded Mo's video from his website, paying the $9.95 and watching it on his computer. It was a lovely combination of music and Southwestern petroglyphs that lasted 15 minutes. Nothing that was related to pencils or swords as far as Sam could tell, and no biblical passages. The credits included two anthropologists, a Dr. John James and Dr. Jack Bloom, a gallery owner named Charles Bloom, and a special thanks to Isabella Graves. A Google search found a Bloom's gallery in Santa Fe, the owner a Charles Bloom.

Sam called the gallery but it went to voicemail after four rings, giving Bloom's store hours and address. According to the website and phone machine, the gallery should be open. Sam left another message.

Four hours went by. No call from Mo. Sam had his captain call Los Angeles and ask a favor: to make a house call and check on Mo. It was explained that if there was no answer, to please look inside. The brothers in blue would follow through. Sam just had to be patient and think. He was missing something and he wasn't sure what. It was eating at him. He had seen another pencil at a crime scene, but where and when? Somewhere in his mind he had made a mental note.

He scrutinized all his wall charts. The charts held the answer, but somehow it was hidden in a veil of mental fog that his observant mind wouldn't release. Finally he decided to try a mental trick he used when he couldn't come up with a person's name. He would start with the letter A and go alphabetically through all the names he could think of with A, then go to B, and likewise complete the entire alphabet until the person's name popped into his head, which it always did.

Today, instead of reviewing the alphabet he started with his own career from day one as a rookie cop and worked his way forward through his memories of work, day by day, year by year. Any case that would make his mind pause, even if for just a second, was a potential answer to what he was searching for. Sam was a verbal person and understood hearing his own voice made him think more clearly. So he recited his cases into his tape machine, one by one. Nothing seemed to stick, then it did. "Mrs. Black!"

His memory kicked in: "The house shoes, I remember those house shoes. The old lady died at her desk. Those shoes were not on her feet. Her lawyer gave a plausible explanation why—her arthritis, gout I think. It seemed logical, but there was something else. What was that something else, what am I forgetting? She was at her writing desk... writing desk... was there a pencil?"

Sam almost fell out of his own chair. His eyes popped open and he scrambled for his case files, stored in meticulous scientific fashion. Sam had kept every one of the cases he had worked on during his entire career as a police officer. He found the old dusty file that hadn't been opened since he signed off over 20 years ago and there was a photograph of the elderly lady collapsed over her desk.

Next to Mrs. Black's hand was a yellow pencil, and it was sharp, very sharp, and it was *shortened*! She hadn't ever written anything. The pencil and her body were planted. Who was that lawyer? Sam dug into the case file like a heroin addict would a fresh stash. "There it is, his name was Scriber. Omigod, his name comes from the German word for writer. Fallon Scriber! Is he my killer?"

Sam's hand was shaking when he called down to the records department to request a complete dossier on Fallon Scriber, and he wanted it to start from his birth. Nearly yelling into the phone, he requested, "Look for any deaths and especially murders where a pencil might have been found on the scene in any town Fallon Scriber has ever lived in."

Then the phone call came in from L.A. It was the police chief. Mo was nowhere to be found and worse, from the preliminary discoveries at the scene, it was looking like foul play was involved. Sam was given an Officer Grundy's cell number at the scene.

"Grundy here."

"This is Officer Sam Hubbard from the San Francisco Department of Forensic Investigation. I understand you're at the scene now, Mo Bandgood's house? Is that correct?"

"Yep, I'm standing over some sheet music that has some interesting items I think you might want to know about."

"Give it to me, I'm taking notes. We may be dealing with a psychopathic serial killer."

"Well there's sheet music. It's marked 'Navajo weavings arrangement' and it's titled in large letters 'Spiderwoman Lives.' Looks like some Native American kind of thing, I guess. The word *Lives* has a line through it and the word *Dies* is inserted."

"Anything else?"

"Yeah, there's a sharpened pencil, we're bagging it now. It says 'live by the sword, die by the sword' burnt into the side. It was laying on top of the sheet music. One other thing, you're going to love this. There's a very worn business card that was found with the pencil and on the back written in cursive it says, 'Are you watching? The killer is right in front of you, dickweed.' Wanna guess whose name is on the front of the card?"

Sam was at a loss but tried for an educated guess. "Mo Bandgood?"

"Nope, Detective Sam Hubbard, Forensic Investigation Department, San Francisco, California."

Sam was stunned. It sounded like whoever had been at Mo's had also met him in the past and had gotten one of his cards. It was likely the killer. All he could say to Grundy was, "Thanks, I'll get right back to you. Please make a copy of the card, front and back, and email it to me ASAP. Also send me an image of the writing that is crossed out that says *Dies*."

Sam Hubbard's mind was working at warp speed. He continued talking out loud, recording his thoughts, letting them flow like a river of consciousness.

Maybe organizing himself with a written list would help. He wrote in bold letters the heading PENCIL MURDERER. "OK, what do I know for sure?" he muttered. He itemized:

-Killer's gotten to Mo probably. Mo is missing, maybe dead, left specific clues.

-Same guy killed Meat, same message on the pencil.

-Is it possible Mo is the killer? He had one of my cards, maybe he's got a multiple personality disorder? Hard to imagine but possible.

Sam underlined the word possible and added a question mark.

-Did I give Fallon Scriber a business card? I can't remember.

-Mo is working on Native American music. The word *Dies* is written presumably by the murderer's hand. Need to check against Mo's handwriting.

-Mo worked on a project about Indian petroglyphs and dedicated it to Isabella Graves.

-The name Isabella Graves was mailed to me as a clue from San Francisco.

-Scriber is from San Francisco.

-My name was used as the last client in Meat's appointment log. The murderer is taunting me to find him.

-Bloom's gallery deals in Native American art and is thanked in Mo's film as is Isabella Graves. Bloom's gallery is closed when it shouldn't be.

-Where is Charles Bloom?

-Where is Mo Bandgood?

-Who and where is Fallon Scriber?

Sam's first call was to the Las Cruces Police Department. He explained that Isabella Graves might be in serious danger and to put a car out in front of her house.

He then called Isabella and explained Mo was missing and it didn't look good and to let him know if anyone contacted her and that she would have police protection for now. It seemed to Sam that the most logical explanation for Mo's disappearance was that he had been abducted. He would work from this premise until proven wrong. He had talked with the man on two different occasions over the years and both times he seemed normal.

Sam reasoned that anyone thanked in the book or on the tape could be in danger. He decided to work harder on tracking down Bloom first, as he wasn't answering his gallery phone, an ominous sign for anyone in retail.

A quick Internet search found Bloom also had a connection to the Toadlena Trading Post in New Mexico. Sam called the post. Sal Lito, the owner, thought Bloom would be at his house and gave him both Bloom's cell and home numbers. Sam called the house number and found Rachael Yellowhorse.

"Yá át ééh," answered Rachael, half expecting Bloom was calling, having stuck her truck in a ditch leaving the Minimart.

"Hello, is Charles Bloom there? I need to talk with him. This is Detective Sam Hubbard from the San Francisco Police Department."

Rachael didn't like that a big city cop had their phone number and was calling her boyfriend. Every time a cop called, it seemed to be trouble for Bloom. Her heart started to race.

"He's out right now. Can I take a message? I'm his wife, Rachael Yellowhorse." Rachael hated to lie to a cop, but figured he might give a wife information that a girlfriend would never merit. Besides, it was just a matter of time before Bloom realized what he had and married her.

"Please tell your husband we have a missing person we are trying to locate. We have reason to believe this individual was kidnapped and by someone very dangerous..."

"Who? What individual?" Rachael interrupted, her heart now pounding in her chest.

"A Mr. Mo Bandgood."

"We both know Mo. Who is the very dangerous suspect?"

"There is one prime suspect. It's a man named Fallon Scriber who..."

Rachel interrupted, "That man's with my husband right now! They met two hours ago. Is Charles in danger?"

"I don't know. We have had a recent vicious murder and significant clues were left that all seem to be pointing toward something Mo worked on, a film about petroglyphs..."

Rachael cut him off for a third time. "My Charles took Scriber to look at those petroglyphs today! That's where they went and it's a very remote area!"

"OK, Rachael, calm down. We don't know anything for sure. Stay put and in contact. I'm calling the local police. I should know more shortly." Sam gave her his cell phone number and hung up.

Rachael sat in her kitchen, tears running down her face, trying to figure out what to do. She thought of another time when she and Bloom had helped Carson Riddly. If she had waited then for the cops, Dr. Riddly would have been killed.

She knew where the petroglyphs were. There was no time to wait. She had to do something. Her faux-husband and friends were in mortal danger from a savage killer, and on terrain she always knew had bad spirit energy.

She went to her pine bureau and retrieved two small pouches. The larger bag's leather covering was slick from wear. Only a very fine yellow ochre color persisted. It was her grandfather Hastiin Sherman's medicine bundle. Inside was a black-chipped stone. It was called a male arrowhead. Its edges were razor sharp with a pointed end like a knife. She was well aware of the power it possessed. It had come from her grandfather, a respected medicine man, and he had left it to Rachael. It would guide her.

The other pouch, which had more of its yellow ochre covering, contained a female arrowhead that her grandmother Ethel Sherman had given to Rachael during her *kinaalda* puberty ceremony. The female arrowhead is also a very powerful stone, but rounded in shape. The two stones together increased their power for the holder.

Rachael whispered a Diné prayer and carefully placed both pouches in her jeans pockets. She would need all the medicine she could gather if she came up against a *chindi* as dangerous as the one the cop had described.

Willy was sleeping in his cradleboard. Rachael grabbed Willy and his baby bag, and headed to the Toadlena Trading Post.

When she arrived in Bloom's old Mercedes, Sal was in the back looking at a rug for possible purchase. Rachael barged in and removed Sal's truck keys from the hook and replaced them with Bloom's key.

She then interrupted Sal in a very un-Navajo way: "Sal, you have to take care of my Willy. Everything you will need is in the baby bag and I'm borrowing your four-wheel-drive truck. Bloom's Mercedes is out front if you need it. If you don't hear from me in two hours, I'm in very bad trouble. Send the police to my mom's old sheep-grazing range. Our families call it Hidden Canyon. It's where that petroglyph wall is. Susie Manygoats can take them there. Two hours!" And with that, Rachael was gone.

CHAPTER 55

IN THE NAVY

Sam was getting ready to go over to search Fallon Scriber's house. Judge Mason was signing a search warrant and it would be ready soon. Then a call came in from the records department.

"Are you in your office? Get your pen out, Sam. We have some new additions for your charts. Your day just got busier." The perky voice on the phone knew she was about to give the well-liked detective information he would love.

"OK, Sandy, I'm ready. I hope this is good," Sam told the pretty young records officer.

"You'll want this, Sam. First, Fallon Scriber was in the Navy stationed at Seal Beach, and he was there the same time and in the same department as Petty Officer Mat Smith."

Sam's hand began trembling as he wrote down Scriber's information.

"Now here's the part you aren't going to believe," she continued. "It even scares me. Scriber went to a middle school in Oakland where coincidently one of his classmates was murdered in the eighth grade. The kid who was viciously killed was a Willy Bellows, murdered. Care to guess how?"

Sam feet were tapping the floor so hard he was having a hard time writing the name *Willy* down. "Tell me it was by a pencil?"

"Two pencils. He was repeatedly stabbed to death with two common yellow number-two lead pencils. It was classified gang related. No murderer ever found!"

"Oh my God, it's Fallon Scriber! He's a psychopathic serial killer!" Sam hung up, checked his weapon, and rushed out to Fallon Scriber's house. The warrant could wait.

CHAPTER 56

DON'T TOUCH ANYTHING

Sam and a dozen police officers converged on Fallon's house, a nice three-story redbrick structure that was post-1906 San Francisco earthquake. It looked to be an expensive place with the luxury of a garage. Walking up to the front door, Sam experienced déjà vu. He was sure he had been at this very house before. He had. It was 20 years ago when it was Mrs. Black's home. Could Fallon Scriber be sending another message? That Mo had missed him long ago when Fallon was right in front of him?

The military dossier on Scriber was chilling. He was an expert marksman, both gun and rifle, had advanced training in hand-to-hand combat, and was a specialist in ballistics. He was a well- trained killer thanks to the United States Military. The bomb squad was here. They entered the house in full protective gear, expecting the worst, booby traps. Sam was right there with them. This was the man who had killed his nephew. It was still personal and always would be.

No sign of anyone on the first floor and no bombs were found. The second floor was where they found Fallon's bedroom, now turned into Mo's torture chamber. Mo was found buck-naked, spread-eagle handcuffed by all fours to the bed. A foul, smelly goo oozed out from around an apparent abdominal wound. There was a small puddle of the fluid that had pooled around his buttocks.

Sam barked at his officers, "No one touch him! He may be booby trapped."

Mo's eyes and mouth were still duct-taped shut. Underneath the tape his pupils were dilated fully, his body experiencing uncontrollable shivering due to fever.

"Mo, this is your old friend Detective Sam Hubbard. We talked about the Zodiac movie, remember?"

Mo carefully nodded yes.

"This is very important, Mo. Is there any reason that you can think that we shouldn't remove the duct tape? The guy who did this to you was a bomb expert." Mo slowly shook his head no then yes, his way of saying maybe.

"Mo, we are going to first look around the bed to make sure there is nothing hidden that might explode before I touch you. I know you're scared and hurting but everything is OK. We just need to do our job first."

Mo slowly shook his head affirmatively.

The bomb crew meticulously reviewed the situation. Then came the words no one wants to hear, especially when you have been impaled and are completely nude and helpless.

"Watch it, there's a live one and it's damn good!"

The underside of the bed was filled with a plastic explosive C4 bomb that was set to explode if there was a weight change of seven pounds. This was a diabolical plan as Mo had already lost at least five pounds from starvation and dehydration during the last two days; he would blow up sometime in the next day or so if the infection didn't get him first.

The next hour was spent defusing the bomb by the best in the business. Mo was kept informed as the defusing process slowly proceeded. Sam never left his side. Mo's mind kept thinking of the "Saturday Night Live" sketch in which MacGruber repeatedly blows up everyone due to his incompetence. The poorly written music of the skit was playing nonstop in his feverish head.

There was no way to remove any of Mo's bindings or even touch him until the bomb was secured. It was the longest 60 minutes of Mo's entire life. The scene sounded surreal. He could hear men scurrying around and orders being barked, and the occasional curse word thrown in. He knew he was nude with a horrible-smelling wound that was incredibly painful and he was thinking about an "SNL" skit. Mo tried desperately to calm himself. Finally MacGruber left his mind and he was able to concentrate on a new composition. He called it "When I Get to Heaven." It was an inspirational piece.

Finally the bed was secured. Mo's mouth was untaped and before they even got to untaping his eyes, he frantically yelled, "Sam, go help Charles Bloom! His family is in great peril. This guy Scriber or whatever his name is, is a sick puppy. He has a huge tattoo on his chest of a petroglyph called 'Fallen Man.' The man is convinced he is some sort of god and I was an evil disciple. He will butcher them all, including Bloom's newborn son Willy, and I gave him the information he needed to take them down."

Mo started sobbing at the thought of people being killed because he helped a serial killer.

Little could Mo have imagined that at the exact time he was telling this to Hubbard, Bloom was about to find out who he was dealing with.

Sam called his captain and got a special order for a helicopter to take him to New Mexico's Hidden Canyon. The Navajo Tribal Police were also notified. Sam tried calling Rachael, but there was no answer. He left a message that he was on his way, to stay put, and Mo was safe.

Sam arranged for an ambulance to pick up Mo and attend to his festering abdominal wound. While they waited, Mo once again drew out a map of the canyon as he had for Fallon, detailing landmarks for the hard-to-find entrance. Sam girded himself to meet the deadly Fallon Scriber in person again. On this encounter he would have no doubt who he was dealing with, a true psychopathic serial killer, the rarest and most dangerous kind of human known to exist. The Navajo language was about to add another word to its vocabulary: *psychopath*, just like the rest of the world.

CHAPTER 57

SHOW TIME

The two trucks pulled into Hidden Canyon just as the rising sun was fully exposing the petroglyphs. Bloom had driven very slowly as he didn't want to skid on the icy snow-packed dirt roads, dinging Rachael's truck or losing his client in a ditch for the day. He wanted to make sure they all got there safely. He had pulled over one time to watch a group of mule deer cross the road in front of him. He pointed to the magnificent animals, thinking his L.A. client would want photos. Scriber gave him a "whatever, let's get going" kind of look.

The two-plus inches of snow that had fallen the night before had completely covered Fallon's footsteps and tire tracks. Fallon was thankful his god had protected him by concealing his tire tracks in an area that people never visit. He was surprised he had not thought of this wrinkle, as he was pretty sure he had divine knowledge at this point, but god provided.

The group climbed out and made their proper introductions. Everyone seemed to like their newest client and each person expounded in great detail about the wall and how special it was. They wanted to make sure for $20K that Fallon felt like he was getting his money's worth. Little could they know he was counting on it.

Fallon was dressed in a large bulky coat, wool hat, and new hiking boots. Surprisingly, he had not brought a camera. This puzzled Bloom. Why would a man pay so much money to see something so special and not bring a camera? He finally asked Fallon, who replied, "It's better if I remember it in my mind. I'm sure you have plenty of cameras to take photos." It was an odd answer, but so was paying $30K to see something you could buy for $9.95 on the Internet and watch in your own living room.

The order of accession up the tricky handholds began with Frank, who scampered up first as if his ancestors had taught him. He was followed by Jack Bloom, Dr. J, Fallon, and finally bringing up the rear, Charles. Frank carried Dr. Bloom's walking cane with him, hanging it around his neck as he scrambled up the rock face. The ascent was hard for the octogenarian Bloom Sr., whose bad hip made it painful, but finally he conquered the cliff with a little encouragement from his associates. As Fallon reached the walking ledge, Frank yelled something in Diné and then in English: "I don't know what this means. Come here, you guys, this is weird and it looks fresh!"

Frank pointed at the Fallen Man image halfway down the wall. The professors closed in, reading glasses poised for inspection. In the lower half of the large iconic image was a human handprint, which had not been there before. It was fresh and for all purposes looked like blood. Frank, who was quite disturbed, began chanting in Navajo. The old men just looked perplexed. Bloom heard Rachael's voice in his head: "It's *chindi*."

It would become quite clear where the blood came from in short order. As the four men's eyes were transfixed on Fallen Man, the fifth visitor, Fallon Scriber, was busy preparing. He had unzipped his coat, removing a portable frog gig that he had telescoped out, in his left hand. In his right, was a .45 magnum. Fallon had no shirt on underneath his coat, and now his symbol of courage and power was visible to all. The still very irritated tattoo of Fallen Man dominated Scriber's chest and abdomen. There was a new addition: a fresh, deep, horizontal cut directly below the Fallen Man tattoo paralleling

215

Willy Bellow's old scars, the apparent source of the new bloody handprint.

When Bloom turned to say something to Fallon he was dumbfounded by the insane-looking spectacle of the man before his eyes grinning at him in an "I'm going to eat you" kind of way.

"Shit! OK, why do you have that gun, Mr. Scriber? Let's just take it easy here," Bloom reasoned.

By this time the other three men were also noticing the horrifying image before them. Fallon blocked their only escape exit.

"Throw me your keys, Bloom," Fallon ordered, "or I'll show you how well I can handle a firearm. Or would you prefer the gig?"

Bloom didn't say a word. He fished out his keys with a picture of his newborn son on them and tossed them to Fallon, who caught them with the gig still in hand.

"Nice picture, Willy, isn't it? I once knew a Willy." Fallon laughed at the thought of his first victim 40 years ago. A lot had transpired since then.

"OK gentleman, this is how it works. You two old guys come over here and face each other." The terrified men did as instructed. Fallon pulled two pairs of handcuffs from his jacket pocket and had them cuff each other's wrists and ankles together. "OK, now go stand under your god, the almighty Fallon Man." For the first time "Fallen Man" became Fallon Man in Scriber's mind. The professors duck-shuffled over to the imposing figure, the iconic image now looking down at two new subjects, his fresh red handprint making him even more intimidating.

"He likes you," Fallon said jokingly. "OK, Bloom, you're next. No hero shit. Get your ass over there, slowly."

As Bloom started to head over to the professors, Frank made a desperate leap for safety. He got a little running start towards the ledge, then hurtled himself off the nearly 20-foot cliff like an Olympic broad jumper, smashing into the frozen ground with a hard thud and a loud cracking sound which was audible to all. He screamed out in agony as he had just broken the largest and strongest bone in his

216

body, his femur. He tried to stand, but fell with another scream and began to drag himself in the snow out of sight from what looked to soon be a death zone.

Fallon yelled out to the badly injured Navajo man, "You could have died like the rest of them in a big blast of rock, much less painful. But because you are going to make me chase you, I'm going to gig you with my spear like a frog and then cook your heart up and eat you. Don't ruin any of that tender meat. Maybe I'll cook it up in a little Navajo baby fat." Fallon said it with such conviction that Frank and everyone else knew it wasn't an empty threat.

What Fallon didn't know was one other person beside his captives had heard his maniacal rant and she had other plans. It was Rachael Yellowhorse, and she was coming for Fallon Scriber.

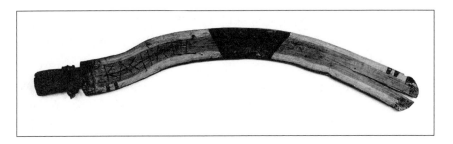

CHAPTER 58

A NEW HAIRSTYLE

Rachael hurried faster when she heard Frank's scream. She had hidden Sal's truck as a precaution and was working her way over to where she figured Frank would try and escape. You don't herd sheep for years in remote canyons and not develop an intimate lay of the land. She found Frank as he was trying to reach a crevice, a horizontal crack in the earth she had named Nap Time Slit because one could just fit into the small crack in the wall and lay prone and watch the sheep, which usually led to taking a nap.

"Frank, Frank," Rachael whispered.

"Leave me alone. I haven't done nothing," the disoriented Frank pleaded in a terrified voice. He gingerly turned himself sideways, expecting the wild man who was going to eat his heart. "Oh, thank god, it's you! We have got to get out of here! There's a guy trying to kill us. We got to go!"

"I heard him. I know he's crazy. He still has Bloom and he will kill Willy and me and anyone else in his way. I have to stop him. Listen, I'll push you up into the crevice. Once you get in, go to the far little back cave. I'll follow you in. I've got a plan but we have to work fast," Rachael whispered.

Rachael, who weighed only 120 even after having had a baby, pushed the skinny young man up into the crevice. Frank put part of his shirt in his mouth and clamped down on it so as not to scream out in pain. His leg was badly broken and throbbing intensely. Once he pulled himself in, Rachael jumped up in one bound, pulling herself up as she had done a hundred times as a teenager. Frank huddled in the remote cave as far in the back as he could go. Rachael took out her iPhone and used it as a light for a quick check for any hibernating rattlesnakes, and then she found what she needed. Lying next to an empty PAYDAY wrapper from the eighties was her dark, pinion-wood Hopi Rabbit Stick, a weapon used for hunting small animals. It had a curve like a boomerang.

The stick had been given to her grandmother by an elderly Hopi man and she in turn had given it to Rachael as a teenager to ward off coyotes. It would probably be considered an antique and would have been quite valuable, except Rachael had carved in her name in big block letters on the entire stick's surface one summer in case any other shepherds had eyes on her family heirloom. Rachael had spent hundreds of hours honing her talents in the use of the weapon and had deadly aim when it came to throwing it, and the courage to match.

"Frank, you need to help me cut off my hair." Rachael put her phone in her mouth with the light pointed downward then pulled out her grandfather's medicine pouch and removed the male arrowhead.

"What are you talking about? We need to get help! Why would you want me to cut your hair?"

"Listen to me! If you want to survive this day, you will do exactly what I say. I have to creep up the cliff on my belly if I want to stop this lunatic and I can't have my waist-long hair getting in my way. Now do as I say. Cut it all off above my shoulders."

Rachael held the phone's light up to her head and Frank did as he was told, grabbing handfuls of Rachael's pristine silky black hair, which had never felt the touch of scissors before. He sawed it off with the black male arrowhead, Rachael chanting a hushed prayer as he cut.

After he was finished, she put a small amount of her shorn hair inside her grandfather's pouch and returned the arrowhead to its housing. Rachael then drew a map in the dirt illustrating where she had left Sal's truck. She handed Frank the keys and her phone.

"I told Sal to call the cops if he didn't hear from me in two hours, and it's been almost an hour. So stay put. If I don't come back that means I'm dead. Use the truck, but only as a last resort." Then Rachael jumped out of the hiding place and scampered off like a fox, wiping out their tracks with a pinion branch as she bolted from Nap Time Slit. Frank started chanting in a low whisper. It was up to Rachael now.

CHAPTER 59

THE BIG BANG

Though Rachael didn't like to get too close to the rock art wall, she did know the terrain very well. There was a secondary entrance to the cliff off the mesa top. It was dangerous and required dropping down into the ledge from above. She hated that route, as she was always afraid her weight would bring down a section of the rock overhang on top of her. Today there was no other option. The hidden entrance to the rock ledge was where the canyon had gotten its name. It was the same entrance the Nasazi had used for hundreds of years.

Reaching the slit in the earth, Rachael held her breath and squeezed through the crevice. She was 13 the last time she had done this and hadn't had breasts to speak of. It was painful but she managed past the seven-boulder obstacle course the gods had put in front of her, acutely aware that too much pressure on any one of them and all the gigantic boulders could give way on top of her. Finally she could see the ledge floor and knew it was in the gods' hands now.

She lowered herself down, hiding behind a large outcropping of rocks that obscured her from the men on the ledge. The first 100 yards of the approach required Rachael to snake along on her belly carrying the rabbit stick in her mouth. She had played coyote many times and knew how to stalk a prey. This time it was for real and the prey was Fallon Scriber. He was an enemy of the Diné and he was on her land.

The three captives were standing next to Fallen Man, listening to the maniacal Fallon.

"You men are the disciples of this demon," Fallon accused, rubbing his skin, creating huge welts. "See how my skin has been made defective by his power? The closer I am to the epicenter of his evil, the more my skin reacts. He doesn't like my blood on him. He knows I have his soul and he will soon have met his match. I will destroy him and all of you in a magnificent final explosion. Your souls will become my property instead of his. You will thank me for freeing you from your bondage and will be happy in the afterlife with me as your master."

Bloom kept eyeing the rock slab lying partially suspended over the petroglyph ledge. He had pushed the flat rock to the edge the last time. Today he hoped he could slide over the precipice on his so-called sled. No fear of the consequences now. The real danger was screaming at him in insane gibberish. How to get Fallon distracted so as to make his escape?

Just as he was considering trying to make his desperate move, praying Fallon wasn't as good a shot as he had bragged, Bloom saw the most magnificent and unbelievable sight.

Bloom's girlfriend and the mother of his child with her long hair now gone was sliding down the opposite side of the rock wall coming to rescue them. Bloom knew what to do.

"Fallon, how long till you become the keeper of our souls?" Bloom figured if he played up to the man's narcissistic ideas of grandeur he would have a better chance distracting him. This usually worked in retail. Have him talk, maybe even get some useful information, most importantly allow Rachael valuable time for whatever she was planning, which he hoped was good.

"Ah, I'm glad to see you are coming around, Bloom. My presence is affecting you in a positive way. Soon you will be free, my son. The time is near," Fallon promised as he pulled out his detonator and pushed the button that started a countdown. "You have three minutes more to suffer in this life. Move to the end. I will say goodbye to my arch enemy and leave for my destiny."

The men shifted away and closer to Bloom's sled. At the same time, Rachael, now standing erect, back against the wall, started inching forward like a cat, stopping once she was in range of her target. She cocked the rabbit stick with her right arm like a big league pitcher in the ninth inning, then hurled the wooden weapon at Fallon's head. The ancient hunting stick hit Fallon squarely on the right temple with a huge crack, crumpling him like a used Kleenex, his body falling hard onto the prehistoric sandstone surface. His front teeth slammed into the canyon floor.

"Rachael," Bloom yelled, "get over here! There's a bomb and the timer's ticking! He's going to blow us all up in two minutes!"

Rachael bounded over the heaped body, retrieved her rabbit stick and ran to Bloom and the two old men, who seemed to be in denial about their perilous position. Bloom pulled his father and Dr. J over to his sled. He pushed the sled's rock nose further towards the edge, then positioned the two handcuffed men next to each other sitting down, facing each other. Their weight once aboard tipped the sled forward and for a minute it looked like it might leave without Rachael or Bloom, but it was too heavy. It sunk further into the mud and snow.

"OK honey, you know what we have to do here. We both push and jump on, you first, me right behind you, and we hold on for dear life! You hold the guys and I'll hold you."

Rachael stuffed her rabbit stick in her pants and the couple dug in with their feet, leaning forward. Like some massive luge, they pushed the heavy sled with all their might. The sled inched onto a snowy spot, moved more easily, and suddenly its weight shifted over the edge. Rachael and Bloom jumped on, not a second too soon, as the earth's gravitational pull reached out for the huge slab of rock that slid over the side for the ride of their lives.

The rock sled flew down the insane incline, picking up speed quickly, no handhold to speak of, just each other's tight grip trying to maintain balance. The riders clung together, their bouncing bodies fighting to stay on the hard rock surface of the sled as it hit the bumpy ground. The ice and snow helped keep the sled from flipping, but added to the speed. All the occupants were screaming as if on an amusement ride, but this was anything but. Then the incline shifted upward and the sled slowed, careening into the side of an ancient downed juniper that lifted the rock pancake to a 45-degree angle, tossing its occupants out onto a large southern-facing snow bank. Miraculously, all of them tumbled out, unharmed.

But as they extracted themselves out of the snow, a new horror confronted them. Fallon stood upright above them on the ledge, his hands still gripping his powerful weapons, his body leaning against the rock image of "Fallen Man" for balance. "I will not let you go, I am Fallon Scriber," he screamed at his escaped souls, lisping badly as he said *Scriber*, his front teeth lying at his feet. He pointed his magnum revolver toward his victims, shakily taking aim.

Just as he did, a huge cataclysmic explosion went off. It blew the ledge to bits, shaking the entire hillside and knocking Charles and his group to the ground. The timer had gone off on Scriber's ordinance, and the overhang, which had protected the ancient petroglyphs for a thousand years, was destroyed in a matter of seconds.

As Charles and the rest slowly clambered to their feet again, the professors still cuffed together, they watched a massive dust cloud dissipate. No longer was there any "Fallen Man" or Fallon Scriber. Now lay a giant slab of sandstone wall that had fallen directly on top of the psychopath killer, his broken arm holding his spear, the only part of his evilness still visible. The survivors looked at each other in amazement, ears ringing from the enormous blast.

Dr. Jack Bloom, the consummate researcher, shouted, "You have to see this." The dazed group looked where he was indicating. It was the underside of Bloom's makeshift sled. There was another large image pecked into the stone, one that had been hidden since it had cleaved off the cliff a hundred years ago. It was an exact copy of "Fallen Man," minus the horns and spear, its face and eyes less ominous. Directly in the middle of the petroglyph's body there was one additional adornment, an ancient red handprint. "A counterbalance to the evil," proposed Rachael. "The goodness was let loose when rightness prevailed."

Charles looked at Rachael and she at him, both with tears flowing down their faces. Then Charles said in his most passionate voice, "Rachael, love of my life, will you give me the honor of becoming my wife? I can't imagine anyone braver or more beautiful to spend my life with... and I love the new hairstyle."

Rachael, looking into Bloom's watery blue eyes, realizing he finally understood who she was and where she came from, replied the only way possible. "Yes," she said, and she did it in Navajo, knowing Bloom could now truly understand what it meant to be Diné.

CHAPTER 60

AFTERMATH

Sam Hubbard was back at work in San Francisco from his unplanned New Mexico trip. It had taken a week to recover the body of Fallon Scriber and had required the help of a huge crane to lift off the monumental slab of petroglyphs that had severely crushed his defective remains, which were now stored at the morgue, waiting for someone to claim.

There was a new calm in Sam's voice and demeanor. His life's work had not been in vain and he felt at peace for the first time. After returning to San Francisco, Sam had closed four charts in one week: those of Bill Sneadly, Mat Smith, Robin Pettipoint, and the Pencil Murderer, Fallon Scriber. The new open space on his wall had come just in time, as he had been sent a small brown-and-white Navajo weaving, a gift from Charles and the Toadlena Trading Post as thanks for his help.

He was looking forward to his scheduled return trip to the rez. He had just gotten his invitation to the Yellowhorse and Bloom wedding, scheduled in a month. The wedding announcement included a photo of the happy couple and their child in front of an orange sandstone wall, all smiling with Willy holding Rachael's antique rabbit stick. The wedding was scheduled for May 7th. The procession music would be "Spiderwoman Lives" conducted live by Mo Bandgood and performed by the Red Lake singers.

Rachael had included a handwritten note in Sam's envelope. It said: "I hope you can come. Isabella Graves has just RSVP'd, I thought you would like to know. P.S. I'm expecting again. It's a girl. I'm going to name her Sam. Love, Rachael."

Sam had been in frequent touch with Isabella by phone and email these last few weeks. Like Sam, she had never married. Family and work had gotten in life's way. Sam picked up the phone and RSVP'd to the party. He asked Rachael to make sure he and Isabella sat at the same table. He was tired of being alone.

The End

STONE MEN

BY MARK SUBLETTE

CHAPTER 1

#35

The stone man's hand trembled ever so slightly as he inspected his precious find. Surging endorphins pulsed through his body, a rare occurrence for an ex-Marine who understood true danger. The catalyst of his excitement wasn't a bullet, but a colorful rock shaped like an oversized deer pellet. It was the moment he lived for, the thrill of finding a new turquoise deposit. It had been two years since his last adrenaline surge. Now he had found the mother lode. His tremulous hand told the whole story.

The President, as he was known in the world of rock hounds, had made a monumental discovery. It was the finest raw turquoise nugget he had ever seen, and a surface find at that. The probability was there were plenty more precious veins of turquoise just underneath the bare Navajo sandstone. The nugget was a harbinger of what was to come. It had taken good detective work, years of experience in the field, but now it was going to pay off big-time. Most stone men, even good ones, would have breezed past, never giving the nondescript pebble a second glance. Not the President. His well-trained eye discerned the glint of importance nestled in a tan sandstone trough, one of thousands of ravines that made up this portion of the Navajo reservation. Here it was in his hand. A magic pill, the panacea for all that ails a hard-lived life. A rough turquoise stone that would transform his remaining days and solidify his standing as the best in the field.

The stone was on Navajo property but private land was less than a quarter mile away. He would just stretch the truth a bit on its location, a specialty of the trade.

The President managed to muster a little saliva, which he applied to the nugget. Its true beauty came shining through. Gingerly he rolled the precious moist stone between his thumb and index finger, instinctively gauging its value. Reticulated silver encapsulations appeared on the rough stone, the same glint that initially caught his attention. To the trained eye its structure was visible even without magnification. It was a flawless gem. The rock's complex metallic matrix deposited in a sea of aquamarine color was an exceptional mix of silver and blue. The stone was no larger than a marble but after cutting and polishing, it would result in two small five-carat cabs. He would realize an astronomical premium, the most any turquoise had ever demanded. He figured out loud, "$1,500 a carat has a nice ring to it," computing what his eyes had confirmed. He already had a name picked out, one he been saving for the ultimate turquoise find. A moniker worthy of his own initials, JFK, also the initials of the 35th president.

"Number 35, my search is over. You will make #8 look like a second-grade gem stone," he told his new stone, laughing at the thought of his new discovery outclassing #8 which up until this point was considered probably the premium-grade turquoise. "I'm going to always price you 10 times the spot value of #8," he planned, his booming voice echoing off the steep white walls of the canyon.

As the last of his voice trailed off in distant Navajoland, the President heard a new sound reverberate through the high desert air. It was the crack of a high-power rife, a noise he knew. The President ducked his head and turned instinctively. A second later he felt an excruciating pain burn through his right triceps, his precious #35 escaping his grip, bouncing one time before plummeting down a bottomless crevice, lost forever to mankind. The only colored stone now was the crimson sandstone slab he was laying on, blood oozing over the rocks he loved so much.

The President hit the ground hard with an audible thud, like a kill shot to a deer. His left thigh bruised and swelled, but his quick action had saved his life. A second shot whizzed 10 inches over his head, ricocheting off a boulder and almost hitting him in the back. He began gasping rapidly. It was hard to focus, but if he wanted to live he knew exactly what he had to do. Two years in 'Nam had taught him how to survive. This wasn't his first go-round at being shot. This time it appeared his arm had a flesh wound. His truck was hidden a quarter-mile away and dusk was in a half-hour. He could tell by the sound of the shots and the time it took to hit his arm and sweep over his head that the shooter must be a fairly long way distant, a good marksman no doubt. It was open range and the assassin couldn't know he was unarmed, so they would be cautious, especially if they knew his history. If the President played his cards right, he could escape. His bruised leg was usable. His arm hurt like shit but the bleeding was slowing and he had full movement. Still a lucky day.

He managed to tuck himself behind two dinosaur-egg shaped salmon-colored boulders. There would be no way the shooter could hit him if he didn't panic. Keeping as low as possible, he flattened his body like a lizard in the cold. A third shot rang out, its distance as far away as the other two, bouncing around, but he was safe. Then his unrelenting trained eye caught the reflection of something... *silver.* The low sun's rays grazed the surface of an unusual rock. His prone position gave him the optimal angle for discovery. If he were the type of man to contemplate his situation he would stay perfectly still, but he wasn't that man. Instead, he eased his left hand out past the protective boulders, expecting to be shot, waiting for a new searing pain. Neither occurred. With slabs for fingers he trapped a golf-ball

229

size stone that was wedged underneath two large sandstone rock formations, quickly retrieving it. Another #35! He couldn't help but smile, admiring the gem encryptions laced with silver. He rubbed it with his blood-soaked shirtsleeve, the deep blue color indisputable even through his own red filter. It would be worth a fortune. Now if he could only figure out a way to survive so he could realize his payday. He tucked the stone safely in his pants, covered his wound, and waited for dark. No one was stealing his claim. No one.

To be continued in STONE MEN, *scheduled for release in 2014.*

Photography courtesy Mark Sublette, unless otherwise noted

Page 1:   *Example of Skin Condition, Dermatographia*, photo by
            Megan Laughlin
Page 6:   *Javelinas*, Tucson, Arizona
Page 10:   *Hampton Inn*, Kayenta, Arizona
Page 13:   *My Hand and Petroglyph*, Northwestern New Mexico
Page 20:   *Navajo Silver, Turquoise and Coral Cigarrette Box with the
            Initials FS*, circa 1960
Page 35:   *Apache Cradleboard, circa 1960*
Page 40:   *Paint Can*, Chuska Mountains, New Mexico
Page 42:   *Toadlena Trading Post*, Newcomb, New Mexico
Page 46:   *View from the Porch*, Toadlena Trading Post, New Mexico
Page 55:   *Petroglyph Wall*, Northwestern New Mexico
Page 59:   *Santa Fe in Season*, New Mexico
Page 68:   *Petroglyphs*, Northwestern New Mexico
Page 88:   *Crashing Water*, Pacific Ocean
Page 131:   *Corner of Canyon Road and Camino Escondido near Bloom's
            Gallery*, Santa Fe, New Mexico
Page 140:   *Sold Weaving Tag by Rachael Yellowhorse*
Page 145:   *Anasazi Pottery*, Northwestern New Mexico
Page 148:   *Spongebob in Vegas*, Nevada
Page 161:   *Winter Cold*, Near Kayenta, Arizona
Page 172:   *Antique Frog Gig*
Page 214:   *Stuck Truck*, Navajo Nation
Page 218:   *Rachael's Rabbit Stick*
Page 221:   *Escape Hatch, Petroglyph Wall*, New Mexico
Page 227:   *Spiderweb Turquoise*